DREAMS

OF

SILVER

OTHER TITLES BY MINA BAITES

The Silver Music Box

DREAMS

OF

SILVER

MINA BAITES

TRANSLATED BY ALISON LAYLAND

amazon crossing

Text copyright © 2018 by Mina Baites
Translation copyright © 2018 by Alison Layland

Previously published as *Träume aus Silber* by Tinte & Feder in Germany in 2018. Translated from German by Alison Layland. First published in English by AmazonCrossing in 2018.

Published by AmazonCrossing, Seattle

www.apub.com

Amazon, the Amazon logo, and AmazonCrossing are trademarks of Amazon.com, Inc., or its affiliates.

ISBN-13: 9781503901254
ISBN-10: 1503901254

Cover design by Shasti O'Leary Soudant

Printed in the United States of America

DREAMS OF SILVER

List of Characters

1963:

Lilian Morrison (Gesa Blumenthal, Lilly Dölling): Born in 1937, translator in London

Sam Flynt: Born in 1935, Lilian's fiancé, primary school teacher

Paul Blumenthal (Peter Dölling): Born in 1910, father of Gesa and Margarethe (Emma)

Lotte Kuipers: Born in 1887, Paul's mother

Dede Achebe: Born in 1941, Lotte's friend and protégée

Friedrich Lükemeier: Born in 1894, an old family friend

August Konrad: Born in 1888, a WWI comrade of Lotte's husband, Johann Blumenthal

Ceara Foley: Born in 1931, Dublin carpenter

Aidan Foley: Born in 1931, Fireman, Ceara's husband

Rhona Ward: Born in 1901, Ceara's foster mother

1995:

Daniel Flynt: Born in 1965, son of Lilian and Sam Flynt

Megan Flynt: Born in 1968, daughter of Lilian and Sam Flynt

Prologue

Hackney, London, December 1940

The late afternoon sun beat down on the Church of St John at Hackney, framed by the leafless skeletons of winter trees. The chimes of the clock striking four alarmed a small flock of pigeons, which flew silently away from the church to find a sunny patch in the adjacent garden.

But the blue sky was deceptive. A biting wind blew over the rooftops of working-class Hackney, making its inhabitants shiver.

In one of the simple houses on Sutton Place, a child sat cross-legged on the floor, listening to the sounds drifting in from the street below. A bent old woman in a winter coat was huddled outside the house opposite, talking to herself. They were changing shifts down at the docks, and a procession of workers, cigarettes hanging from the corners of their mouths, streamed by. As they passed the old woman, she ranted and raved. No one took the slightest notice of the child who appeared at the second-floor window. The cropped hair and too-small jacket gave no indication of whether this was a boy or a girl. Only the fine, curved eyebrows suggested the latter.

Frowning, the child watched a long-legged spider creep from a crack in the wall and make for her legs. She edged toward the spider, but it scuttled behind a threadbare curtain that divided her makeshift sleeping area from the combined living room and kitchen. A pot lid rattled, and her nostrils were full of the unpleasant smell of boiling cabbage. The girl could only bear the steam from the kitchen if she kept the window open, so she wore a woolen scarf around her neck. To avoid having to think about food, the nine-year-old closed her eyes and daydreamed about happier times. Times when the winters had never seemed so cold because she could snuggle up to the people she loved the most, people who had warmed and comforted her. It seemed that, here in this house, every day was cold, and the nights were full of terrifying dreams.

Lost in thought, she felt around in her sagging jacket pocket. Until a short time ago, a time that seemed as far away as the moon, she had kept a special treasure there—a silver music box that her grandpa had made for her papa many years ago. Oh, it was so pretty, and it even had a secret compartment. But her favorite part had been the little bird that jumped up from the lid and twittered whenever she pulled a tiny lever.

Now her jacket pocket was empty. But if she shut out the street sounds and concentrated, she could still feel the weight of the music box and trace its contours with her fingers. Its feet were shaped like leaves, and it had hearts engraved on the sides. She wiped a hand over her cheeks, a sad smile on her lips. She wouldn't feel so alone if she still had Grandpa's music box. She could write down her thoughts and hide them in the secret compartment, and she would have something to keep her fingers occupied whenever her fears returned. The little girl sat on the bed with its moth-eaten woolen blanket and stared into space.

"My name is Emma. Only Emma," she murmured.

The rest was a big secret she must reveal to no one—her father had made her promise. She couldn't remember Mama and him ever talking so urgently as they had that morning in Lübeck. She missed Mama, the most beautiful woman in the world—Papa had thought so, too. She could still see him in her mind's eye, and she would never forget the way he'd cried when they parted. *Be brave, both of you. Look after each other. I'll come and fetch you as soon as I can.*

Not a day had gone by since without her standing at the window, waiting for her father's footsteps approaching the front door. He would have to be careful that no one saw him.

The wind carried the voices of people talking outside, but her father's was not among them. Her lips pressed together in a thin line, she turned from the window.

"My name is Emma," she whispered again into the icy air. "Only Emma." Her father's voice echoed in her mind. *We'll be back together soon, my darling.*

But when was *soon*? She paused on hearing a sound. A black-and-white puppy with floppy ears pattered into the room and stood looking up at her, tail wagging. He had belonged to the family for a few weeks and often crept into her bed at night. She put on a stern expression, picked him up, and ruffled the soft fur behind his ears.

"Jack, you vagabond, don't let them catch you. Otherwise there'll be trouble."

The puppy understood her. He didn't care that she hardly ever spoke a word of English. He licked her cheek and snuggled up to her as though he knew full well all the things she was missing. The doctor who lived with his wife on the ground floor also understood her. He was nice and sometimes spoke to her in German. Emma planted a kiss on the puppy's head and, since she knew he liked it, hummed one of the songs she used to sing to her baby sister when she cried or couldn't get to sleep. Her sister couldn't even walk yet when the train had brought them to England. At the time, Emma hadn't known where this *England* was. Now she was wiser: it was a place with a forest of chimneys and poor people wandering the streets and fighting when they'd been drinking beer. Hackney had nothing at all in common with Altona or Lübeck.

William popped his head around the curtain. He was a few years older than Emma and had a pimply but friendly face. There were also two other boys and a girl in the family.

"Come and wash your hands. Supper's on the table. You know Aunty Daisy doesn't like waiting."

She's not my aunt. Emma hugged the puppy and shook her head.

"Have it your own way." William fixed her with his gaze. "You've got to eat soon, or you'll look like an old skeleton."

Emma folded her arms across her chest and crawled into a corner. She felt William's eyes on her back for a brief moment longer, until the curtain rustled and she was alone again.

The family mostly left her in peace. Maybe they could have won her over if they'd talked to her the right way. Maybe they'd tried but eventually given up in the face of Emma's stubbornness.

So she sat there unmoving, pressed against the little puppy's body for warmth as the sun sank below the rooftops and darkness descended on Hackney.

Jack's closeness reminded her of the moment when she had hugged Lilly for the last time. The little girl had thrown her chubby arms around her sister's neck as if she'd never let go. Her mouth had been distorted in silent pain, and a few small tears had rolled down her cheek.

The head warden of the home had finally pried the toddler from her.

"For Lilly," Emma had said, as she handed over the music box and left with the lady who'd come to take her to her new foster parents.

A bloodcurdling howl jerked Emma back to the dark room. Not again. She felt like she couldn't breathe.

Jack flinched, too, and ran from the room with his tail between his legs.

"Air raid warning! Into the Tube station. Quick!" Uncle Alfred barked out.

There was no time to put her shoes on. Emma picked them up and, with her jacket still unfastened, ran with the rest of the family out into the open.

"Run, for God's sake! The Germans are coming!" William cried.

She stumbled, her knees threatening to give way. He slung her unceremoniously over his shoulder and hurried down the crowded staircase to the Tube station where they always took shelter. It was already filled with an ocean of people.

The siren screeched in Emma's ears. She whimpered as she felt other bodies pressing against her. The smells of fear, sweat, and urine hung in the air. Someone was laughing hysterically.

Dust motes danced in a dim beam of light.

A hush spread through the crowd as they listened, wide-eyed.

"Why do the Germans drop their bombs and destroy everything?" Emma asked William, who was sitting on her right.

"Are you stupid? Because they want to reduce the whole of London to rubble and ashes."

Her heart was beating in her throat, and the hairs on the back of her neck stood on end. She looked sidelong at him. Even though he acted all clever and grown-up, she saw in his eyes the same fear she was feeling herself.

Emma looked around in the semidarkness. She recognized a few familiar faces among the strangers. There were the Browns with their elderly parents and five children, whom people often called their tribe. Then there was pretty Lisa Harris with her friend Mike, the Clarks with their twins, and that lout Taylor, who was unemployed and sat around the park drinking beer. Lisa was holding her cat tightly on her lap, and the poor creature mewed constantly.

Emma suddenly turned ice cold. Jack! Where was Jack? A cry on her lips, she dashed toward the steps.

"Come back this instant! Are you mad?"

But she was already bounding up the stairs. *Jack! My God, Jack!* Emma hardly noticed the distant humming in the air as she looked around. The street was deserted, not a soul in sight. She heard crows nearby, their caws more insistent than usual. *He must be under my bed,* she thought as she crossed the street as fast as her legs would carry her.

She was in luck! In the rush, Aunty Daisy had left the door ajar. Emma ran through the house, calling the dog. A pitiful whimpering reached her ears.

Jack! The puppy was cowering in a corner of the kitchen. He jumped into her arms, and she tucked the trembling little dog inside her jacket.

She stopped at the front door, beads of sweat forming between her shoulder blades. The eastern sky was stained red. She could make out points of bright light that rapidly increased in size and intensity. Emma ran toward the Tube station. The next time she drew breath, the lights seemed to be directly over her head. Only a few steps to go.

A shrill whistling suddenly rent the air. Emma was thrown violently upward as though by invisible hands. The world seemed to explode. The last things she knew were Jack's whimpering and a bright flash in front of her eyes before darkness enveloped her.

Chapter 1

Lilian

Sea Point, Cape Town, South Africa, July 1963

Her bathrobe pulled tightly around her slim body, Lilian Morrison paused by the wide-open French doors opening out onto her grandmother's terrace and watched in fascination as the early-morning mist swirled, cloud-like, around the distant Table Mountain. It was cool on that South African winter morning, and she could even see a sprinkling of snow on the mountain peaks.

Once again, the young translator wondered in amazement at the sudden turn her life had taken only a few months ago. The previous winter, when she had still been living in London as the daughter of kindly civil servants, she had believed she knew what her future held, and although her relationship with her parents was always a bit distant, she had loved them both.

Lilian liked her job—and she liked Sam even more. He was her best friend, the light of her life, her rock, and was soon to be her husband.

Unbidden images from the last few months played through her mind like a movie. The death of her parents; the copper box they had left her, its contents turning her world upside down; the discovery that Steve and Heather Morrison had adopted her yet never broached the subject with her. Lilian's shock and bitter disappointment had long since faded, and she understood that they'd truly believed they were protecting her from the pain of confronting her origins. How much easier it would have been if they'd talked it all through calmly. Maybe then it would have been easier for Lilian to come to terms with her Jewish roots and the fact that her biological parents were deemed missing. But that was all in the past, and no amount of recrimination or acceptance would bring her adoptive parents back to life.

Lost in thought, Lilian watched the sun breaking through the mist. Wasn't time a strange concept? Clueless and blind, people stumbled through the years, deceiving themselves that they had enough time for everything. But that was a dreadful mistake.

Rays of sunlight fell on the silver object in her hand, highlighting the little box's filigree ornamentation in all its glory. Lilian's Jewish grandfather, Johann Blumenthal of Altona, had made the piece fifty years ago for his son, Paul—her biological father—as a parting gift when, in 1914, Johann had volunteered to fight for his homeland. The music box had been Johann's final legacy; he fell in the First Battle of the Somme in 1916.

Lilian's parents, Paul and Clara Blumenthal, had two daughters. Her older sister, Margarethe, was born in 1931; she herself followed in 1937 and was originally given the name Gesa. Her father had cherished the silver heirloom for many years. When her parents had been persecuted by the Nazis and Paul had despaired, the gift had given him hope and strength. He later passed it on to Margarethe.

Lilian held the treasure up to the light and felt the mixture of awe and sadness that stirred in her every time she looked at it. If she looked at the engraved image closely, she could see that the little boy with his notebook and conductor's baton was smiling. The toy, with its light traces of use, had become so much more to her than an heirloom, a pretty trinket to keep on the shelf. Lilian ran her fingers over the lid thoughtfully. The silver music box was the key to her past. It was her talisman, binding her in a very special way to her family, only some of whom had survived the Holocaust.

She heard soft footsteps behind her. Sam appeared and kissed her gently.

"You're up early this morning," he said as he handed her a mug of steaming tea.

She set the music box down on the table and took the mug gratefully. "I couldn't get back to sleep, and I didn't want to wake you."

Sam regarded her with a frown. "You're worried about leaving your family, aren't you?" He drew her into his arms, and she looked up at him. "It should only be a few weeks before we're back in Cape Town, Lil. Then we'll celebrate our wedding with the whole family around us."

In two days' time they would be flying back to London, where Sam intended to give notice at the primary school where he taught. They would also sell Lilian's adoptive parents' flat, as they intended to live here in Sea Point.

"My mum and dad said in their last letter that they'll book their flight as soon as we've fixed a date," he added.

Sam's parents had moved to the Channel Island of Jersey years ago because of its mild climate, so the family only got together occasionally. But there was no way they were going to miss their son's wedding.

Lilian snuggled up to him. It was true, she was worried about the imminent parting. After all, she had only been reunited with her father and her grandmother in Cape Town for a few weeks, after months of searching. Before that, she hadn't even been aware of their existence. In that short time, they had become so dear to her that the thought she would have to leave them again so soon—even temporarily—tore her apart.

She looked into Sam's beloved face, which she could read like a book, and felt her mouth go dry. "I've got something to tell you."

He motioned her to sit and took his own place opposite her. "Fire away."

Lilian reached for the music box and weighed it in her hand. If only she knew how to begin. She licked her lips, unable to meet his eye. "I need a little more time, Sam."

His expression changed. "Time for what? What do you mean?"

She saw the sudden fear in his eyes and indicated the heirloom in her hand. "You know, I thought I had the music box to thank for the fact that I've found my real family. But that's not strictly true."

Sam's bewilderment showed on his face. "You're speaking in riddles."

"It's really my sister I have to thank," she continued. "If she—if she hadn't given me the music box, it would never have ended up in the box my parents left to me." She fell silent.

"That's true," Sam said. "I've always been amazed that your sister let her favorite toy go like that. But however tragic it might be, she died in the war. I know it's difficult, but you've got to get used to it, my love."

Lilian shook her head. "I can't. Not until I've learned everything about her life, up to the moment she died. Can you understand that? All I have of her are the registration papers from the Hampshire Court children's home, a fading photo, her death certificate from 1940, and a few postcards she sent to Papa."

It still pained Lilian to think of the circumstances that had separated her seven-year-old sister from her when she was not even two. Her parents, Paul and Clara Blumenthal, had been German Jews living in Altona, where her father managed the local branch of the renowned Blumenthal & Sons. A skilled jeweler, Paul had even designed his own collections. After Adolf Hitler came to power, Paul and Clara had converted to Christianity in the hope of being able to live in peace in their beloved homeland. But the Nazis had persecuted the young couple, whom they branded non-Aryans. Within the space of a few years, they had taken everything from the Blumenthals—their business, their home, their dignity, and even their identity. Her parents had fled that hopeless situation using forged passports. They had been heading for Cape Town, where Paul's mother, Lotte, and Aunt Martha had emigrated several years before. But fate had other plans for the family, then hiding under non-Jewish names: Peter, Charlotte, Emma, and Lilly Dölling. During Kristallnacht in November 1938, Clara was gunned down by SS officers before Paul's eyes. Fearing for his daughters' lives, he had sent them to England on the Kindertransport. After a brief time in Hampshire Court, the sisters were separated and placed with different foster families. Little Gesa had been adopted by Steve and Heather Morrison and baptized with the name Lilian, while Margarethe's trail had been lost in the confusion of war. Paul had lived in South Africa ever since, his identity hidden so completely that even his own mother called him Peter.

Frowning, Lilian drew a photo from the secret compartment of the music box. Her sister had beautiful chestnut hair, similar to her own. Around her mouth were defiant lines; amid all the suffering, her seven-year-old sister had held her head high. Lilian gently stroked the old photograph. It had shaken her to the core when she learned her mother had been shot, but to have lost Margarethe as well, the big sister who had reportedly watched over her as she slept in the children's home, was a deep wound that hurt afresh every single day. She wondered as she so often did what her sister would have looked like now.

"What good would it do you to search for more details of Margarethe's life?" Sam asked, steering her carefully back to the present. "Leave the past in peace and look forward to the future. To our future."

Lilian sighed and tucked the photo back in its place. "I will. But first I need closure. And I can only have that when I've found out everything I can about her." She reached across the table for his hand. "When we get married, I need to be free inside for our new life."

Sam remained silent for a long while, playing with her fingers. When he raised his head, Lilian read disappointment and vulnerability in his face. "I understand what you're saying, though I must admit I'd imagined our trip to London rather differently." He kissed the palm of her hand, and her heart leapt. "After all, the actual date we get married isn't so important. What matters is that we belong together." Sam cleared his throat. "What are your plans?"

He listened carefully as she told him what she wanted to do. "Do your father and your grandma know?" he asked when she'd finished.

"No. I wanted to tell you first."

"Very well." He pulled her to her feet. "Then it's time to talk to them."

The whistling of a kettle sounded from the kitchen. Lilian smiled briefly—Lotte Kuipers already knew exactly what her granddaughter liked.

A little later, the family was gathered around the long dining table. It had become their custom to begin the mornings together. Her grandma sat across the table, her thick, gray-streaked hair as immaculately styled as ever. It was a mystery to Lilian how she managed to look every inch the lady even in her simple housedress. Although her seventy-some years had clearly left their mark on her features, she sparkled with energy and joie de vivre. Her grandma's decision to emigrate to Cape Town soon after Hitler came to power had proved wise. Under the South African sun, the painful memories of what had happened in her homeland gradually faded, and after the death of her second husband, Antoon Kuipers, she had found a new purpose in life: Lotte had founded the Blue Heart drop-in center to provide food, education, and support to young single mothers and their children, giving them hope and affection. Lilian admired her unreservedly and helped her as often as she could. The work made Lilian happy.

Lotte must have felt Lilian's eyes on her, because she passed her the sugar with a wink.

Friedrich Lükemeier sat on Lilian's left. Formerly a tenant farmer on an estate near Lübeck, he had helped Peter, Charlotte, and Emma—as he had known them—when they were on the run by allowing them to work for him and then hiding them when needed. They had become friends, but his farm girl had betrayed the Jewish family to the SS, and they'd been forced to flee. Then the war had broken out, and as the family was wanted by the police, it had been impossible to stay in touch with Friedrich. But the tough pensioner with a big heart had never given up hope that he would one day see his friends again. Lilian smiled as she recalled the wonderful sight of Friedrich and her father falling into one another's arms at the airport after more than twenty-five years. If Friedrich had not recognized the silver music box in the photo that had accompanied her missing-persons ad, who knew whether she would ever have seen her family again.

Lilian caught a look that passed between the widower and her grandmother, who had hit it off immediately. Friedrich's eyes sparkled whenever he looked at Lotte. He had originally intended to travel back to Europe with Sam and Lilian, but had now decided to extend his stay. "We're not getting any younger—let's all enjoy each other's company while we can," he had declared. Lilian suspected there was more to his decision than a desire to spend more time with his old friend.

Lilian's father was sitting next to his mother, pouring tea. His melancholy smile went straight to her heart; it had an amazing way of making the jeweler look so much younger. There was something about him—Lilian couldn't quite put her finger on it—that immediately endeared him to everyone he met. Maybe it was his warm, friendly voice, or maybe it was his fine features that revealed every emotion. Whenever Lilian looked at him, she was struck by how much she resembled him.

"Do I have shaving cream on my chin? Why are you looking at me like that?" he asked as he handed Sam the basket of Lotte's home-baked, braided bread.

"Sorry, Papa. I was just thinking," she replied.

Silence fell as they all suddenly looked at her.

"You're miles away today. What's the matter?" Lotte asked, gently but firmly.

"If you stir your tea any more, you'll wear the glaze away," Friedrich added good-naturedly.

Caught in the act, she put her teaspoon down.

"Come on, darling, out with it," her father said.

Lilian took a deep breath and told them about her plan. "I have to do it," she concluded. "I want to know what Margarethe's life was like, whether she had any friends, whether she felt at home in England before she died."

Peter's cup rattled slightly as he set it down. "What if you can't find anything?"

"Then I'll accept things as they are," she replied calmly. "But I have to try. You've got your memories of Mama and her. You were there when Mama died. But I don't know anything about my sister's last years." She looked into his eyes. "Don't you ever wonder what things were like for her?"

"Of course. Every single day," he said. "After we were parted, I went to sleep worrying about you both, and my fears woke me in the night. But I couldn't leave Cape Town for a long time." He laid his napkin on his plate. "By the time I did, Margarethe had been killed and, as you may remember me saying, your adoptive parents wouldn't allow me to see you because they were worried about your spiritual well-being. I was helpless in the face of the adoption laws."

Out of the corner of her eye, Lilian noticed the silent exchange that passed between Friedrich and her grandma.

"I know," she said. "But surely you tried to trace Margarethe's adoptive family while you were in England?"

He wiped his mouth with a napkin. "I didn't dare stay any longer than necessary or travel much while I was there. I was afraid that I'd get into trouble because of my forged passport. After the Germans took away my citizenship, I was stateless for many years. I never even dared to use my real name." He paused, turning a mug around in his hands.

The bitterness in his voice pierced Lilian to the heart. He clearly still found it difficult to talk about those times. Her eyes came to rest on her grandmother. "Can I ask you something?"

"Of course," Lotte said.

Lilian folded her hands on the table. "You loved your homeland, and you had deep roots there. Now a couple of decades have passed since those dreadful times. Haven't you ever considered returning to Germany?"

Lotte and Peter were taken aback.

"I do miss dear August," her grandmother said.

Gregor Oetting and August Konrad had been comrades-in-arms of her first husband, Johann; the three had served together in the Great War. After Johann was killed, Gregor and August had stood by Lotte and her family in their darkest hours and helped smuggle them out of Germany under their new identities. Gregor had died in the Second World War, but August was now in his eighties. A few months ago, his daughter, Friedel, had moved her family to Regensburg, her husband's hometown, and August had moved to be with them. He wanted to spend his remaining time with his grandchildren, Uschy and Monika. Since Lilian and Sam had found him, they, as well as Lotte and Peter, had called every week.

"Sometimes I miss the north and the clear air after a rain shower," Lotte continued. "But what I miss most is our language. I'm delighted every time I meet German people here. You know, I feel at home whenever I can speak my mother tongue." She smiled apologetically. "But I digress. No, Lilian." Fine lines showed around her mouth, giving her features a certain hardness. "I'll never set foot on German soil again. I'll always be grateful to those who stood by us, but I could never forgive nor forget the evil done by the Nazi regime."

"Going back is out of the question for me, too," her father said. "I'd have to start all over again there, you see, and I'm too old for that."

Lilian laughed. "Oh, Papa. You're anything but old."

"Nevertheless," he said. "Now, back to Margarethe. Of course, we searched, too. We asked for assistance from the International Tracing Service once we'd exhausted all the other possibilities. But I'm afraid it's been to no avail. A lot of documents were destroyed or lost during the war. But a few days ago, I did receive confirmation that they received my application to use the name Paul Blumenthal again."

Lilian's heart leapt. "Oh, that's wonderful, Papa! Why didn't you tell us right away?"

"There's no telling whether the application will be granted, and if so, when."

"Why are you doing it now, Papa? Your customers and neighbors all know you as Peter Dölling."

"Because we found you," her father said simply. "Because it would mean a lot to me to be myself again. Paul Blumenthal, son of Johann and Lotte, father of Margarethe and Gesa, widower of Clara."

Lilian recalled the dedication her grandfather had engraved on the base of the silver music box. *Johann Blumenthal, Altona 1914. For Paul, with love.*

Her father looked at her affectionately. "Don't cry, Lilian."

"I dream about my sister almost every night, Papa," she said quietly.

Tears shimmered in Peter's eyes. "I'm not surprised. She loved you very much. There was a strong bond between you."

"Everything's still so new," Friedrich said in a soothing voice. "The dreams will stop one day."

Sam looked from one to the other. "I want to help Lilian with her search."

"Good," Peter said. "And I'll come with you."

Lilian felt warmth suffuse her. "That's really kind of you, Papa. But Sam will have to go back to teaching soon, and I've got a translation job waiting for me. You'd be on your own a lot."

Peter shook his head slightly. "That could be good. While you're working, I can track down some leads. You don't think I'll sit around in Sam's flat doing nothing, do you? We're talking about my daughter here. I'll call Robert as soon as we've finished talking and ask him to take care of the business while I'm away."

"Well, if you mean it," Lilian said, "it'd be wonderful to have you there. Wouldn't it, darling?"

Sam smiled. "Amazing."

Friedrich turned and looked at Lotte through his rimless glasses. "What do you think?"

She had been following the conversation thoughtfully. As she met Lilian's gaze, a shadow crossed her face. "You surprise me. I don't have the courage to stir up the past again," she admitted. "I'd find it unbearable. I needed to draw a line under it at the time, otherwise I'd never have found peace. But you're cut from the same cloth as my Johann." Her voice trembled slightly. "May Adonai guide you and bring you home soon. I hope you find what you're looking for."

Chapter 2

Lilian

Cape Town and London

That Sunday morning, the three of them called a taxi. Friedrich had offered to go with them to D. F. Malan Airport, but Lilian turned him down. She found it so hard to leave, not knowing when they would see each other again. Though the curtains in the house were drawn, Lilian thought she could make out the silhouettes of her grandma and Friedrich by the window. They left Sea Point in silence, and Lilian looked out of the window as the taxi driver skillfully negotiated the quiet, winding streets to the airport.

She was surprised to hear her father talking quietly to the black driver in Afrikaans. He had clearly adapted to his new homeland in matters of language, too.

Sitting next to her on the back seat, Sam kissed her brow. Lilian felt the outlines of the music box through the fabric of her bag. The others probably thought her hopelessly sentimental or at the very least eccentric for bringing it with her. But not Sam, who had secretly visited a leather goods store to have a new case made and surprised her with the gift. Yet Lilian could not bring herself to throw the old one away. Her father had told her that Margarethe—Emma—had made it in haste before the Kindertransport. That explained the uneven stitching, which Lilian had wondered about when she first saw it.

The three of them spoke little as they went through passport control. Lilian was relieved that her father did not have to face any further questions. In the waiting area she caught him staring at his newspaper without reading a word. His nervousness rubbed off on her and Sam.

When they finally took off, cirrostratus clouds were streaked across the blue sky. With mixed feelings, Lilian watched as the plane rapidly gained height. The white houses by the coast and the green terraced fields at the foot of Table Mountain shrank to tiny dots until they finally disappeared from view.

She closed her eyes and tried to compose herself. Her life in London seemed an eternity away, and for the first time she failed to feel the excitement that had always gripped her on returning home. London would soon belong to the past.

Her brooding inevitably called up thoughts of Margarethe. Lilian suppressed them firmly, distracting herself by picking up the book on gardening she was supposed to translate from German. But it wasn't long before she put it aside in favor of a bloodthirsty thriller, the only book that wouldn't put her to sleep before she reached the end of the first page.

Late that evening, London greeted them with pleasant temperatures and a warm breeze. On the way, they had decided to stay at Sam's, since he had a guest room. As a bonus, the landlord had just installed telephone lines. After a brief call to her grandmother, Lilian prepared supper. All three were bone-tired after the long journey and soon went to bed.

Lilian lay awake for a long while, however, going over and over her next moves, checking that there was nothing she had forgotten.

As they sat on Sam's terrace the following morning, drinking cups of strong tea, Peter asked, "Where shall we start?"

"I need to arrange to see the headmaster to talk about leaving my job, and I've also got to set about finding a new tenant for this place," Sam said. "Flats with gardens are really sought-after in London, so it shouldn't be a problem."

"That's good." As Lilian spoke, she pushed a yellowed document toward her father. "But let's talk about Margarethe. I suggest we concentrate first on the information provided by her death certificate."

Peter glanced at the piece of paper. "It shows the address of her foster parents in Hackney and the name of the doctor who issued it."

"Exactly," Lilian said.

"We could make inquiries with the British Medical Association," Sam suggested. "Their headquarters is about halfway between here and Hackney."

Lilian looked at the name. "Good idea. Let's ask them about Dr. Ernest Cook. With any luck, he'll still be alive and might have some information for us."

"It's only a half-hour trip on the Underground from Paddington Station," Sam said.

Peter clapped his hands. "Then let's not lose any time."

A little later, they arrived at the venerable building with its richly ornamented façade. They were asked to wait in the reception area, and Lilian felt transported back a few months to the Lübeck records office, where she had walked down an apparently endless corridor with similar impatience. She had been trying to trace Alma Schott, the resolute housekeeper who had loyally served Lilian's great-uncle Max. Max Blumenthal—her grandfather's handsome brother, who had loved women as much as he did Cuban cigars. Her father and Lotte often spoke affectionately about him. One night, when his beloved home city of Lübeck was being bombed, he had taken his own life. Lilian deeply regretted never having known him.

She took a deep breath. From the experience tracking down her family, Lilian had learned that finding this Dr. Ernest Cook could prove to be like looking for the proverbial needle in a haystack.

An elderly man in a neat suit invited them into his office and listened to their request.

"Of course I'd be pleased to help you, but I'm afraid that not every British doctor is a member of our association."

"We realize that," Peter replied. "But we'd be grateful for any information you might have on Dr. Cook."

The official stood. "I'll check the archives. Could you come back around noon, please? It'll take some time."

Lilian thanked him. On the way there, she had noticed a real estate agency, and she decided to use the time to put the flat she'd inherited from her adoptive parents on the market. The agent promised to inspect the property as soon as possible and get back to her.

By half past eleven, the threesome was sitting once again in the waiting area of the BMA. Another hour passed before the official returned with a few files under his arm.

"Here he is! Dr. Ernest William Cook, born 1892 in Exeter. During the war, he worked as a registered general practitioner in Fulham. Shortly after the war ended, he terminated his membership with us. He'd probably retired by then." The man scribbled something on the page of a notepad and handed it to Lilian. "This is his last address known to us. Does it help you?"

"It certainly does. Thank you very much for your efforts," Lilian replied.

"Good luck."

As they left the building, Sam put an arm around Lilian's waist. "Show me." He studied the piece of paper. "Since Chelsea's in the opposite direction, let's go and look for Margarethe's foster parents in Hackney first."

They reached Sutton Place three quarters of an hour later. Lilian gazed at the soot-blackened houses against a background of soulless concrete blocks and empty warehouses. She shivered despite the summer sunshine.

"A dismal place," her father said as he looked for the house number.

"It certainly is," she replied. "I've been warned about this area; it's supposed to be dangerous at night."

They stopped in front of a brick house, and Peter rang the bell.

An elderly woman in slippers and an apron opened the door and stared at them through thick glasses. "What do you want?"

Despite her air of suspicion, she listened patiently to Lilian, then gave a hollow laugh.

"I'll tell you this for nothing: those damned Nazis didn't leave a single wall standing here in Hackney! They turned the whole street to rubble. Those who survived had nowhere to live. You won't find anyone left here from those times."

The woman made to shut the door, but Lilian raised her hand. "Please wait a moment. I'm looking for the Jackson family. Alfred and Daisy Jackson. They had a foster daughter. Do you know them?"

The old woman appeared to be thinking. "Jackson," she muttered under her breath.

"They lived at this address until 1940," Lilian prompted cautiously.

"I don't remember. My memory isn't what it was, you know. Anyway, I moved away before the war broke out and didn't come back until the fifties." She blinked. "But my younger sister lived through the Blitz. She never forgets a thing. Just a moment."

Lilian watched the old woman shuffle into the house. A few moments later, she returned with a torn-off corner of newspaper. "This is Helen's telephone number. She might know something. She lives in Surrey."

"Thank you very much."

As the door closed, Lilian looked at her companions. "Better than nothing, I suppose. What shall we do now?"

Peter rubbed the tip of his nose. "Let's have lunch. We need a break."

Lilian kissed her father's cheek. "Great idea."

That afternoon, after a fortifying lunch, they set off for Chelsea.

On the train, Lilian hugged her bag tightly. The weight of the silver music box had a calming effect on her. She gave a slight smile. It would have made her grandfather Johann happy to know the huge significance of his gift to her and the rest of the family.

"Don't you agree?" Her father's voice interrupted her thoughts.

"Sorry, I wasn't listening. What'd you say?"

Sam grinned. "The fact the man's a doctor could make our search easier. People will probably know him."

"Let's hope so," Lilian replied.

Outside Dr. Cook's last-known address, the busy noise of the city was muted. Lilian looked around. Between some new houses and a row of older façades, she saw some Victorian buildings that had apparently survived the war without any serious damage. She double-checked the piece of paper and pointed to a two-story house on the right. "It must be that one."

There was an insurance office on the ground floor, but the owner had only been there a year and had never heard of Dr. Cook.

"You'd better ask upstairs. I think the Allister family's lived there for quite a while."

Lilian rang, and the door was answered by a lady in her thirties with long, fiery-red hair tied with colorful ribbons.

"Dr. Cook? I've no idea. Can you wait a moment? I'll ask my parents."

"That's very kind of you. We'll be happy to wait," Sam replied.

They soon heard voices from inside. Lilian found it hard to control her impatience.

At last the red-haired woman returned, accompanied by a bent, elderly man who leaned heavily on a stick. She went back inside, leaving him to stare at the three of them with curiosity.

"Are you related to the doctor?"

"No, my sister was a patient of his. It's really important that I speak to him," Lilian said quickly. Although it wasn't exactly a lie, she felt uncomfortable not being entirely straight with the kindly-looking man.

"I see. Yes, Dr. Cook used to live downstairs. But that was ages ago. He must have moved out not long after the war. We ran into each other a few times after that, but he wasn't much of a talker."

"Do you know where he moved to?" Peter asked.

The old man snorted. "No. He never told us anything. He was a strange fellow. Every morning he left the house at seven on the dot, not a minute before or after. He always wore a suit and hat, even in summer. No one ever came to visit him. It was as if he had no friends because he was always so stiff and formal—he was an odd man. Then he vanished overnight, without giving notice. Our landlord had to have the flat cleared."

The three visitors exchanged a puzzled look.

The man beckoned Lilian closer and lowered his voice. "If you ask me, something wasn't right." As he spoke, he revealed a set of decaying teeth. "But we never managed to get the story out of our landlord."

Lilian gave him Sam's address. "Just in case you think of anything else. Would you be so kind as to tell us where we can find your landlord?"

"But of course. His name is Malcolm Jones, and he lives just a few streets away, at 60B, Sloane Avenue." The old man took a card from the hall table. "Office hours Monday and Wednesday, three to five p.m." He gestured back inside. "You'll have to excuse me now. My wife's calling, and it's a well-known fact that a man should always keep his better half happy."

"Very wise. Thank you for your help," she said.

Lilian and her companions were back on the sidewalk outside.

Sam was the first to gather his thoughts. "What do you make of that?"

"It certainly sounds mysterious, if you can believe the neighbor," Peter said, opening his umbrella against the drizzle that had just begun.

"Why shouldn't we believe him? He's got nothing to gain from lying," Lilian said, pulling up her hood. "I just wonder why someone like Cook would vanish into thin air."

"You're right." Sam hooked his arm through hers as they hurried toward the nearest Underground station. "But we ought to talk about it back home."

They settled down in Sam's living room. Lilian stretched out her legs and rested her aching feet on a footstool. "Maybe the doctor had an accident."

Peter sipped his lemonade. "It's possible. But if it had been fatal, they'd have informed his family."

Sam frowned. "But the man said no one ever came to see him. What if he didn't have any family?"

"Under those circumstances, the police would inform the landlord," Peter said.

Lilian nodded. "Probably so. But he could have been living under an assumed name—you do, after all."

"You think he might be Jewish?"

"Why not, Papa? Maybe he was the only one in his family to escape the Nazis!"

Sam smiled. "That seems highly improbable, Lil. If he were Jewish, the doctor would have gone into hiding before the war began."

Lilian drew up her legs and said nothing. It looked as though every trail would lead nowhere.

Chapter 3

A few days went by. Sam went back to teaching, having handed in his notice, and agreed with his head teacher that he could leave after a few weeks. Lilian sat at her desk, working on the translation of the gardening book. One dull morning, she couldn't stop thinking about the mystery of Dr. Cook.

The telephone rang.

"I thought I'd pay a quick visit to the post office and call you before I open up the Blue Heart," her grandmother said over the crackly line. "Can you hear me?"

"Barely." Lilian pressed the receiver to her ear. "How are you? Is there any news?"

Every time Lilian heard Lotte's voice on the telephone, she was reminded of that fateful day a few weeks ago when her life had been turned upside down. The search for her family had dragged on fruitlessly until her great-uncle's former housekeeper gave her his address book, which she had hoped would reveal her family's whereabouts in South Africa. Max had indeed noted Peter and Lotte's address, encoding it cleverly so that no one would uncover their disguised identities. Lilian would never forget the moment when she heard her grandmother's voice for the first time on the other end of the telephone line.

"Come home, little one, and we'll explain everything," Lotte had said. "You've made an old woman very happy."

Smiling at the memory now, Lilian told her grandmother what had happened since they parted. "Do you have any idea who we can ask about Dr. Cook?"

"Wait a moment, I think something's occurred to Friedrich. He's standing right here next to me. Just a minute."

"The Red Cross," Friedrich said. "They could have members who remember working alongside him in the past."

"Thanks," Lilian said. "We hadn't thought of that."

"Keep in touch, little one. We've both got our fingers crossed."

As soon as she hung up, Lilian called the Red Cross and told them what she knew. They promised to look into it.

A little later, Lilian sat contemplating the music box on her desk, running her fingers over the intricate, lovingly crafted scene and the little boy on the lid. Strange though it may seem, simply touching the beautiful object made her feel connected to her grandfather, whom she only knew from a few photos, but who seemed to have poured so much of himself into crafting the piece.

Lilian turned back to her work. Sam was on a school trip that afternoon, and her father was visiting Chelsea again to talk to Cook's old landlord.

The sun was low over the rooftops, and Lilian was covering her typewriter when Peter returned and sat down beside her.

"What's up, Papa?"

He looked at her. "I can't believe how much you resemble your mother."

"So everyone keeps telling me. You know, I miss Mum and Margarethe, even though I can't remember them. Is that crazy?"

"No, Lilian, it's your heart speaking," he replied, pain clouding his features.

"Last night I dreamed of the two of them." She picked up the music box and pulled the little lever. A small bird sprang from the lid and twittered joyfully. Then the lid snapped shut.

They sat in silence together for a few long minutes. Then Lilian told him about Friedrich's suggestion, and how the Red Cross had been willing to help.

"That's great," Peter replied. "Oh, and Cousin Robert sends his regards. He says the shop's surviving fine without me. I also phoned August. He's happy to be living with his family and spending so much time with his grandchildren. He loves Regensburg. It's much nicer than Hamburg, he says."

Lilian smiled and pictured August, standing upright despite his injury. *I wonder if he'll teach the little ones to ride a bike on that crazy bicycle he adapted for himself.*

"August wishes us luck. He only regrets that he can't help us in our search."

Lilian smiled again. Knowing her father's and grandfather's old friend, even his stiff leg wouldn't have stopped him, if the doctors hadn't forbidden him from making long journeys. "I can believe it. But why didn't you call from here?"

Peter waved her away. "Long-distance calls cost too much. I've been putting money aside to cover our calls to Cape Town—I wouldn't want to leave Sam with a horrendous bill."

"You don't need to worry about that, Papa." She looked up at him. "Perhaps we can visit Regensburg on our way home. I'd love to see August again. I'm sure he'll want to know everything we've been doing."

"Yes, let's do that, love," her father said softly. "I wouldn't miss any opportunity to see him. Who knows how much time we have left."

"Too true. Did you find anything out in Chelsea?"

He smiled. "I thought you were never going to ask."

"You look pleased with yourself."

"I am. It was a trip worth making."

"Out with it, then! What have you found?"

"It's only a tiny detail, but it could make all the difference."

Lilian elbowed him in the ribs. "What do I have to do to make you tell me?"

"Very well." Peter turned serious. "About a week after Dr. Cook vanished, Mr. Jones, the landlord, was visited by two police officers."

"Police officers?" she echoed, dumbfounded.

"Yes. They asked if he knew where Cook could be."

"The police were searching for the doctor?"

"That's right. I told Mr. Jones about Margarethe—Emma. He also lost a daughter in the war, and I think that's why he confided in me about the police. He says he doesn't like to talk about it much, since rumors about Cook could harm his reputation."

"I can understand that." Lilian looked away. "Did the police tell him anything?"

"No, that was all he knew." Peter stood. "But we can ask the police to help us."

"Yes, in theory," she said pensively. "But I doubt they'll just turn over information if we don't have anything specific about Cook."

"You're right," Peter said. "We'll keep putting the pieces of the jigsaw together one by one, and it'll make sense in time." He brushed her cheek with his finger.

"I really hope so. I don't think my dreams of Margarethe will stop haunting me until I've done all I can to shed light on the last years of her life."

He raised her chin. "We've found each other already. Don't forget that, my strong, stubborn daughter."

"It still amazes me."

"Later, I'm going to ring the sister of that old woman in Hackney. But I'll leave you in peace for now. I've kept you from your work for long enough."

Lilian watched him walk to the kitchen for a bite to eat. Her father's simple presence in the next room sent a wave of happiness through her.

That evening, they discovered that Helen Stanton had known the Jackson family a little. Her husband and Alfred Jackson had worked at the docks together for years. After the night of the bombing, the Jacksons had moved to Stratford, to Mr. Jackson's late parents' house. Mrs. Stanton couldn't remember the exact address, only that it was on Langthorne Road. "You'll need a good deal of patience if you're just going to knock on doors till you find them," she had warned Peter on the phone.

Lilian was thrilled to have a real lead. She went with Sam and Peter to Stratford the next day. Fortunately, a summer storm had cleared the muggy air, which lightened their steps.

Mrs. Stanton hadn't exaggerated about Langthorne Road's length, and they knocked on a dozen doors until someone finally gave them the right house number. They stopped in front of a plain brick house with Tottenham Hotspur team scarves adorning an upstairs window.

A man in his sixties opened the door. His gray hair was combed neatly back, and his shirt stretched over a generous paunch. "Can I help you?"

Lilian introduced herself and Sam. "Are you Alfred Jackson?"

"I am. What do you want?"

"This is my father, Peter Dölling. My sister lived with you for a while in the late thirties. I believe you knew her as Emma. Could we ask you a few questions?"

He considered her coolly. "All right. If you don't mind keeping it short. We're expecting visitors."

"Of course. We won't disturb you for long," Peter said with his most charming smile.

As they entered, they were struck by the smell of old smoke and mildew. Alfred Jackson showed them in and invited them to sit at the dining table. A young man in a suit, whom Lilian estimated to be in his midthirties, rose from the sofa, disturbing three tabby cats that had been sleeping next to him.

"Daisy, come in here!" Alfred called to his wife. "This is our son, Billy."

The young man tucked a chin-length strand of hair behind his ear, gave them a friendly smile, and joined them at the table.

The lady of the house entered the room. She had obviously been preparing dinner. She wiped her hands on her grubby apron and looked inquisitively at each of them in turn.

"These good people are looking for information about Emma," her husband explained.

"Emma who?"

"Emma Dölling. You know, the little girl who was killed during the Blitz."

She looked past them out of the window. "Oh yes, that poor little thing from Germany. What do you want to know?"

"She was my sister," Lilian replied firmly. She took the old photo from her purse and laid it on the table. "This is her. Please can you tell me everything you remember?"

"We've raised twenty-one children. Some of them lived with us for a few years, others only briefly," Mr. Jackson said. "Besides, it's an age since then, Miss Morrison."

"I realize that." Lilian stroked a cat that was rubbing up against her leg, then turned to Mrs. Jackson. "But please try. It would mean such a lot to me."

The woman took the photo and studied it for a long moment, while Billy peered over her shoulder, his face showing not the slightest emotion. Lilian clutched the bag containing her music box, which she had anxiously stowed in there before leaving the house.

"If I remember rightly," Mrs. Jackson said, "Emma was very reserved and for a long time refused to speak English. If she was in a bad mood, she wouldn't eat for a whole day. She could understand us full well; she just didn't want to talk to us."

Goose bumps ran up and down Lilian's arms. She exchanged a look of consternation with her father.

Sam took up the thread. "How did she do at school? Did she make any friends?"

"What do you think, Mr.—?" Mr. Jackson folded his arms across his chest.

"Flynt. Sam Flynt."

"What do you think, Mr. Flynt?" he repeated. "It was hard for the children from Germany to fit in; they didn't speak our language when they first arrived. On top of that, most of them were Jews. It stood to reason that our English kids didn't know where to begin with them." He shook his big head. "None of us could get much out of her."

Lilian had a vivid mental image of her sister, and it was nothing like the picture painted by her former foster father. Her eyes filled with tears. "Did she—did she die right away, or did she suffer?"

"Emma would have felt nothing. It all happened so quickly," Mr. Jackson said. "When the sirens went off, we all went to the Underground station. She suddenly ran back up the steps. I yelled at her to come back, but the girl took no notice of me."

"She wanted to rescue our dog," Mrs. Jackson said quietly. "He always used to sleep close by her."

Lilian searched the woman's face in vain for any sign of sadness, or at least a show of feeling, and immediately chided herself. The child's death was a quarter of a century in the past.

"Just a moment." She heard a hint of sharpness in her father's voice. "Didn't you run after her?"

"How could we?" Mr. Jackson said. "The first bombs were already beginning to fall. And Emma wasn't our only foster child at the time; we had three others to look after."

"Of course," Lilian replied, trying to stay calm. "Tell me, do you remember Dr. Ernest Cook?"

Mr. Jackson's face froze. "Uh, no. Who's that?"

"He's the doctor who registered Emma's death," Peter said. "You must have spoken to him."

"I had to go and identify her, sure," Mr. Jackson said, "and the doctor there offered his condolences. That was it. We didn't know him. Is there anything else?"

"Yes, if you don't mind," Lilian said. "I'm sure you must still be in touch with some of your foster children?"

Mrs. Jackson's features softened. "Yes, a few of them. It makes us happy, of course." She looked lovingly at her son, who was following the conversation in silence.

Lilian turned her attention to Billy. "Do you remember anything about my sister?"

"Sorry," he replied after a slight hesitation. "I don't recognize the girl in that photo."

"That's a pity. I'd hoped so much—" She had a sudden idea. "I'd really appreciate if you could give me the names and addresses of the children who were living with you at the same time as Emma."

Mr. Jackson drummed his fingers impatiently on the table. "No way. We don't give their addresses out. It wouldn't be fair—we don't know whether the children would want it."

"It's a matter of principle," his wife insisted.

Lilian took a deep breath. "Does Emma at least have a grave we can visit?"

Mrs. Jackson's cheeks took on an unhealthy red color. "After that dreadful night, the streets of Hackney were strewn with corpses, Miss Morrison. Lots of people were killed by the Germans, and the bombings went on for weeks afterwards. There was no time for grieving or proper funerals."

An ice-cold hand gripped Lilian's heart. "She was thrown into a mass grave?" she whispered.

"Like all the others," Mr. Jackson replied. "They wanted to prevent disease from spreading." He looked at his watch. "Is that everything? We're expecting guests."

"Yes. Thank you." Lilian placed a card on the table. "Here's my contact information in case you remember anything else."

A short time later, Lilian, Sam, and Peter were sitting at a table outside a café across the street, staring pensively at the Jacksons' front door.

"Strange people," Sam began.

"Their cats seemed better cared for than they did themselves," she said.

"I can't believe it," Peter said sharply. "How is it they didn't make any attempt to stop her? If they had, she could still be alive today."

Sam nodded. "In their defense, they probably didn't have time. It was probably chaos with the bombing."

"Parents act instinctively if their child's in danger," Lilian said. "Even if it costs them their own lives."

"Real parents, anyway," her father said.

"She was in their care," she said vehemently. "Nothing else matters."

They remained sunk in thought for a while before Lilian gave voice to a thought she couldn't drive from her mind. "Papa, can you imagine Margarethe as a stubborn, unfriendly girl?"

He smiled in that way that always pierced her to the heart. "To an extent. Your sister was strong-willed and knew exactly how to wrap us around her little finger. But she was clever about it, and was always open and friendly to everyone."

Sam shook his head. "Something doesn't feel quite right to me. Open children are interested in making friends, and don't take long to get their bearings in a new environment." He gulped down the rest of his juice. "Though I'm sure the tragic circumstances affected her behavior."

"What did they do to you, Margarethe?" Lilian said with a moan, burying her face in her hands.

"Come on, Lil. Let's go home." Sam placed a few coins on the table.

"We've done enough for today," her father added. But she could tell from his expression that he was plagued by similar thoughts.

Chapter 4

On the way home, they said little. Once at the house, Lilian made straight for the kitchen, eager to keep her hands busy with cooking. The sounds of "Twist and Shout" by Brian Poole & the Tremeloes blared from the living room. She was about to pour beaten eggs into a pan to make an omelet when the doorbell rang.

"I'll get it," Sam called.

A moment later, she heard a third man's voice. Lilian switched off the stove and hurried into the living room.

She came to an abrupt halt. "Hello, Billy," she said to the Jacksons' son. "What brings you here?"

"I thought I'd stop by on my way home. I told my parents I had to babysit our baby son this evening," Billy said, looking at each of them in turn. "Can I have a quick word with you?"

Sam indicated the sofa. "Of course."

Lilian watched their guest, forcing herself to stay calm. Contrary to the impression he had given an hour and a half ago, he seemed nervous.

After they'd all sat down, he gave a crooked smile. "I wasn't totally honest with you, Miss Morrison."

"In what way?"

"My parents don't like people poking around in their private lives, so I kept my mouth shut when you were asking about Emma."

Her pulse quickened. "You did know my sister?"

"I did." He shrugged. "I was already living with the Jacksons when she came."

Lilian caught her breath. "You're not their biological son?"

Sam offered Billy a drink, but he declined. "I'm their foster son. My full name's William Field. When I was ten, the police took me away from my home and sent me to live with the Jacksons. It was a relief, I can tell you." He gestured dismissively. "But that's got nothing to do with this."

Wondering what it would take to make a child glad to be taken from his family, Lilian exchanged meaningful looks with Sam and her father. "Did you also come to England with the Kindertransport?"

"No, I'm a Londoner. But there were a few Jews from Germany in my class at school, and I had some idea of what they'd gone through. I felt sorry for Emma."

Her father fidgeted anxiously. "Please tell us everything you know."

William crossed his legs. "I don't think my parents ever understood Emma. It hurt my mother's feelings that the little girl rejected every attempt to get close to her."

A shadow passed across Peter's face. "What do you mean? That doesn't sound like my daughter at all."

William thought for a moment. "She was traumatized. We all found her a bit strange." He began telling them about the girl's habit of huddling away in corners for hours. If anyone tried to entice her from her hiding place, she'd scream. If they tried to comfort her, she'd scream more. William described the family's helplessness in the face of such peculiar behavior. "We thought things would get better with time, but they didn't. I sometimes heard her singing German songs to our little dog. And then—"

"What?" Lilian broke in.

William cleared his throat. "Sometimes Emma had a really vacant expression; she'd go to her room and say the same sentences over and over again. I was learning German, and I could understand her."

"What did she say?" Peter asked breathlessly.

"My name is Emma. Only Emma."

Lilian suddenly remembered her father telling her how difficult it had been to impress upon the child before they fled that she was no longer called Margarethe Blumenthal, but Emma Dölling, and her parents were Charlotte and Peter. It must have been painful for the adults to give up their identities and assume the role of strangers, but a child like Margarethe must have been overwhelmed and bewildered. "My God," she said, overcome by horror.

Her father had turned white as a sheet.

"She'd say it again and again for minutes at a time, as though she was learning lines by heart," William continued. "Sometimes I tried to talk to her, because it scared me. But she never responded." He looked at Peter. "Does that make any sense to you?"

"It certainly does," Peter murmured, pain hardening his features.

"Because of her strange habits, our brothers and sisters kept out of her way," William said. "They were glad when she crawled off to her room. But she trusted our neighbor on the ground floor more, maybe because he spoke German. It all made me feel so sorry for her; she was so homesick."

All at once, Lilian found the air in the room hot and suffocating.

"What made you think that?" Sam asked into the silence.

"She'd stand for hours at the window," William replied. "I suppose she was waiting for someone to come and fetch her."

"Excuse me a moment." Peter rose stiffly and hurried out.

Frowning, Lilian watched him go. "This is very hard on my father."

"I understand. Is there anything else I can do to help you?"

"Yes," she said. "Please tell us honestly, did the Jacksons care for my sister despite everything?"

He looked serious. "It's hard to say. I think they wanted to like her. She was an awkward child, unlike me." William told them about his childhood tendency to want to do everything right for his foster parents, out of fear that they might send him away. "They made no secret of the fact that I was their favorite, both of them. It made me feel uncomfortable—the other kids were jealous because I got away with more than they did. But I was grateful to my parents for what they did for me."

"Are any of the other children who were there at the same time as Emma still in touch with the Jacksons?" Sam asked.

Peter returned, looking more in control of himself, and sat down close to Lilian.

"Not really," William replied. "One of my brothers visits them at Christmas; the other lives and works in Wales. And my sister, a year older than me, hasn't had any contact with them for years. But I'm sure she'd remember Emma." He took a piece of paper from his jacket pocket. "She's a legal secretary. I've written her phone number down here. And there's my address, too."

Sally Russell, Lancaster, Lilian read. She looked up and saw William was smiling. "This is very kind, thank you."

"No problem. It's time I went, though. My wife will be waiting for me."

"Of course. Can I ask you one last question, William?"

"Fire away."

"How did the family cope with Emma's death?"

"No one missed her," he said regretfully. "Except me, perhaps."

Chapter 5

Ceara

Dublin

Sunlight sparkled off the previous night's rain on the rooftops, sidewalks, and trees of the leafy city. Schoolchildren sat in the parks, enjoying snacks. In the Temple Bar district, tourists wandered the ancient streets or sought respite from the summer heat in shady spots along the Liffey. Hardly any of this activity spread as far as the peaceful suburb of Ballygall, a little outside Dublin. Apart from a few determinedly crowing cockerels and the notes of a folk song drifting from an open window, no sound, not even a car engine, disturbed the peaceful noon stillness. The front yards of the neat little houses were well kept, and everyone knew everyone else.

The outbuilding of one of the houses on Collins Row had a striking red wooden door with a sign, "Ceara's Furniture," to indicate this was more than a garage.

Dust motes and specks of sawdust danced in the warm air of the workshop as Ceara Foley carved a claw-foot for her latest creation. The oak table, inlaid with an African-inspired design, was a custom order for one of her regular customers. When the young cabinetmaker had finished, she paused and blew from her brow a reddish-brown lock of hair that had worked loose from her braid.

As he did every lunchtime, Buzz O'Reilly stuck his head through the window.

"Good day to you, Mrs. Foley," he lisped, betraying a gap in his teeth.

He continued on his way without waiting for a reply. She watched as the old man with his weather-beaten face went on his way. Every day at the same time he ran into Mrs. Kinney and her two dogs on the other side of the road. Ceara suspected he timed it to the minute so he could enjoy chatting with the widow. The two of them saw her watching and waved. Later that afternoon, Mrs. Kinney's teenagers, Brenda and Cayden, would come home from school, bickering at the tops of their voices until their mother gave them the sharp end of her tongue.

Ceara found herself smiling. She liked these scenes that repeated themselves over and over in the lovely rhythm of everyday life. She was even more fond of the warmheartedness of her neighbors, although she avoided getting too close. Their unshakable warmth was one of the reasons she could never imagine leaving her homeland.

Ceara looked around her workshop. It had belonged to her foster father who, for forty years, made practical wooden furniture for ordinary customers. This had not been enough for Ceara, and so, after his death ten years ago, she had begun to make bespoke pieces alongside the everyday items. She paused and studied her claw-foot with satisfaction.

Ceara's eyes stung with fatigue. The previous night, she had wandered through the house as she so often did. She couldn't remember for how many years she had woken in the night drenched in sweat, not daring to go back to sleep because of the recurring dream. It shook her to the core; she still felt as though something powerful was hurling her through the air and dropping her at incredible speed.

The dream always began like a fairy tale. Ceara was running through a meadow of grass and sweet-smelling flowers beneath a silvery sky that shimmered with a hint of the deeper blue of the hour before dusk. Somewhere in the distance she could hear a child's carefree laughter, which took her under its spell and drew her onward. The chubby-cheeked boy, sitting on his usual fallen log, suddenly appeared. On his lap he was holding a thick book with a silver cover. Laughing, he raised a conductor's baton and waved it in the air. As if following some silent command, a few birds appeared from nowhere and flew around him, twittering brightly. In the dream, Ceara always stood in fascination, wondering what this strange boy was doing there. He beckoned her closer, and she realized that the birdsong formed a lively melody—a melody that made the blood surge through her veins. Her legs moved unbidden, and she tapped out the rhythm with her feet, turning in circles and feeling lighter than she ever had before. She sang along with the birds, her arms thrown wide. But the earth suddenly began to vibrate as though the god of the underworld was angry with them. The birds vanished, and her own frightened cries cut discordantly across the harmonious tune. There was a rumbling in the air, coming nearer. A bloodcurdling blast sent waves of pain through her body. The world around her seemed to explode . . . That was the moment she always awoke, terrified.

Ceara's thoughts wandered back to 1940, when she had woken, seriously injured, in a Dublin hospital. She still recalled with horror the sight of her seriously cut and injured body, and the tears that refused to dry up. She would have scars, the doctors told her as kindly as possible. The bombing had brought down an iron girder that pierced her lower abdomen. It was only thanks to the doctors' swift action that Ceara had been saved by an emergency operation, literally at the last minute. She should be grateful to have survived.

All Ceara could remember was compressed down to that blast wave in her dreams. The day she came to, an unfamiliar woman had come to sit by her bed and taken her hand. Her parents had died in the bombing, the dark-haired woman had told her cautiously. She, Rhona Ward, and her husband, Brady, were now her foster parents and would take good care of her. And they had done exactly that. They had always been by her side when she cried in her sleep or tried desperately to remember and come to terms with her scarred body. After the Wards had done all they could and it was still not enough, they consulted the best specialists. The phenomenon was not a new one, of course: many war victims suffered from nightmares, terrors, and amnesia. The Wards were given advice on treatment methods that Ceara had been unable to pronounce. But even now, twenty-three years later, none of their efforts had brought back her memory or stilled her fears.

Muttering a curse, Ceara brushed a mosquito from her hand. That had not been all. Shortly after her recovery, she'd been told that they'd had to remove her uterus and that she could never have children. As a nine-year-old, she had failed to take in the significance of this fact, but now the painful realization struck her every time she looked in the mirror.

Ceara switched the radio on to drive away her gloomy thoughts, and measured the second table leg. There was something incredibly satisfying about working with tools and watching her skilled hands gradually transform wood and nails into something unique.

Ceara hummed along to the music as she sanded down the edges. She was suddenly whirled around and found herself looking into Aidan's brown eyes.

He looked exceptionally handsome in his fireman's uniform, and even after five years of marriage, he still made her pulse quicken.

"I wanted to give my lovely wife another kiss before I go to work," he said with a gentle smile.

She threw her arms around his neck and kissed him tenderly. The wood shavings that fell into his hair and onto his jacket didn't seem to bother him in the slightest.

"Are you going to wish me a quiet shift?" he asked as he stroked her cheek.

"Very quiet. Take care."

The bell over the door rang and Caitlin Dunn, the daughter of Aidan's coworker, came in with her small son on her hip. "Hello, you two! Is our rocking horse ready?"

"Ready and waiting for its new owner."

Ceara went to fetch it and handed it over to her customer. The little blond-haired boy gave a whoop of joy when he caught sight of what Ceara was carrying, and reached out his chubby arms toward the colorful cap she always wore when working. She sat him on the rocking horse and smiled, but felt a knot in her chest.

Aidan drew her briefly to him. "I've got to go. See you later." He turned to Caitlin. "See you on Saturday at the Shamrock?"

The Shamrock was Aidan's favorite pub. Whenever time allowed, he'd go to the weekend jam sessions there with his friends Lugh and Padraig. Aidan played the banjo and sang, Lugh was a virtuoso fiddle and guitar player, and Padraig embraced his uilleann pipes like a lover.

"You can be sure of that," Caitlin said. "What do I owe you?" she asked Ceara once Aidan had left.

A little later, Ceara was on her own again. She turned the radio up and forced her attention back to the table she was making. Why were her hands shaking, for God's sake? She certainly couldn't do any delicate work like this.

Since Aidan would be home late, she spent the evening with Rhona, who lived next door. To look at the lively pensioner it would be impossible to tell she was well into her sixties, even though fate had not always been kind to her. Since her husband's death, Rhona had lived modestly, as Brady's workshop had provided her with just enough for the necessities. But she had never lost her sense of humor, and her optimism could often conjure a smile onto Ceara's face.

"You're thoughtful today, my love," Rhona said. She turned down the sound on the new television that Ceara had bought for her birthday.

"I'm a bit tired, that's all," she said. "But I want to wait up for Aidan. I don't like going to sleep till he's home."

When the detective drama ended, she stood and kissed Rhona on the cheek. "See you tomorrow."

Ceara went inside the little house she and Aidan had moved to when they married. She didn't turn the light on but lit a few candles in the living room, picked up her notebook from the table, and looked at her design for the inlay. It wasn't long before Ceara threw the notebook aside and stared darkly into space.

That was how Aidan found her when he came home. Without speaking, he served himself a bowl of the stew Ceara had made for him, opened two bottles of beer, and came to sit by her. Ceara laid her head on his shoulder and accepted the beer he held out.

"There was an explosion over in Ballymount," he said. "Probably a gas leak. It's lucky no one was hurt."

Ceara murmured agreement.

"Then there was a kitten that had climbed high into a tree in Phoenix Park and didn't dare come down." Aidan laughed. "The little beggar kept us busy for a whole hour. Davy's hands look like he's been fighting a tiger."

Ceara stared out of the window. "Kittens are lively."

He took her face in his hands. "Is something wrong?"

"Everything's fine, love," she said absently and put her beer down.

Aidan's expression darkened, his lovely lips narrowing. She hadn't seen him so angry for a long time.

"I don't want to play anymore, Ceara. I've had enough!"

The coldness of his voice made her shudder. "What's the matter, Aidan?"

Even the candlelight couldn't soften his stony expression. He put an arm around her shoulders. "I can't watch you tormenting yourself any longer. It's been like this as long as we've known each other."

"Well," she said, more sharply than she intended, "what do you suggest? That I pull myself together? If that was possible, I'd have done it ages ago!"

"I know." He shook her gently, worry clouding his eyes. "But look at yourself. You're getting thinner by the day. You don't eat or sleep nearly enough."

She avoided his intense gaze.

"I've understood for a long time," he continued more calmly. "You want to erase your past. But it's got to stop."

"What's that supposed to mean, Mr. Smart-Aleck?" Ceara was seething. "You sound like Dr. Hamlin." Her foster parents had consulted the psychiatrist shortly after she had come to live with them, but despite their attempts to persuade her, she had always refused any kind of treatment. "Why should I be bothered with the same old nonsense?" Her voice faltered. "I want to live in the here and now, with you and Rhona, not rummage around in the past."

"You don't get what I'm saying, do you?" He stood abruptly and paced up and down the living room. "Dr. Hamlin has been recommending therapy for years. With his help, you might succeed in overcoming your fears."

"I don't want to remember what happened before the bombing, Aidan! Especially not my family. They're dead, and the less I know about them the better."

"You're deceiving yourself, my love." He drew her into his arms. "It's time to face the truth."

Chapter 6

Lotte

Sea Point, Cape Town

The man at the post office had a hard time trying to reach Lotte's family in London. It took several attempts before she heard her son's voice telling her the news about Dr. Cook's unexplained disappearance and the conversations with the Jacksons and William Field. She could tell from the way he spoke so rapidly that he was trying to hide his feelings.

But she also knew there was no point pressing him about it. He probably didn't want to upset her.

"You've already found out quite a lot." Lotte tried for a lighthearted tone. "I can't wait to hear whether William's sister remembers any more about Margarethe."

"Neither can we, Mama. How are things at the Blue Heart?"

Lotte assured him that everything was running like clockwork both at the women's drop-in center and his shop, and that all was quiet. "You'd best put Lilian on quickly, or this call will get expensive."

"I will. Speak to you soon, Mama."

Peter passed the receiver to Lilian.

"Hello, Grandma," she said. "I'm so looking forward to seeing you again and playing with the children at the center. I do feel for them."

"Oh, my dear. I do miss you." Lotte looked outside without seeing. "Little Michael's been asking about you. But can I ask you something? What's the matter with your father?"

Her granddaughter sighed. "Papa didn't tell you everything."

As Lilian quickly filled her in, Lotte leaned heavily against the wall that shielded the post office telephone from curious eyes.

"Oh God, our poor little Margarethe." A sob rose in her throat, and she had to swallow several times before she could speak. "Not to be missed by anyone is the worst fate I could imagine. Her name would be forgotten forever if we didn't grieve for her. Children and grandchildren should never die before their parents."

Lilian agreed.

"It must have affected Peter badly."

"He's deeply shaken, Grandma."

Lotte's heart felt heavy. "I wish I was with you."

"I know, but the women at the Blue Heart need you. Don't worry. I'll call again at the end of the week, and for now I'm sending you a hug. Give Friedrich my love, too."

"I will. Speak to you soon."

Lotte walked, stiff-backed, from the post office onto Regent Road. A few passersby with broad-brimmed hats nodded to her. They were Boers like her late husband Antoon, but unlike him, they believed they belonged to a ruling class. Lotte turned away. Lilian's news had thrown her, even though she had never known Margarethe, as her granddaughter had come into the world after Lotte had left Germany for Sea Point. But Peter had brought Margarethe to life for her with his detailed descriptions. How tragic to learn that such a bright, loving child had remained an outsider in England right until she died.

Lotte walked briskly along Main Road with its bright, multistory buildings, past cafés and ice cream shops, before turning onto leafy St. John's Road, where she admired the magical view of Signal Hill. She was used to making the half-hour journey on foot—it kept her joints and muscles supple—but today she was pleased to leave the busy street behind. After emigrating, she had lived near here with her sister-in-law, Martha, and Martha's husband, Hermann. She soon reached the low-rise, sky-blue building on Clifford Road with its palm trees and purple-flowering jacarandas. This was where her drop-in center was housed, a good quarter hour's walk from the cozy house on the Atlantic that Antoon had bequeathed to her. A few inviting tubs of flowers and colorful stone statues with children's faces guided people to the welcoming center. It had formerly been Antoon's restaurant, but she had converted it after his death.

Lotte busied herself preparing a casserole in the Blue Heart kitchen, since she knew from experience that a few of her charges would turn up hungry at lunchtime. Offering meals was also a good way of encouraging the women to talk. Since the introduction of apartheid, black South Africans had been forbidden from spending time in the whites' residential districts. They were treated like scum, which inevitably invoked memories of Nazi Germany in Lotte. It was horrific. She treasured her contact with the locals from various ethnic groups and always saw it as an enrichment of her life.

A sudden sound tore her from her thoughts: Friedrich clapping his hands as he entered the kitchen. "I'm bored. Can I help?"

"You must be a mind reader," she said warmly. "If you could chop the meat and vegetables, I'll go and see to the guest rooms that were vacated yesterday evening."

"Gladly," Friedrich said as he tied an apron around his middle. "Off you go; I can manage this."

By the time Lotte had finished and was bringing the dirty linen to the laundry room, just over an hour later, the house was filled with the alluring smell of frying meat, garlic, and onions.

As they were setting the table in the dining room, a young black woman approached the entrance. She was wearing a colorful but dusty kaftan, and her hair was bound up in a skillfully wound turban. She couldn't have been more than twenty, but her face was lined with exhaustion. She staggered, caressing the head of the little child she was carrying at her breast, and kept looking around anxiously.

The woman's wide eyes turned to Lotte. "May I come in, *meesteres?*"

Lotte was taken aback at hearing the respectful Afrikaans word for mistress. She glanced around outside, then waved the woman in. "Go through to the back. Quickly, before anyone sees you."

The baby, who looked around two months old, made smacking sounds with its lips as Lotte showed the woman to a room, where she set down the fabric bundle that was clearly her only luggage. "You look tired. Rest here before you do anything else. We can talk later."

The young woman seemed too exhausted to reply, as she immediately stretched out on the bed with the baby in her arms. *"Dankie,"* she murmured. Her eyes closed, and Lotte tiptoed out.

Friedrich had been watching, and now led her into the kitchen, shaking his head. "Are you out of your mind?" he whispered as he glanced around to make sure they were alone. "You can't allow any blacks in here. What if someone saw you?"

"But no one did," Lotte said, trying to pacify him. "Don't get so worked up, Friedrich. What's wrong with allowing the poor thing to rest here for a few hours? No one but you knows—unless you intend to betray me."

"Certainly not," Friedrich said. "But you have to send her away as soon as possible if you don't want any trouble."

A few other visitors now found their way to the drop-in center. Among them were two girls, scarcely more than sixteen, one of them heavily pregnant and the other with a six-month-old. They sat down at a corner table, keeping to themselves. Lotte guessed they must be runaways. She turned out to be right; their families had thrown them out, and since then, they had been living on the streets, trying to get by on their own. They were finding it hard, to judge from their neglected appearance. Lotte showed them to the bathroom and offered them clean clothes, then she washed the baby. The young mother might be in need, but the little one was well fed. Later, she discovered that the young woman had fallen in love with a black man and was no longer accepted by his or her own family. Lotte frequently heard stories like this. Maybe she was particularly moved by the fates of such people because she had experienced hatred and rejection herself. Shortly after meeting her, Friedrich had asked why she didn't settle down to enjoy her autumn years with her feet up rather than choose such a difficult, exhausting occupation. Her reply was simple: she wanted to do something useful with her time, something fulfilling.

When the other visitors had finished eating and the mothers of older children had gone to the playroom, the smell of food drew the young black woman from her room, the baby sleeping in a wrap on her chest. Lotte beckoned her into the kitchen and watched with a smile as she ate enthusiastically. She noticed the woman kept glancing toward the playroom. "I'm sorry about the secrecy. But we both have to be very careful."

"Don't worry, Dede will not be a problem for long," the woman said, blithely mixing heavily accented Cape Town English with a smattering of Afrikaans.

She made as if to rise, but Lotte stopped her. "That wasn't what I meant. Please stay. My name is Lotte Kuipers. Please call me Lotte. What's your name?"

"My *naam* is Dede Achebe. But she is not a good-for-nothing kaffir begging for handouts, in case that is what you're thinking."

Lotte flinched at the slur and cut her short with a wave of her hand. "You wouldn't be sitting at my kitchen table if that's how I thought." She smiled. "So, you've given me a good idea of who you aren't. But who *is* Dede Achebe?"

Her guest raised her chin. "She is a Zulu from KwaZulu and one of the few black women who have studied at university."

"That's amazing," Lotte said. "But then they forced you to do menial work, am I right?"

"Oh yes, the government has forbidden us from training for a profession and from studying. They have destroyed our settlements in the townships, but you know that, yes? Dede's parents married her to a much older man three years ago." The young woman snorted. "They said he can offer her a better life and drive all the nonsense from her head."

"Nonsense? What do you mean?"

"They think Dede is a bad woman because she asks difficult questions and stands up against injustice."

As Dede gesticulated, her kaftan slipped to reveal part of her shoulder. Lotte saw a swollen red scar that looked like a stab wound. "I see. And your husband didn't like it, I take it?"

Dede nodded and rocked her baby, who had begun to whine softly.

"Things got very bad when our Madiba was arrested last year."

Lotte was aware of the nickname used for Nelson Mandela, his Xhosa clan name.

"Since then, Dede campaigns with the resistance for the release of Madiba, against her husband's wishes. During their last argument, five months ago, he kicked her in the stomach."

Five months ago? Lotte's blood ran cold. "You must have been heavily pregnant at the time."

"She was in her seventh month." Dede's lips quivered. "She ran away from the house that same night. She is a strong woman, but she wept from pain and from fear that he killed her baby. She came to the Jewish quarter in Cape Town, because she had heard good things about the people here. To be honest, she hoped she could rest with you for a while before moving on."

"Of course you can," Lotte said reassuringly. "But Dede, you talk about yourself in the third person. Why?"

Dede suddenly looked shy. "That man—my husband required it. I must break this habit. Dede—I should not be telling you all this, but I sense I can trust you."

"You certainly can. We'll find a way." Lotte poured her a glass of juice. "What did you want to do for a living, originally? Do you have any special skills or talents?"

"Oh yes, lots," the young woman replied eagerly. "I can cook, I'm skilled in a number of crafts, and I love children. I used to want to be an infant nurse."

"Well, for now you can stay in the summerhouse," Lotte said. Friedrich had been staying there, but since the others had left for London, Lotte had given him a guest room in the main house.

Dede beamed. "Thank you very much. I won't stay long."

Lotte showed Dede to the light timber-clad summerhouse with its sparsely furnished but cozy interior. "You even have your own bathroom. I'll bring you a cot, too, later. Come in for supper at around seven."

Dede thanked her quietly.

When Lotte returned to the Blue Heart, Friedrich was pacing restlessly up and down the kitchen. "Is everything OK in the playroom?"

"There were a few harsh words between the two girls from the street, but apart from that all was calm." He took her by the shoulders. "Where's the black woman now? I didn't see her leave."

"She's in the summerhouse. She's staying the night with us."

"I beg your pardon? Are you crazy?"

Friedrich usually had a healthy tanned complexion, but now all color had drained from his face.

"Don't get overexcited. It won't do your blood pressure any good." She stroked his cheek. "She'll be staying with us for a few days until she's strong enough to be on her way."

"Oh yes, and where will she go then?"

"I didn't ask." Lotte smiled. "It's only for a little while. Don't look so grim."

"I don't like it," Friedrich muttered. "I have every respect for your kind heart, but this is bordering on madness!"

Lotte laughed out loud. "So speaks the man who kept Peter's savings safe for decades? Who harbored my son and his family for months when the Nazis were after them? The same man who hid them when the SS came banging on the door and let himself get beaten up rather than give them away?"

He drummed his fingers on the table. "That's exactly why. I nearly lost my best friends, and I don't want to be visiting you in prison. It seems I have to look out for you—you're too careless."

Lotte tipped her head to one side. "Dede's the one in great danger, not I." She relayed what the young mother had told her. "Her husband's a violent man. She could have lost her baby."

"That's despicable." Friedrich stroked his neatly shaven chin. "All right. But tell the woman she's got to stay on the property, out of sight."

"I'll talk to her." Lotte looked at him affectionately. In the short time they had known one another, he had already become an essential part of her life. Friedrich was as steady as a rock. But in a few weeks, he would be returning to Germany, and there was no guarantee they would ever see each other again.

Chapter 7

Lilian

London and Lancaster

Early the following Saturday morning, Lilian, together with Sam and her father, made the three-hour train journey from Euston Station to Lancaster. She had arranged a meeting with Sally Russell, William's older foster sister. In Lancaster, as Sam's infallible sense of direction took them straight to the stone house with its pretty flower borders, she felt butterflies in her stomach. On their arrival, a girl of around twelve with innumerable freckles invited them into the sunny yard.

Sally Russell came out to meet them, and it was clear from whom the girl had inherited her appearance. She was in her forties with blonde hair bound in a loose braid. As she approached, she smoothed her flowered dress and greeted them with a friendly smile that instantly banished Lilian's trepidation.

"Will's told me about you. Please make yourselves at home. Can I get you anything?"

The daughter and younger son brought some iced drinks.

"It's very kind of you to spare the time for us," Lilian began cautiously.

"I'm glad to," Sally said. "Years ago, I searched for my birth mother—she gave me up soon after my birth. I still haven't managed to find her, so I understand your situation, and I'm pleased to help." She smiled sadly. "Will tells me you're looking into Emma's final years?"

"That's right," Lilian replied. "I was reunited with my birth family recently, but I've only been able to find out the bare minimum about my sister. William managed to shed a bit of light on her for us."

Sally's expression was one of regret. "I'm sorry. I must admit I never managed to get through to Emma, though I admired her."

Lilian, her father, and Sam exchanged a look of surprise. "In what way?" Lilian asked.

"Well, we foster children were all war orphans or else came from broken families. Each of us had our tale of woe, and it showed, for example in our performance at school. But not with Emma. She had an inquiring mind, and although she couldn't understand our language at first, soon she was one of the top pupils in the whole school." Sally swirled the ice around in her glass, deep in thought. "When she was reading or doing homework in her room, she wasn't the same girl as the one who crouched in corners and cried out."

The only thing Margarethe could rely on in those difficult times was her keen intelligence, Lilian thought. She cast a furtive glance at the bag on her lap, thinking of the music box, which had once belonged to her sister, the little girl whose thirst for knowledge had provided her with an escape from harsh reality. Lilian had gazed at Margarethe's photograph so many times that she knew every detail of her face. She could visualize her sister now, almost as though she were alive and Lilian could reach out and touch her. Was that a look of delight at meeting again she saw on her face? Once again, Lilian felt the sharp pain of their early separation.

"My daughter had a serious nature," Peter said, tearing Lilian from her thoughts.

"And the next moment she could be fearful and stubborn," Sally said. "I was struck by how determined she was to keep our foster parents at a distance."

"What do you mean?" Sam said.

Sally leaned back in her deck chair. "To be honest, we'd never have admitted it then, even to ourselves—on the surface, the Jacksons took good care of us. But deep down"—she tapped her chest over her heart—"there was something lacking. While the rest of us competed for their attention, Emma gave the Jacksons the cold shoulder from the very start. In truth, I wanted to be like her."

Her words shook Lilian. "William said you're no longer in touch with the Jacksons."

"That's right. I moved to Lancaster around twenty years ago and met my husband here a few years later. You know, I've always sensed that Will's the only foster child they really loved."

"No child should feel like that," Lilian said. "But do you think my sister made her life unnecessarily difficult by rejecting them?"

"It's possible," her father said. "But she'd never put on an act or do anything that would turn people against her." He sipped his drink. "Well, that was how I knew my daughter as a seven-year-old. But who knows how being in a strange country may have changed her?"

Sally smiled a little. "I don't think it did. Emma didn't refuse to eat because she wasn't hungry, but because she felt people didn't understand her. If only I'd understood that as a child. Looking back, I think she stayed true to herself."

"Emma was born into a loving family," Peter said thoughtfully. "She suffered when she was separated from us and had to carry secrets with her that were too great for her to bear. I'm afraid my wife and I were unable to spare her that."

Lilian silently placed a hand on her father's arm.

Sensing that they needed a moment to process it all, Sam took up the conversation. "Can I ask you a personal question, Sally, about the Blitz?"

"Of course. Patrick, Cathy," she called to her children, who were playing with a ball. "Go inside and help your father."

They both made a face, but did as she asked. Once they were out of earshot, Sally asked, "What do you want to know?"

"I know it's hard to speak about those times," Sam said, "but what do you remember about the bombing?"

"I don't mind," she said dismissively. "It was half a lifetime ago." She gazed at the apple tree, its heavily laden branches swaying in the wind, although Lilian could swear Sally wasn't actually seeing her surroundings in that moment. "That afternoon, I'd gone to meet my best friend. We preferred to play at her house, because it was a much more cheerful and peaceful place. I had to go home at five to help Aunty Daisy—my foster mother—bake the bread. Later I went into the playroom to read. Then the sirens sounded . . ."

Lilian listened as Sally described the events in much the same way William had.

The horror of that night was written on Sally's face. "It all happened so quickly. Emma suddenly disappeared. I only noticed when Uncle Alfred yelled at her to stop. There were several explosions, and we were dreadfully afraid. The last bomb damaged the entrance to the Underground station. The men spent the whole night clearing the debris with their bare hands."

Sally's words conjured up an image of people with dirt-smeared faces and eyes wide with fear, crying out and pressing close to one another for comfort. Lilian's throat was tight.

"Early the next morning we were finally able to leave our shelter," Sally continued, "and we made our way through rubble and dust into the open air. I remember asking everyone about my friend, but no one had seen her. I wanted to go and look for her, but Uncle Alfred held me back. I cried and shouted at him to let me go, but he wasn't having it." Sally fought down tears. "I'm grateful to him now. While we were struggling through mountains of rubble, and the doctors and firemen were clearing the way—" She paused. An ominous silence hung between them.

"So there I was, standing with Uncle Alfred and a few people from the emergency services. Among the debris I saw a severed arm with red-painted fingernails." Sally shuddered. "Uncle Alfred yelled at us, 'Eyes forward! No looking to the side!' Aunty Daisy stood beside him in silence, rigid with shock. I suppose they found more body parts scattered among the ruins that we weren't supposed to see. Our street lay in rubble and ashes, and we children were crying. Some of the houses were still on fire. The smoke made it hard to breathe. Then we saw something bright among the bricks, metal scraps, and broken furniture—my friend's red gingham scarf. 'Don't touch it,' Uncle Alfred said. 'Look away!'" Sally had turned pale and took a quick gulp of her drink before continuing. "He told me later that my friend was missing. At first I thought she'd been rescued with her parents, but she was never found."

"That must have been awful for you," Lilian said, quietly grateful that she had been spared experiences like that.

"I'll never forget the sight of that severed arm. Something like that burns itself into your mind, you know?"

"I can imagine," Lilian replied. "How—how did you find out about Emma's death?"

"We wandered around in a daze. Aunty Daisy was calling Emma's name and asking everyone we met if they'd seen her. 'Reddish-brown hair, slight build, nine years old.' Then she went over to two men. One of them was a fireman, the other didn't have a uniform. He introduced himself as a doctor."

"Do you remember his name?" Lilian asked.

Sally frowned. "Sorry, I don't. There were people from the emergency services all over the place that day."

"Yes, of course," Lilian said. "What did the doctor look like?"

"He was rather small—I remember the fireman had to look down at him. He wore round glasses and—" Sally's face suddenly brightened. "Yes, I remember now! I stared the whole time at his old-fashioned curly beard, because I thought it was so ugly."

From the corner of her eye, Lilian saw that Sam was taking notes and flashed him a grateful smile. "Thanks for that, Sally. I'm sure it'll help. Please go on."

Sally nodded. "So, the doctor asked Uncle Alfred to follow him. When they returned, the doctor said they'd found Emma's body. I remember him giving us his condolences." Sally gazed into space. "Oh, what was the man's name? I recall Aunty Daisy saying she knew a neighbor with the same surname—she asked if they were related. Ah, that's it! Cook, if I'm not mistaken."

Lilian let out her breath with a hiss, forcing herself to stay calm. "Did you ever see him again?"

"Not as far as I know." Sally toyed absently with her straw. "I heard something about him later, but I can't remember what it was in connection with. It must have been many years ago, anyway. Maybe he practiced here in Lancaster for a while."

Peter broke in. "No. At the time of the bombing he had a practice in Fulham, and he retired shortly after the war ended."

"Then I must be mistaking him for someone else," Sally said. "Sorry. Anyway, we left Hackney shortly after that. Friends of the Jacksons put us up until we were able to move into the house in Stratford." Sally lowered her head. "Afterwards, I often felt ashamed because I was more concerned for my friend than I was for Emma."

"You were little more than a child yourself," Peter said. "What was your friend's name?"

"Ceara. Ceara Doyle." Sally looked up.

"Are her parents still alive?" Sam asked.

"I've no idea. Anyone who lived on our street had to find a new home. In the confusion we all lost touch with each other."

"Do you remember Ceara's address and date of birth?" Lilian asked.

"I certainly do. She was my best friend."

Sam handed her a pen and a notebook.

"What do you intend to do now?" Sally asked Lilian a little later.

"We'll ask around after Ceara's family. Maybe they'll remember a few more details about my sister."

Sally nodded. "You don't want to leave any stone unturned."

The three of them said goodbye.

"Good luck. Don't give up." William's foster sister smiled. "It's good to have some certainty. It makes it easier to come to terms with the past."

Lilian returned her smile. "I know. All the best to you and your family, too."

Peter, Lilian, and Sam made their way home in silence. As they waited on the platform for the London train, Lilian sensed Sam's questioning gaze.

She turned, and he took her hand. "Penny for your thoughts."

"Our conversation got me to thinking. Let's talk about it later," she said quietly, so her father couldn't hear. "Papa's been upset enough for now."

"I understand." He laid an arm around her shoulders, and together, the young couple climbed into the train with Peter.

Lilian stared through the window of their carriage, watching the landscape flash by. Her mind worked incessantly, considering everything that Sally had said. Peter, too, said little.

After supper she made the excuse of a headache and went to bed early. When Sam slipped under the covers a little later and laid his head wordlessly on her chest, she grew gradually calmer.

She ran her fingers through his hair. "My mind won't stop racing. There was something strange about what Sally said, and I couldn't put my finger on it. But I can see it clearly now."

Sam sat up and looked at her.

"Do you remember what she said about Dr. Cook?"

A narrow crease formed between his brows. "I do, but what was so strange about it?"

"She said that, many years ago, Cook might have had a practice in Lancaster."

"Yes, that's what she said. But so what?"

"I mean that Cook must have made a lasting impression on Sally."

"Makes sense. After all, he was the one who broke the news of Margarethe's death to the family."

"Sure. But she obviously remembered his appearance more than his name. My instincts tell me she didn't see him again after that encounter. Otherwise she'd be able to remember him better."

"Sally said she heard something about him many years later," he replied thoughtfully.

"Exactly! Not until she was living in Lancaster."

"Hang on, Lil." There was excitement in his voice. "Are you suggesting that Cook didn't really retire after the war?"

"Bingo!" She kissed the tip of his nose. "I'm going to talk to Papa tomorrow."

He drew her closer. "Have I already said that I can hardly wait until you're my wife?"

Lilian raised her head. Sam was always affectionate, but he rarely actually spoke about his feelings. "No, you haven't. But I feel the same way."

"Let's go to sleep," he murmured in her ear.

That was easier said than done. She listened as his breathing grew deeper, but her inner turmoil kept her awake for hours.

Lilian got up early with Sam and saw him off to school. After breakfast, Peter listened quietly as she shared her theory.

"We should definitely follow up on it," he said. "But, love, the doctor would be over eighty by now, so you need to be prepared for the possibility that he might have died."

"I hope not."

"Has your grandma been in touch?"

"No. I don't want to talk to her again until we've got some definite news, or she'll worry unnecessarily. Poor Friedrich has a hard enough time with her as it is," Lilian said with a smile. *Papa's also sleeping badly,* she thought. He had dark shadows under his eyes. "I've no idea what we should do next."

Peter fell silent.

Through the window, she watched a few schoolchildren in uniform crossing the street, laughing and hopping as they went. "Papa, where do you think Sally could have seen Dr. Cook, if not in Lancaster?"

"Good question. In a photo, perhaps?" He put on his reading glasses and picked up the newspaper.

She jumped up. "Why didn't I think of it before?"

He narrowed his eyes. "What, sweetheart?"

She moved behind her father and kissed him on the cheek. "In the papers! Sally could have seen the doctor, or read about him, in a newspaper. An article about his retirement, for example."

Peter lowered his own paper. "That's a possibility. So what are you going to do?"

"I'm going to search the archives of the national papers."

Her father clapped his hands. "Very well. Let's get to work. I'll make inquiries in the church registries about Cook and Ceara's family. We might find some clues there." A shadow crossed Peter's face. "The Doyles and the Jacksons must have known one another if their children were friends."

Lilian nodded. "I'll keep my fingers crossed for you." She stared at the lines of sorrow around his mouth. "Sometimes I worry that all this is too much for you."

He patted her arm. "There's no need," he said softly. "I'm only going through what all parents do when they're grieving for their children and looking for answers. Just a few decades late."

"I never thought of it like that, Papa. But really, if at any point it gets to be too much, we'll stop immediately."

"It's fine, darling. Is there any news about your flat?"

"There've been a few viewings, but no one's made an offer yet." She looked up at him. "Are you OK if I leave you now? My translation work's waiting, and I need to draw up a list of the national papers."

"I'll see to that. You get on with your work."

A little later, Peter laid a piece of paper on her desk, then set off for Hackney and Chelsea. Lilian studied the list. *The Daily Telegraph, The Guardian, The Daily Mirror, The Times,* and *The Sunday Times.* She made appointments for the end of the week with *The Daily Mirror* and *The Sunday Times,* and decided to start with *The Telegraph* archive. She wrote a quick message to say she'd be back that evening, and put it on the kitchen table.

At Paddington Station, she took the Tube to Blackfriars, then walked to the Daily Telegraph Building on Fleet Street. She knew the way, as she'd been there to do an interview for a reference book she translated once. After being shown to the archive, she completed all the formalities and began her search through the old editions, beginning in January 1941, looking for references to Dr. Cook.

In an edition from February 1941, she found a group photo showing a number of smartly dressed doctors posing for a photo to celebrate the twenty-year anniversary of a general practice surgery. A caption underneath identified one of them as Dr. Cook. Lilian looked closely at the photo. His graying hair, handlebar mustache, round glasses, and the cheerless smile on his face reinforced her impression of a stern man who revealed nothing of himself or his thoughts. He seemed not to be an easy person to get along with either, as his colleagues all maintained a slight distance from him. Lilian continued her search, but apart from this brief mention, she found nothing. She obtained a copy of the page and made her way home, feeling she had made at least a small step forward. Her father was less successful; there had been no documents relating to Dr. Cook in the church registry, although he had found the death certificates of the Doyles in Hackney; it appeared that they had died along with their daughter in the air raid.

Chapter 8

Ceara

Dublin

It was an unusually hot Friday afternoon at the end of August, and Ceara's blouse clung uncomfortably to her skin. She would have given anything to be working in her cool workshop. Instead, she was sitting in Dr. Hamlin's stuffy treatment room, making every effort to hold her ground before his penetrating gaze. She had no choice; she had promised Aidan she would visit the psychiatrist and at least listen to what he had to say.

"I'm glad you've come to me, Mrs. Foley," he said. A stocky man in his midsixties, he had a receding hairline and a receding chin. "I suggest we work together to try and recover your lost memories. In order to do that, we need to explore your unconscious mind. There's a reason why your conscious mind has stowed these memories away in a safe place, and we need to be very careful when we look behind that concealed door."

Ceara bit her lower lip.

The doctor spun a pencil in his hand without taking his eyes off her. "For a treatment to be successful, it's essential that you're ready and willing, and that you trust my work."

At least he doesn't beat about the bush. Ceara shuffled in her seat. "Understood. What therapy are you proposing?"

"Analytical psychotherapy. In your case, I think it's the most promising method for plumbing the depths of your unconscious mind. It works like this: you'll lie on the couch while I sit behind you, out of your field of vision so you can concentrate entirely on your regression. And then we wait to see what enters your head. You'll use free association until we come to a point where it would be worthwhile to look more deeply, to see whether the door to your unconscious mind has opened sufficiently wide. I can't make any promises about how soon it will begin to work. In certain circumstances it can take a long while, but if memories push their way to the surface, things can move quickly. Your own subconscious will take control and will only reveal as much as you are able to process at the time. Do you agree to it?"

She thought hard, staring at a fat fly buzzing around an artificial orchid on the windowsill.

"Very well," she said after a pause. "Let's try it."

"Good. Please can you fill out a few forms before our next appointment? They'll give me a better understanding of your past."

A little later, Dr. Hamlin gave her the papers and dismissed her with a firm handshake.

Relieved to have escaped the oppressive atmosphere of the therapist's consulting room, Ceara drove home.

She was alone. Rhona was out shopping with a few friends, and Aidan was rehearsing with his folk band for a session that evening at the Shamrock.

Once home, she looked around the house hesitantly. The stillness played on her nerves, so she went out to the workshop. She usually closed for the weekend, but that was only to the public; she didn't keep to regular hours herself if she felt that a piece she was working on was calling to her.

If a stranger could have seen her at that moment, they would have witnessed a young woman pacing the workshop purposefully and setting to work with an expression of concentration, as though she were in a great hurry to finish. But anyone who knew her would see the tension in her body, the lines around her mouth, and the gleam in her eyes.

Ceara was not aware of the beads of sweat blending with dust motes and sawdust to form a film that coated her skin and hair. It was not until the last piece of marquetry for the table lay beautifully finished before her that she looked up with satisfaction. It was after five. She'd lost all track of time.

She mused over the offcuts of wood. What could she do with them? Ceara loved the delicate grain of old oak, and it pained her to throw away the offcuts. The wood was too good for simple mats or coasters, and too small for furniture making. She weighed the two pieces in her hand and ran her fingers over the smooth-planed surfaces. A slight smile twitched at the corners of her mouth. It would be enough to make a jewelry box or something similar. With a few inlaid ornamentations, it would look lovely in her display window as it waited for a new owner.

She tucked her sketchbook under her arm, picked up the wood, and went over to the desk, where the light was better. She looked with pride at the telephone that had been installed only a few months ago.

Sometime later, she held the little box up to the light to examine it. It could also make a good container for playing cards. She took last year's sketchbook from a drawer, but couldn't find a design she liked. She wanted a children's motif suitable for both boys and girls. Suddenly, as if taking on a life of its own, the pencil in her hand began to fly across the paper, and as the scene unfolded on the page before her, Ceara felt an inexplicable elation rising inside. The picture at her fingertips was of a chubby-cheeked boy sitting on a log, waving a conductor's baton. On his lap was a thick book with a cover that she shaded carefully with pencil strokes to look like silver. The boy was wearing shorts and a shirt, which had come slightly untucked as he played. His curly hair followed the movement of his head. A row of trees in the background swayed in the wind. A few birds and notes of music, and the image was complete.

Ceara stared in amazement at the scene from her dream, scarcely able to believe what she had drawn. How wildly she always danced when she was in that scene, rays of sunshine gently warming her skin; how free and happy she felt, before the ground began to shake and she was hurled into the air—sadly, she was unable to capture these joyful feelings in the picture. But it nevertheless seemed perfect for the little box.

Inspired by the sketch, she decided to engrave the image with a burin, one of her favorite tools that she used to give pieces an antique feel. It would take a while, but there was no hurry. She cut notches in the sides so the little box closed better, and sanded it smooth. When she had finished, she drew the image onto it lightly in pencil, placed everything she needed for the next stage into an old box, and left the workshop.

At home, Ceara made tea, glaring at the forms on the kitchen table as she added the milk and sugar. She wondered why Dr. Hamlin insisted on knowing her life story even though Rhona was sure to have told him everything in the minutest detail.

Gritting her teeth, she set to work. After her second cup, she paused, having managed to answer half the questions. She set the papers aside in frustration before warming the vegetable soup Rhona had left near the stove. Aidan always ate at the Shamrock when he was playing there.

That morning, he'd made her promise she'd be there. Her conscience plagued her because she always looked for excuses not to go with him to his music sessions. She loved traditional music and felt unreserved awe at his talent, but she hated crowds, and the proposition of a pub full to bursting unsettled her.

Ceara took a leisurely shower, slipped into her new, colorful summer dress, and allowed her chestnut hair to fall loose over her shoulders.

She applied a little blush to her cheeks so Aidan wouldn't see how pale she was.

As she reached the pub door, the old, melancholy strains of "The Curragh of Kildare" drifted out to her. Aidan began to sing, and she stood stock-still. His deep, warm voice always cast a spell on her.

"The winter, it is past, and the summer's come at last. And the birds, they are singing in the trees. Their little hearts are glad, but mine is very sad. For my true love is far away from me."

As the instruments took over, Ceara entered the room. The pub welcomed her with its lively murmur of voices. She wondered briefly whether anyone would notice if she turned around and went home. But a promise was a promise. The air in the Shamrock was heavy with the smells of whiskey, smoked meats, and pipe tobacco. The walls were adorned with pictures of musicians who had played there in the past, along with a collection of old guitars and bodhrans. She saw a free stool by the bar next to old Buzz O'Reilly and headed for it, imagining the other customers' eyes on her back.

"Hi, Ceara. Over here!" Caitlin and her husband, Bernie, called from their table tucked away by a window. Not wanting to appear rude, she greeted the couple and stopped to exchange a few words with them.

"Come and sit with us," Bernie said, a pint of Guinness in front of him.

Ceara forced a smile. "That's kind of you, but it's a bit crowded for me here. I'd rather sit at the bar."

"Whatever suits you." Caitlin turned back to her husband.

Aidan had spotted her and winked as he began the second verse and strummed his banjo.

"The rose upon the briar, by the water running clear, brings joy to the linnet and the deer . . ."

Lugh coaxed sweet notes from the fiddle, then Padraig joined in on the pipes.

Buzz O'Reilly beamed when he saw Ceara and patted the bar stool next to him. The creases around his eyes deepened. "Will you give me the pleasure of your company, Mrs. Foley?"

Ceara raised her voice so he could hear her above the music. "The pleasure's all mine," she said, echoing his lighthearted tone as she discreetly wiped her damp palms on a handkerchief. Her anxiety usually only lasted a few minutes, and she told herself that once it had passed, things would get easier.

"Logan!" The old man called to the owner, who was polishing glasses behind the bar. Logan was the latest of four generations of O'Sheas to run the pub, a popular venue for weddings, baptisms, and funerals. They were well known in the local area for their good food and the whiskey they bought from a distillery in the north. On top of all this was Logan's love of live music, which brought in many young traditional musicians on the weekend.

"Please get this pretty young lady whatever she'd like to drink," Buzz said. "Beer or whiskey, madam?"

"A single malt, please," Ceara replied without hesitating.

Buzz O'Reilly nodded. "Excellent choice."

He raised his glass to her. *"Sláinte!"*

Fortunately, he was more interested in the next traditional melody that Lugh struck up than he was in her. Ceara had never understood why she felt so uncomfortable in public. Buzz's carefree attitude did her good, however, and she began to relax, savoring the whiskey as it slipped down her throat and swaying to the music. Sometimes she thought her heart would burst with happiness when she watched Aidan.

She vividly remembered their first meeting, over ten years ago. Her foster father, Brady, had still been alive. He had a pressing deadline and had sent her to the builders' merchant with a shopping list. There, she saw Aidan coming toward her, with long sideburns and a despairing expression. Thinking she worked there, he asked her advice on how to protect a parquet floor from wood beetle infestation. Ceara still wanted to laugh whenever she thought about it; she would never forget the perplexity on his face as she explained it all in minute, jargon-packed detail.

She must have made an impression on Aidan, because he came to the workshop a few days later. When she asked how he knew where she worked, he smiled and indicated the company logo on her overalls, adding that he lived in the neighborhood. Ceara did all she could to turn down his overtures kindly but firmly, though the twinkle in his eyes never failed to faze her. He didn't seem particularly concerned by her reserve, though, and began to visit the workshop more and more often. Later, he confessed that the shelves, boxes, and furniture he'd ordered often swallowed half of his wages—and they'd only been an excuse to see her. Years went by before they met for the first time outside the workshop.

Ceara watched Aidan engrossed in his banjo playing, wondering how she had been able to live without him. He was the best thing that had ever happened to her.

He looked up and searched the crowd to catch her eye.

When Lugh played the introduction of "The Rising of the Moon" on his fiddle, a murmur passed around the pub. The ballad told of the struggles of the eighteenth-century Irish rebellion, and its lively melody ensured it was a staple at any session or gig.

Logan's younger sister, Fiona, who worked behind the bar at the Shamrock on weekends, finished serving her customer, picked up a bodhran, and joined the musicians to rapturous applause.

Buzz nudged Ceara gently. "What would you say to a little dance?"

Ceara stared at him. He really meant it. Before she could gather her thoughts, the wiry pensioner had already dragged her out onto the dance floor. It was ages since she'd last danced, but Buzz spun her around skillfully amid a shower of compliments. Aidan smiled. If the truth be known, they were as different as chalk and cheese, Ceara thought, yet they went together so well. Of course, she knew what people whispered behind their backs—that a cheerful soul like Aidan should have a similar partner.

The dance floor had filled up, and she let the rhythms drive her feet. Spinning around made her slightly dizzy, and the feeling was intoxicating, like in her dream when she danced with her arms outstretched.

When the song ended, Padraig announced they were taking a break, and Buzz let her go.

Aidan came up to her and stroked her warm cheeks. "I'm so glad you're here."

She kissed him.

A few minutes later, Lugh asked for silence. "Padraig, Aidan, and I have a surprise for you good people."

"Tell us!" someone called from the back.

"Are you going to propose to me at last, Paddy?" shouted forty-year-old Suzy, who never failed to turn up to a party since her children had grown up.

Everyone laughed.

Aidan took hold of the microphone. "That wouldn't be a surprise for anyone, Suzy! But it's not that." He waited till the murmurs died down again. "You know we're always on the lookout for old, forgotten songs. A while ago, Lugh and I discovered a particular treasure. It was originally a piece for the piano, and we've arranged it for our instruments. It's called 'Dolly's Dream and Awakening.'"

Ceara cocked her head in surprise. He hadn't dropped any hints about a new piece. She didn't recognize it at all.

The new song began with a delicate melody on the fiddle before Aidan joined in on the banjo. Ceara listened entranced. She felt she had heard the piece somewhere before. But where? When Padraig began on the pipes and the instruments wove around each other, Ceara suddenly heard a roaring in her ears. The dancers faded to shadowy, moving silhouettes, as though there were a curtain of fog dividing them from her. The roaring suddenly stopped. The music seemed to transport her to another place: a place where there was a silvery shimmer in the air and the instruments were transformed into birdsong. She was running with bare feet on dew-wet grass. At the far side of the meadow she saw the boy with his conductor's baton and waved madly. As she spun to the rhythm, laughing, she heard a girl's voice carried on the wind from afar. She moved nearer and became aware of an echo in her body. Ceara's heart suddenly beat faster. All at once she knew that it wasn't a stranger's voice singing, but her own. And as she followed the notes, the song blended with the heartbreaking crying of a little child. Until an earsplitting explosion tore the ground in two.

Chapter 9

Lotte

Cape Town

Lotte stood by Dede and watched her washing her baby son and changing his diaper.

"My family tried to force me to give up the campaign for Madiba's release so that I could take better care of my husband." Her dark eyes gleamed brightly as she continued. "*Nee!* I told them that if we did not stand up for the man who's languishing in jail because he wants to free us from apartheid, we will lose everything. All the native people must be out in the streets, *meesteres*. Every man and every woman. It is the only chance we have of ending oppression."

"I know exactly how you feel." Lotte looked into the streaming sunlight that reflected on the windowpane and threw bright stripes on the stone floor. Decades had passed since the horrific events in Germany that had driven her into exile. *The worst memories fade with time; only the good ones stay in the memory. Whoever said that was wrong.*

The young black woman kissed her son. "That's why I wanted to come to you. You are a good woman, *meesteres*." She laid the baby in a basketwork crib and covered him. "Will you tell me what happened to you?"

Lotte led Dede down the corridor from the room next to the laundry room. "I don't like to talk about those times. I had to leave part of my family behind. Things were so dreadful in Nazi Germany, and even though I was safe in Cape Town, worrying about the loved ones I'd left behind was a sheer nightmare."

"Were you reunited with them?"

"Not all of them."

"That's so sad." Dede shook her head. "We will leave when Niam wakes up. You've hidden us here for four days; it is time to move on now."

"Where do you intend to go?"

"*Meesteres* must understand," the young woman said with a fierce gesture, "Dede and Niam are at home anywhere. We'll manage."

"I wouldn't be so sure of that." Lotte lowered her voice. "Listen. I have an idea."

Dede looked at her attentively.

"I'm snowed under with work looking after the house and garden here. I'm not as young as I was, and I could use the services of a maid." Dede made to speak, but Lotte cut her off. "But I don't do things in half measures. If you agree, I'll employ you officially. The government allows you to do that kind of work. I can't pay you as much as I'd like, but you'd both have a new home."

Tears filled Dede's eyes.

Lotte moved closer to her. "What do you think?"

The young woman waved her away. "Nee, you cannot do that, *meesteres*. I do not want to cause trouble for you. Why should you risk that for me?"

"Because you're in the right," Lotte said simply. "I want to support you in your campaign for Mandela's release. Apartheid is an appalling crime against the black population, and Mandela's dedication to the cause is amazing. If I'm honest, I feel too old to demonstrate with you or get involved in the resistance movement, but this is one way I can support you." She smiled. "You could have the summerhouse."

"And what if someone comes after me?"

"Let me worry about that. Now, about my job offer: your working hours would be from eight until one. We can discuss the other details if you accept."

Lotte held out her right hand, and Dede hesitated briefly before shaking it.

"Thank you. I'll never forget what you've done for me," she said, then slipped into the room from where the baby could be heard crying.

Lotte listened as Dede's singsong words soothed the child. Then she returned to work. On two mornings a week she gave lessons in reading and writing, as she had once done in the Jewish community in Altona with Dr. Nathan Fisch. He had been Clara's father and Peter's father-in-law, and all his life he had devoted himself to the needs of his people. Lotte often thought about him and his tragic fate. His loyalty and his refusal to abandon his patients had ultimately cost him his life. He died in 1942 in the Jungfernhof concentration camp.

Lotte pushed the sad memories aside, went into the classroom, and looked around. While it had originally been used by schoolchildren seeking help with their homework, for a while now a variety of illiterate people had been coming to benefit from her help. There were young women like the two girls from the streets—still little more than children, whose parents had robbed them of their homes and their prospects for the future. Lotte put a board up by the window, scattered cushions on the floor, and distributed the writing implements.

She never knew how many would turn up for the lesson. Some women attended two or three times, then never came again. Others kept at it, including a few whom Lotte would not have expected to.

That day, though, she waited in vain for pupils. Only a few young mothers with children turned up at lunchtime, and they left as quickly as they had appeared. Lotte closed the center early that Friday afternoon.

The Blue Heart was always closed on Shabbat. She had invited her friend Ewa Tulinski and a few other members of the Jewish community to celebrate with her.

Outside, she breathed deeply. There was a hint of spring in the cool air. The camphor trees in the neighboring garden were magnificent, with insects humming and buzzing around the delicate yellow flowers. Buds were already appearing on the passion fruit vines that grew in abundance outside many of the houses. Every year, Lotte was amazed all over again to see how rapidly the plants changed after the rainy season into a scented sea of flowers. But despite the cheerful colors and the clear blue sky, she was pensive that day.

Friedrich was raking leaves in the garden. When he saw her, he set aside his rake and wheelbarrow.

Lotte smiled. "What would you say to a little drink?"

"I'd love one." The look in his eyes sent warmth through her. "You're starting early today."

"You're right, I am. I'll just go and get changed." She went into the house, slipped into a comfortable housedress, and draped a woolen shawl around her shoulders. A little later, she came back out to the terrace, carrying a tray of cheese, bread, red wine, and glasses. The Atlantic was turbulent with white-capped waves, and in quiet moments, they could hear the waves breaking on the rocky shore below.

"Have you seen Dede today?" she began carefully.

"Yes, she's in the summerhouse with the baby." Friedrich reached for a piece of cheese. "So she's going to be here again tonight?"

"Starting tomorrow, Dede will be working for me as a maid," Lotte said firmly. "She deserves to be given an opportunity."

"For goodness' sake, Lotte! You know that black servants and their employers are strictly observed."

"I know," she said, unperturbed. "So be it. I'm certainly not going to throw the girl back out on the street. If she does her job well, she can stay."

Friedrich filled their glasses. "With all due respect to your kindness, maybe it would have been better to make sure you have all the information and to consider everything properly before making a decision."

"You may be right, but that's not the way I am," she replied emphatically. "I've listened to my gut feelings my whole life, and that's not going to change now."

"Dede's a resistance activist."

"That's precisely why I'm giving her my support." Lotte laid her hand over his. "She's a brave woman whose strong will and sense of justice remain unbroken despite all the dreadful things she's experienced. We need more women like her, who won't be silenced by anyone."

"I'm not disputing that." Friedrich's brows knitted together. "But why do you have to be the one to get involved? You'd be better off leaving it to the young people."

His strong reaction astounded her. "On the contrary. As a young woman I had to keep my mouth shut, since a careless word could have cost my family their lives. Now that I'm an old woman, I want to make the most of my freedom to take a stand."

Friedrich looked her over thoughtfully. "You hardly know the girl. What if you're wrong about her?"

"Oh, stop it," she said more sharply than she intended. "I'm not going to close my eyes to injustice. Never again!"

She could see him struggling to stay calm. "I understand. But I still don't like it, if you want to know my opinion."

"But I'm not asking you," Lotte said as gently as possible. "You've become a dear friend, and I'll never forget what you did for my son and his family."

Friedrich held her gaze. "But?"

"But I'm not answerable to anyone," she said calmly. "I make my own decisions."

His face froze. He stood. "I didn't mean to step on your toes. Of course you're right. If you'll excuse me now."

Lotte watched him go. She stared at her plate, then pushed it away, her appetite gone. She decided to go shopping for the Shabbat meal. Lotte loved the market with its extensive jumble of colorful stalls, housed in a historic quayside building on Nobel Square. She bought two fine butternut squashes, lamb, cabbage, sweet potatoes, and vegetables. Friedrich loved braised lamb; maybe his favorite dish would soften his mood.

Back home, she looked around, but Friedrich was nowhere to be seen. Her friend probably thought her both stubborn and reckless. He was a kind man, but he sometimes behaved as though she were made of porcelain. Lotte glowered at the squashes before chopping them to make soup. She had to have finished her preparations by sundown, when Shabbat officially began.

Today, Lotte drew no satisfaction from the occasion, which she had loved since childhood. She set the table ceremoniously, polished the cutlery, and arranged everything on the counter in the kitchen. She was just putting the roasting pan in the oven when she heard a noise behind her.

Friedrich ran a hand through his thinning hair. "Can I do anything to help?"

"Thank you, but everything's done."

He came closer. He was wearing a new shirt and had just shaved. "I want to apologize. I behaved like an idiot earlier."

Lotte raised a hopeful eyebrow. "Anything else?"

"You're a woman who knows her own mind; I must have forgotten that. I'm sorry. I only wanted to protect you, but, really, I was unforgivably patronizing." Friedrich gave a crooked smile.

"I can't deny it," she said. "You must trust me, Friedrich. I know what I'm doing."

"Yes. Now, there's something I want to talk to you about."

"Gladly." She untied her apron and sat across from him at the kitchen table.

His expression was open. "What are your plans for the thing with Dede?"

"She'll work on probation for a week, then I'll give her a proper employment contract. The authorities will be keeping an eye on us." She didn't like the thought, but Friedrich didn't have to know that. "Once they're convinced we're doing everything properly, they'll leave us in peace."

"Yes, probably," Friedrich replied, then narrowed his eyes. "Correct me if I'm wrong, Lotte. The fact that the whites control the blacks and use them as cheap labor is a sad fact of life here in South Africa. But why do you want to employ Dede of all people? The girl has a degree and deserves something better. You're up to something, aren't you?"

Lotte smiled. "Yes, her employment here is merely a cover. I'm going to give her practical experience in keeping accounts and looking after young mothers and their children, as well as pass on what I've learned over the years. If she agrees, of course. Maybe someday she could run a place like this herself."

Friedrich's changing feelings showed on his face. "So that's the way the wind's blowing. Just be careful."

"Of course. But Dede's young, and she has her whole life before her. One day, the specter of apartheid will be a thing of the past."

"We all hope for that."

"We certainly do. And when it is, I want her to be able to take up a career that makes the most of her talents and enables her to feed herself and her child." Lotte was suddenly transported back to the time, at the beginning of the 1930s, when they would no longer serve her in the shops and she had to fight for the bare necessities. She caught Friedrich's eye. "Dede should never have to demean herself again."

Friedrich said nothing, and she could see his mind working behind his broad brow.

"Why her in particular?"

"Because Dede reminds me of myself," she said. "She needs something to do, an aim in life. Otherwise she'll become withdrawn and lose herself."

"Like you once did, Lotte?"

"Yes, like I did after Johann's death. Peter was seven when he died. If it hadn't been for him and my work in the community, my life would have been empty. I don't know if I'd have had the courage to move to Cape Town after Peter's wedding. But I'm glad I did, since I met Antoon and enjoyed a few lovely years with him."

Friedrich's expression softened. "And if you hadn't, we might never have met. Good God, what I would have missed!"

Lotte laughed. "Flatterer."

"It's true," he said seriously. "But please make it clear to Dede that she should take a break from her political activities for a while, at least until the authorities turn their attention elsewhere. She'd only put your plan at risk."

Lotte nodded. "I can't argue with that. Very well, I'll talk to her. And what about you? Now that you know the full story, can I count on your support?"

He winked cheerfully. "Always. And if I start getting overprotective again, just tell me to back off."

A burden fell from her shoulders as she saw the mischief in his eyes. "I certainly will."

Friedrich slapped his hand down on the table. "Oh, I almost forgot! Wait a moment."

Frowning, Lotte watched him hurry from the kitchen and return almost immediately with a shoebox-sized package, which he set down on the table. The first thing Lotte noticed was the foreign stamps.

"Postmarked in Israel?" she asked, reaching for her reading glasses. "Herzel Fisch, Tel Aviv." Lotte gasped. "Fisch?"

Friedrich leaned over her. "What's the matter, Lotte?"

"I used to know a Dr. Nathan Fisch." Memories stirring within her, she looked at the beautifully ornamented seven-branched candelabrum, which her people called a menorah, that had taken pride of place on her sideboard ever since she had left home. Johann had made it, and they had once given an almost identical piece to the doctor. "He was Clara's—Charlotte's—father. I was close to him. He was a good man."

Friedrich nudged her gently. "What are you waiting for? Open it."

Chapter 10

Lilian

London

Sam's optimism was proving well founded. A young man his age was desperately looking for somewhere to live and even wanted to buy some of Sam's furniture, so that was another obstacle out of the way of their moving to Cape Town in October.

On Friday, Lilian's grandmother called. Sam was still at work, due home midafternoon. Lilian listened with growing excitement to her grandmother's news.

"You've received what?" she said.

Her father also pressed his ear to the receiver.

"A package from Israel," Lotte repeated. "From a man called Herzel Fisch in Tel Aviv."

"Fisch? Is he related to my father-in-law? What's in it, and how did he get your address, Mama?" Peter asked.

He exchanged a look of confusion with Lilian.

"Wait, let me read you the letter. Oh, I don't have my glasses. Will you do us the honor, Friedrich?"

"Gladly." They heard paper rustling, then his sonorous voice.

Dear Frau Kuipers or relations,

You're probably surprised to receive mail from a stranger in faraway Israel. Actually, we're distantly related, as I'm Dr. Nathan Fisch's nephew, the son of his brother, Yosef, and cousin of your daughter-in-law, Clara Blumenthal. I came to Jerusalem back in 1920, met my wife here, and stayed. She has given me four wonderful children, and we now have eight grandchildren.

Sadly, I only saw Uncle Nathan rarely, but I admired him greatly. In my package, you'll find his notes from his time in the Jungfernhof concentration camp. A few days before he was shot—suspecting he was going to be executed—he entrusted them to a friend named Janusz Wiczorek, asking him, should he survive, to send them to my father. In his letter, Uncle Nathan asked Janusz to find Clara and give her the diaries, but she was officially recorded as missing. After Father's death a few years ago, I inherited the notes and called on the services of the International Tracing Service. From them, I found out that my cousin Clara had been shot by the SS, and that you and Clara's youngest daughter were searching for family members. They kindly gave me your address. If Clara's husband or children are still alive, please pass these notes on to them. In the hope that this finds you and your family well. Yours sincerely, Herzel Fisch.

"That's it," Friedrich said.

There was a long silence on the other end of the line.

"I'm surprised my father-in-law wrote about his experiences," Peter said hoarsely. "Dr. Fisch never minced his words where the Nazis were concerned. Imagine if they'd found it!"

"He was a realist," said Lotte, also on the line. "He probably realized earlier than his fellow prisoners that they wouldn't leave the concentration camp alive, with or without diaries."

Lilian finally found her tongue. "I wish I'd known him, Grandma. I'd have loved him, I'm sure."

"And he'd have loved you, too," Peter said gently. "He always enjoyed making your sister laugh."

"You know what I find most striking?" Lilian continued. "The fact that my grandfather's diaries have found their way to us after all these years. From his fellow prisoner to his brother, from him to his son, Herzel, and now they've come to you."

Lotte agreed.

"Have you read them yet?" Peter asked.

"No, my son. The package is on the sideboard, still tied up. We didn't want to open it until we're all back together."

"I'd be far too curious to resist," Lilian said with a smile.

She and Peter then told them what had happened since their last telephone conversation. "We've got an appointment this afternoon. Papa and I are going to search for Cook in *The Sunday Times*. Keep your fingers crossed for us. We've got to trace this doctor."

"We will," Friedrich said. "If your grandmother was there, she'd be sitting in the archive this very moment, with every employee in the place at her beck and call."

"You can be sure of that," Lotte said.

A little later, Peter and Lilian took the Underground to *The Sunday Times* offices, where they were shown to the archive. Silence reigned throughout the reading room, broken only by the occasional rustling of papers. While her father looked through editions from 1941 to 1945,

Lilian concentrated on the postwar years. The news then was dominated by the destruction and reconstruction after the war.

Lilian's eyes began to smart, and she yawned behind her hand. A look at her watch told her that she had been poring over old news for at least two hours, and she began to wonder whether the search was a waste of time. In frustration, she considered asking an employee to help her, but decided against it.

She felt a hand on her shoulder and turned to see her father's face. "Come here—you've got to see this!"

Lilian, suddenly wide awake, followed him to his desk. He pointed to a news item on the third page.

> Sunday, October 7, 1945. Doctor missing! Has anyone seen Dr. Ernest Cook? £1,000 reward for any information on his whereabouts!

Lilian quickly scanned the missing-person notice issued by the police. The general practitioner with a reputation for reliability had vanished in August 1945 as if swallowed by an earthquake. "Maybe Sally saw this notice back then," she whispered.

"She may well have. How's it going with you?"

"I've found nothing, and there's only an hour left until the archive closes."

He kissed her brow, and they continued.

Lilian finally finished looking through all the articles from 1945 and started on the next year. Her father was making faster progress, probably because newspapers were printed less regularly during the war. There was a report from March 17, 1946, about Auschwitz commandant Rudolf Höss, whom the British had arrested in northern Germany. She read about the first Leipzig Trade Fair since the war and then, in June, *The Sunday Times* was dominated by photos and reports about the London Victory Celebrations. The images of the jubilant crowds celebrating the victory over Nazi Germany left a bitter taste in Lilian's mouth as she thought of the millions of innocent people who had lost their lives in the Second World War. Innocent people such as Margarethe, her mother, her grandfather Nathan, and her great-uncle Max. Lilian took a deep breath. She was about to set the latest old newspaper aside when an article caught her eye.

> Sunday, July 21, 1946. Chelsea doctor arrested! General practitioner Dr. Ernest Cook was on the run for eight months until his arrest yesterday on the outskirts of Leeds. The pensioner is accused, among other things, of adding to his income in at least nine cases during the war by producing forged documents. Further information cannot be revealed at this stage due to the ongoing legal proceedings.

Beneath the article was a photo of Cook from 1942. Stunned, Lilian stared, first at the bold headline, then at the photo, before reading it again. She felt the blood drain from her head. Cook was a criminal? She tapped her father's shoulder agitatedly.

Her expression must have spoken volumes, because he didn't say a word, but came and scanned the report. "Good heavens!"

They exchanged a charged look.

"You'd best get a copy of that."

Lilian nodded, dazed. At least nine cases of forged documents. What had Cook done? They left the building a little while later. Her father led her to a nearby café and pressed her into a seat at an outside table.

"Stay here. I'll go and order us a drink."

She watched him. Forged documents. Her hands shaking, she took the music box from her bag and felt for the secret compartment, in which she kept some beloved photos.

But her fingers were damp with nerves, and the music box slid from her hands. With a cry, she tried to catch it. She was too late, and her treasure hit the ground with a crash.

Lilian gave a moan of horror. A sob rose to her throat as she saw that the secret compartment lay in pieces, scattered around her feet and between the chair legs. The wind rustled the photos. A gust caught them and blew them into the road. At the last moment, Lilian managed to grab them, then gathered up the pieces of the music box. Still crouching, she began to cry inconsolably.

She was still in tears when Peter found her. He set the coffee cups down and hugged her. "What happened?"

Sobbing, she pointed to the music box and the broken pieces of the secret compartment on the café table.

"I can repair it, don't worry." Peter handed her a handkerchief.

His voice sounded muffled to her, as though he were speaking through cotton wool. Lilian sniffed and swallowed, but the sight of her damaged treasure upset her again. "I'm sure you can, but it'll never . . . be the same ever again."

Lilian drank her coffee without tasting a thing.

After examining the toy from every angle, her father looked up. "The walls of the secret compartment have come apart—that's all."

"And there's a dent on the lid, right next to one of the engraved birds," she said.

"I'll repair it as soon as we get home," Peter said. "Or do you want to take it to a jeweler in London?"

"No, we're not letting it out of our hands."

"Very well. Then you'll just have to be patient." Peter lowered his voice. "Listen to me, now. This music box is almost fifty years old, and each of its owners left their mark on it in one way or another." He took her hands. "Not because they weren't careful with it, but because they loved it so much that they took it with them everywhere. Accidents happen. I think it makes the music box even more valuable."

They were silent for a while.

"I think we ought to go to the police," Lilian said then. "If Cook was charged, they must know something about where he is."

"Good idea." He winked.

"We're not going to give up, Papa. Not ever," she said with a crooked smile as she wiped the tears from her face.

Chapter 11

Ceara

Dublin

The oppressive heat had dissipated, and the late summer Sunday looked like it would be lovely. Aidan was still asleep after returning home at five from a night shift. Ceara sat in her overgrown garden, grateful for the morning stillness. Next door, Rhona was watering flowers, tunelessly whistling the latest pop hit. Normally, her cheerfulness would elicit a smile from Ceara, but today she muttered a curse and bowed her head over Dr. Hamlin's questionnaires, which she had put off filling out until the last possible moment.

What event puts you under the greatest stress? she read with growing resentment.

Insomnia and a recurring dream, Ceara wrote, brushing away a twig the wind had blown onto the table.

It seemed the dream had now worked its way into her waking life. Plus, there had been some new, bewildering additions. Ceara couldn't remember ever having heard her own voice in that scene before. She was most shaken, however, by the pitiful child's crying that accompanied her singing before the dream world sank into chaos. Even now, in the bright morning light, Ceara could almost hear those despairing tones, even as she watched a few butterflies fluttering around a lilac bush. The sounds were strangely familiar, carrying a profusion of feelings with them to the surface.

And to top it all off, she had to faint on the Shamrock dance floor in front of all those people, coming around to face their inquisitive looks. She would never forget storming out of the pub with her cheeks flaming red. Even her superfit husband had struggled to catch up.

The prospect of recalling the experience for Dr. Hamlin's questionnaire stirred her resistance. Deep in thought, she chewed her pencil and knocked over a glass of lemonade, lingering over clearing it up before returning to the task.

The first she knew of Aidan's presence was when he crept up behind her and tickled the fine hairs on the back of her neck. "There's fresh tea in the kitchen," she said after greeting him affectionately.

He was wearing shorts and a T-shirt, his brow still creased from sleep. "Do you want something to eat? I'll make breakfast."

"Thanks, but I'm not hungry," she replied absently.

He left and, a little later, returned with two plates of scrambled eggs on toast, which he placed on the table.

"Don't look at me like that, Ceara," he said. "Eat it, or I'll report you to Dr. Hamlin."

"You wouldn't dare," she replied flatly.

Undeterred, he began eating and carefully sipping his tea. "I'd do some much meaner things if it made you see sense."

He held her gaze steadfastly until she gave in and ate a forkful of scrambled egg. Aidan slid a piece of tomato onto a morsel of bread and pushed it into her mouth, taking no notice of her protest.

Ceara looked at him darkly, a look he also ignored.

"Are you ready to tell me what happened at the Shamrock? Do you remember why you fainted?"

She brushed a gnat from her knee, took a deep breath, and handed him the questionnaires.

Aidan let out a whistle as he read the headings.

"I've written it all down," Ceara said. "Although I'd prefer to delete that evening from my memory."

He concentrated on reading, and she watched his every movement.

When he raised his head, the cheerfulness had vanished from his face. "You've never told me your dream in such detail. Why not?"

"Do you think that I, a grown woman in my thirties, want to be teased by you because of a childish dream?"

The corners of Aidan's mouth twitched. "As if I'd do that."

"Whatever," Ceara said, mostly to herself. "I think the last few images were memories." She felt goose bumps along her arms. "I know the child who was crying, and the song I was singing was your new piece."

Aidan choked on his tea. "Would you believe it? Your early memories are coming back, my love. It's a step forward."

"If you say so. But I can't deny it's unsettling me."

"Let's try to find out more about the piano piece. Wait a moment—Lugh, Padraig, and I jotted down some information about the composer. Perhaps it'll help you." He dashed into the house and returned a few moments later with a notebook. "Here we are! The composer, musician, and music teacher Theodore Oesten lived in the nineteenth century, came from Berlin, and was known for his melancholy pieces. The composition we played, 'Dolly's Dream and Awakening,' was originally a children's song."

"I sang along with the piece even though I don't know it at all," Ceara said.

"At least, you don't remember that you know it," Aidan said.

"You've hit the nail on the head."

"Old Sigmund Freud would have been like a pig in clover analyzing your dream," he said with a shake of his head.

"I fear the same could be said of Dr. Hamlin." She looked past him and rose from her chair. "I'll ask Rhona. Maybe she can tell me something useful."

"Good idea. I'm just off for a rehearsal at Lugh's." He looked deep into her eyes and kissed her. "See you later."

Her foster mother was cutting flowers to arrange in a vase and looked up with a smile as Ceara entered the garden. "Everything OK, love?"

"I don't know. Can you spare a moment?"

Rhona wiped her hands on her apron. "Come and sit down. What's up?"

Ceara took a seat between two tubs of flowering oleanders. Hesitant at first, the words flowing more freely as she spoke, she told her foster mother of her dream and the piece of German music. "What do you know of the time before I came to you? Who were my parents? Do I have any brothers or sisters?"

Rhona's eyes widened. "You're asking me this for the first time after all these years?"

"I didn't want to know anything about my past before."

"Which I can understand, under the circumstances. How come you've changed your mind?"

Ceara hadn't told her about what happened in the Shamrock, so as not to worry her. "My dream's changing. A child was crying, and I was singing a song I don't know. I think they could be buried memories. Anyway, please, could you tell me what you know?"

Rhona studied her thoughtfully, but didn't ask anything else. "So, you know how much Brady and I wanted a child. We'd approached various adoption agencies before the war. But no one wanted us—we were too old, and our finances weren't solid enough. But then a private agency got in touch and asked if we'd be prepared to take in a war orphan."

Ceara smiled weakly. "I'm so grateful to you both for everything. If you hadn't been there . . . Did you keep the papers?"

"Of course." Rhona reached out and stroked her cheek. "Come on, let's see what we can find. Help yourself if you want a drink."

Ceara poured herself a glass of water and followed her into the living room. Rhona took a folder from a cabinet. Along with medical reports and details of Ceara's injuries, she saw her school certificates and a large envelope containing paintings she had done for her foster parents' birthdays. Ceara was moved to see that Rhona had kept every little memento.

Rhona took a second envelope from the folder and handed her a formal letter from an organization in Limerick with the evocative name Light and Hope, which confirmed Brady and Rhona Ward as legal guardians of Ceara Doyle, born June 18, 1931 in London. There were also her release papers from a hospital in Cork in early February 1941.

"We went to fetch you from there."

"I know. But what about before that? The people at the organization must have told you something about other members of my family."

Her foster mother shrugged.

Ceara's eyes bored into her as she gripped her arms. "Please try to remember, Mum. Please!"

Tears glimmered in Rhona's eyes. "Mum? You've never called me that."

"Today's a special day," Ceara replied warmly. "But you've always been my mother, even if I've never been able to express my feelings like you or Aidan can." She studied the paper on her lap. "Did you find out anything about my birth mother? Please think back."

"I am," Rhona said with a gesture of helplessness. "They said your parents died in an air raid. I don't know any more than that."

"What about brothers or sisters?" Ceara said. "Could the child crying in my dream have been my brother or sister?"

"I've no idea. Maybe we'll find something among the papers."

The two of them bent their heads over the documents again. Ceara noted her natural parents' names and the dates of their births and deaths, but her embryonic hope of discovering possible siblings came to nothing.

"What will you do now?" Rhona asked after putting the folder away.

"I'll contact the Red Cross and see if I can find out more," Ceara replied. "Something's got to change. I've been in a bit of a mess these last few days. On Friday I got some measurements wrong and wasted a whole morning's work. I can't carry on like this."

"When's your appointment with Dr. Hamlin?"

"Tomorrow morning, before I open the workshop. I must admit I'm not at all comfortable with the idea of bringing my innermost feelings to the surface."

Rhona passed her a plate of homemade cookies. "Dr. Hamlin is supposed to have helped a lot of patients."

Ceara grimaced. "Glad to hear it. But I for one don't trust the shrink." She pushed the cookies away. "What are you doing today, Mum?"

"I've arranged to see Lucas." Rhona winked. "He claims to be a good cook—well, I'll judge for myself this evening."

"Who's Lucas?"

"I met him at our recent cultural evening. He's a nice chap," Rhona said, widening her eyes in innocence.

Ceara laughed. "Do you flirt with him?"

"Of course, but only a little. If he turns out to be a good dancing partner, I may see him more often."

"Quite right." Ceara kissed her cheek. "Aidan won't be home until this afternoon. If you need me, I'll be in the workshop."

"Where else?" Rhona replied with a shake of her head.

Ceara planed and sawed in her refuge, her mind constantly drawn to the little playing-card box. She would have preferred to abandon the turned table legs and work instead on the ornamentation of the toy's lid. But time was short—she had to finish four chairs by the end of the following week, to give to the Camerons for their golden wedding anniversary.

When the second chair was finished but for the protective coat of varnish, she put everything away in the storeroom she reserved for her commissioned work. Her foot brushed against the chest that contained the little box, and she picked it up without thinking.

Ceara looked at it pensively from all sides. There was something missing. If only she knew what. The pattern was correct, depicting her dream scene perfectly and, once painted, would make a lovely Christmas or birthday present for someone. She examined each pencil stroke of her sketch and the two half-finished wooden panels. The interior looked plain and needed a few cheerful details. Ceara traced the grain with her finger, recalling her last dream. She looked up as if electrified. No, she wouldn't paint the box; the wood was too fine to hide it with paint. But she could color the interior silver, like an old treasure chest that only reveals its value when opened, and decorate it with the actual notation of a real tune. A melody crept into her mind. Why not Oesten's 'Dolly's Dream and Awakening'? The future owner of the little box need never know what its symbols and paint actually meant to her. Her thoughts made her heart beat faster—whether from sadness or joyful anticipation she couldn't tell.

Chapter 12

Lilian

London

Back in Sam's apartment, Peter brought together the references from *The Sunday Times*.

"I also found this Wanted notice for Dr. Cook in *The Daily Mirror*," Sam said, laying a photo on the table. "So Cook turns out to be a criminal. What a surprise!" He looked at Lilian, who was unusually silent, staring at the damaged music box on the table in front of her. "A penny for your thoughts."

She raised her eyes. "I keep wondering whether Cook's offense has anything to do with Margarethe. Papa and I talked about asking the police if they can help us."

"You think Margarethe's death certificate could have been forged?" He held her gaze. "What could Cook have changed on the document, Lil? Even if the time or cause of death were wrong, what difference would it make?"

"Sam's right," Peter said. "After the air raid, the place was swarming with people from the emergency services who had to recover the bodies and take them away. Anyway, Sally confirmed that her foster father identified her."

"I know that," Lilian said. "Call me crazy, but I want to look into it, especially as it could be our only chance to ask the police about Cook. If the doctor is alive, I'd like to talk to him."

"OK," Sam said. "Let's give it a try."

"Thank you." She looked at them both affectionately. "I really must send off my translation tomorrow, and I'm behind. I need to work at least two more hours."

"No problem. I'll see to supper," Peter said.

In Sam's bedroom, she put the music box in its usual place on the desk, gave it a thoughtful glance, and turned to her work. As the light gradually faded, she switched on the little lamp and brushed a lock of hair from her brow. It was well past eight by the time Lilian removed the last page of her translation from the typewriter and packed it carefully away.

After supper, they were all still too agitated to rest, so they decided to go for a walk along Regent's Canal. Lilian and Sam loved this little corner, not far from Paddington Station, where colorful boats danced on the water and the leaves of the weeping willows were reflected in the moonlight on the surface of the canal. By day, the place was a lively bustle of activity, but in the evenings, they saw a few dog walkers at most.

The fresh air chased away Lilian's tension. On their return, Peter opened a bottle of vintage Bordeaux, and she soon became sleepy.

"Tomorrow's going to be a big day," Lilian murmured later as she lay in bed and snuggled into Sam's arms. It was to be his last day at school, and she had an appointment with a potential buyer for her adoptive parents' flat.

"And let's not forget our visit to the police." He kissed her, and she was soon listening to his deep breathing before she fell asleep herself.

The next morning, Peter called August, who wanted to know all the latest developments. Meanwhile, Lilian showed the buyers around the flat; they were delighted with it, and she returned, satisfied, at lunchtime.

Now all that stood in the way of her new life in Cape Town as Sam's wife were the many questions surrounding Margarethe—and Dr. Cook.

Sam came home early, and she could tell from his expression that leaving his pupils had been difficult.

That afternoon, the three of them went to the Metropolitan Police headquarters at New Scotland Yard. On the way, they hardly spoke, each sunk in their own thoughts.

A police officer at the reception desk led Lilian and the others to a large open-plan office on the first floor and introduced them to a middle-aged, uniformed officer with sparse red hair.

"Inspector Wilson. How can I help you?"

Lilian outlined her situation. "I'd be grateful for any information about my sister, Emma Dölling, and Dr. Cook—whether a case was ever brought against him, and where we can find him." She gave him a pleading look. "I don't know who else we can turn to."

The policeman closed a file. "I hope you'll understand, Miss Morrison, but we can't give out internal information."

"We understand that," Lilian said. "But we can't leave without at least trying. If anyone can help us, it's you."

"Is there a specific link between Cook and your sister?"

"No," she said quietly.

"What year was the reported case against the doctor?"

"1946."

"I'm sorry." Wilson shook his head. "I can't help you any further. I only took up this post a few years ago, and I'm not personally familiar with the case. In 1946, Chief Inspector Lewis was responsible for the department. He's retired now." He rose and buttoned his jacket. "But I'll see what I can do for you, and I'll call if I have any news."

Lilian handed him her card. "That would be good. Thank you for your time."

Sam's hand was warm in hers as they left the office.

Outside, she rummaged in her bag for her half-empty packet of emergency cigarettes. She instinctively felt for the music box, but found only an empty space. With a heavy heart, she had obeyed her father's suggestion that she should leave the damaged treasure at home. She lit a cigarette and inhaled deeply while Sam and her father waited in silence.

Lilian had no sooner stubbed it out than she caught sight of Inspector Wilson heading straight for her.

"I've finished work, so I'm no longer officially on duty." He handed her a piece of paper with a meaningful look. "This is strictly confidential information."

Peter spoke for his daughter. "We'll handle it with the greatest discretion."

"Thank you." The police officer wiped his brow; it was still warm for early September. "A few months ago, I met Chief Inspector Lewis at an office party—he was the guest of honor. We talked for a while. He belongs to the old school of police, for whom it's a matter of honor to solve every crime." Wilson nodded at the note in her hand. "He'll be able to help you more than I can."

Lilian glanced at the hastily scribbled note. "This is very kind. Thank you very much."

"You're welcome." Wilson touched his hat. "Good luck."

Frowning, the three of them watched him go.

Peter peered over Lilian's shoulder, and his eyes widened. "He's given you Lewis's address!"

Sam whistled softly. "Where does he live, then?"

"In Brentford," she read.

Peter looked at his watch. "It's after five. How far is it to Brentford, Sam?"

"It'll take us quite a while," he replied.

Lilian shook her head. "We can't just turn up unannounced at his door. He has a telephone. I'll give him a ring."

"All the better," Sam said.

A little later, they were on the Underground heading for South Kensington station. Lilian was amazed at how uncomplicated the call to Chief Inspector Lewis had been. He told her he had arranged to meet a few friends at eight o'clock in a wine bar near the Victoria and Albert Museum, and he would be pleased to meet them there around seven. Lilian grew increasingly tense the closer they got to Kensington. Sam was regaling her father with anecdotes about his last day at school, but her thoughts returned obsessively to the imminent meeting with Lewis.

They couldn't miss the wine bar; the sweeping yellow letters of its sign were visible from the Tube station. The bar smelled of pipe tobacco and aftershave, a pianist was playing evergreens, and candles on the tables created a cozy atmosphere. Lilian looked around, but she saw only couples.

Then they became aware of a tall man approaching from a table in an alcove hidden by the bar.

The three of them exchanged a look of surprise, and Lilian's bewilderment grew. Silver-gray hair, a tan, a sporty physique—not at all like she would have imagined a retired chief inspector to look.

"Lewis. Miss Morrison?"

"That's me. Thank you for seeing us at short notice."

Lilian introduced him to the others, and Lewis invited them over to his table. He ordered a round of wine and mineral water, then folded his hands on the table.

"You told me on the phone that you're looking for information about Dr. Cook because of your sister, Emma Dölling."

"That's right," Lilian said.

"We were wondering whether he might have treated my older daughter before she died," Peter said. "If he did, it might help us to understand and come to terms with her death."

"Of all the cases I dealt with, this was the one that stood out for me," Lewis said. "In 1946, Cook was sentenced to two years in jail for nine cases of forged documents and at least two illegal abortions. His license to practice medicine was also revoked. He committed suicide before he could be imprisoned."

There was an awkward silence.

"Why did he do all that?" Lilian asked. "What was his motive?"

"Cook refused to explain himself in court. Sadly, he took his secrets to the grave." Lewis leaned across the table. "But there's something I want to tell you, Miss Morrison. Cook's tragic end meant that his name and that of your sister have stayed in my mind. I have a personal interest in the case, and I wanted to talk to you as soon as possible."

His words sent a shot of adrenaline through Lilian's veins.

"The case is one that I wasn't able to solve completely, although we moved heaven and earth trying. I don't mind telling you that it bothers me to this day."

"Please tell us everything you know," Sam said.

"Gladly. As I'm sure you're aware," Lewis continued, "since the end of the war, the Federal Republic of Germany, together with the victorious Allies, has made every effort to trace missing persons and reunite families who were separated during the Nazi period. That's why Cook's file remains open."

"But what does Cook have to do with reuniting families?" Lilian asked.

"The documents he was found guilty of forging were all children's death certificates."

"I beg your pardon?" Lilian noticed a few heads around the room turn and lowered her voice. "What information did Cook falsify, and how did his accusers know he'd done it?"

Lewis looked at her gravely. "Three sets of parents stated that the children who'd been declared dead were still alive."

Lilian pressed her hand to her mouth to suppress a scream.

"These parents had death certificates with all the correct information about their children?" Sam asked, aghast.

"They did," Lewis said.

The blood drained from Peter's face. "How could that have happened?"

"One couple said that the Red Cross had found their child, slightly injured and disoriented, and sent for them to come and pick him up. At first, they attributed the false death certificate to the frenetic rescue work. They were just happy to have their boy back."

"That sort of thing shouldn't be allowed to happen," Lilian said in a choked whisper.

"You're quite right, Miss Morrison," Lewis said. "But the story doesn't end there. The same thing happened to a lawyer whose child was hospitalized, but not fatally wounded. He was angry and went to ask the Red Cross, where he heard of a third case in which the death certificate had also been issued by Dr. Cook. The lawyer encouraged the other two families to bring a lawsuit against the doctor. The Red Cross later confirmed their statements."

The three of them stared at Lewis. Innumerable thoughts whirled in Lilian's head, but she was unable to grasp any of them.

"You said nine forged certificates. What about the other six families, Chief Inspector?" her father asked.

"Some died in the war. Others didn't want to stand up in court. We're missing a few important pieces of the puzzle, which is why we've never been able to close the case once and for all."

Lilian tilted her head. "You said my sister's name had stuck in your mind. How was she involved?"

"It's a long, complicated story, and I'm afraid we don't have time now. But how does this sound to you? We've got some witness statements recorded on tape. I'll have a word with Inspector Wilson and see if I can get you permission to listen to them." Lewis smiled. "The recordings will answer some of your questions, and who knows? Maybe you can help us get nearer to closing the case."

Chapter 13

Lotte

Cape Town

Lotte threw on a kaftan and found her slippers. She had been lying wide awake for four hours and knew she wouldn't get back to sleep. Moving quietly so as not to wake Friedrich, who was asleep in the guest room, she slipped into the kitchen for a glass of orange juice. Her gaze fell on the sideboard, where the packet containing Dr. Fisch's papers lay. Sometimes she felt her fingers itching to open her old friend's diary, but she knew the memories it triggered would be painful. It was right to wait and read it when the whole family was together. Lotte turned away.

She stepped outside and looked up at a clear, strikingly beautiful starry sky. The air smelled damp. She drew the kaftan tighter, gazed up at the stars, and thought about the Shabbat dinner a few days ago. Once the last guests had left, she had sat with her friend Ewa Tulinski, gazing in wonder at the stars. Lotte thought back to their first meeting, when they were both newly arrived in Cape Town. The traumatized young girl who had miscarried during the difficult ocean crossing from Germany had been transformed into a self-confident woman. An administrative employee, she had never married, but whenever she had time, she would come and look after the playgroup at the Blue Heart.

Ewa's warmth was particularly evident when she was with the little ones. It was such a shame that she had remained childless, but she seemed satisfied with her life. Lotte had no reason to worry about her.

It was a different matter with her own son. Lotte's thoughts turned again and again to Lilian's call the previous evening. The news that Cook had been arrested had shaken her, but the despair in Peter's voice affected her more deeply. It must have been a hard day for him and Lilian.

That night Lotte felt her age in all her bones, and she wondered if it wouldn't be better to leave the past well alone. Neither her son nor her granddaughter would be helped by finding out the disturbing details of Cook's life, and it certainly wouldn't bring Margarethe back to life. Lilian was tougher than she realized, but Lotte was worried about Peter. The impression he gave others was always one of calm self-control. But Lotte knew how things really were with him and what the years spent alone, in the dark about the fate of his children, had cost him.

Much to Lotte's regret, Peter seemed immune to feminine charms. How often had she seen the way women looked at him, but their attention simply bounced off him unheeded. Of course no one could ever take the place of Clara, just as Lotte would never find a second Johann—their love was forever anchored in their hearts—but Peter was a mature man now, and he needed a woman to bring some joy to his everyday existence. She knew full well, however, that children never listened to their parents' advice, even though she was an excellent example of how it was possible to have a fulfilling relationship at a ripe old age. Lotte smiled fondly at the memory of Antoon. He had not only put her in touch with the Jewish community shortly after her arrival in Cape Town, but the sprightly Dutchman had told her every day how he felt about her and showed her that it is the present that counts. That you can't have a single moment of your life back. Antoon had taught her to laugh again. And when he died a few years later, her gratitude for their time together outweighed her grief.

Lotte knew Peter's heart's desire was different. He longed to have his birth name back—Paul Blumenthal, widower of Clara, son of Lotte and Johann, father of Margarethe and Gesa. But that decision lay in the hands of bureaucrats who had no idea what it meant to have to deny your own identity.

She felt a knot in her stomach as she stared at the sky.

The Atlantic murmured. *He cares not for the concerns of men.* Mingling with the constant roar of the waves was another noise. At first, she couldn't place it. It sounded like the bleating of a goat, but there weren't any nearby. Lotte stood, felt around for the flashlight that hung on a hook by the door, and shone it out over the garden and the neighboring property. She could see nothing unusual.

There it was again! She suddenly realized—Dede's son was crying. She sat down, relieved. Maybe Niam was cutting his first tooth, as the wailing soon grew to a sustained scream. He normally fell silent as soon as Dede took him in her arms. Lotte waited for the calm that followed when Dede nursed her son. But she waited in vain; the screaming became more insistent.

Shining the light before her, she made her way to the summerhouse. She had often noticed that the young mother switched on the bedside lamp when the baby woke her, but that night, the cabin was in darkness.

She knocked. "Dede? Is everything all right?"

Nothing.

An uneasy feeling crept over Lotte. She opened the door, which led straight into the bedroom. Dede's bed was empty. Where on earth could she be? She quickly picked Niam up and wrapped him in a warm blanket. She found a pacifier on the bedside table, which she gave to the baby before looking around in alarm. Dede never left her son alone. Lotte hugged him to her, went outside, and with her free hand shone the flashlight along the back of the summerhouse.

She stumbled. Looking down, she saw a crumpled figure lying unmoving before her.

Lotte shook her shoulder. "Wake up, girl! Oh my God!"

When Dede failed to react, Lotte turned her onto her back. She let out a scream, ran back across the grass, and hammered on the door of the guest room. "Friedrich! Help!"

A moment later, he opened the door a crack and blinked sleepily in the harsh light of the flashlight. "What's the matter?"

"Dede's been hurt! Here!" She pushed Niam into his arms and hurried away.

She fetched a first aid kit and hurried back to Dede, who gritted her teeth and opened her swollen eyes. "*Meesteres.*"

"Yes, I'm here. What happened?"

The young mother curled into herself, her hands pressed into her left side. Her chin and eyes were already showing bruises. "Two men . . . They were masked." Moaning softly, she raised her head, but let it sink down again. "Niam."

"He's fine. Those thugs beat you?"

Dede nodded. "With . . . wooden batons."

Lotte quickly moved to support the injured woman's head. Apart from a small graze, which was beginning to swell, she couldn't see anything too worrying there. "You've got to come into the house and get warm. Can you stand? I can't carry you."

"I'll try."

With Lotte's help, Dede finally managed to stand, her face screwed up in pain.

Friedrich hurried toward them.

"Where's the baby?" Lotte asked, a supporting arm around Dede's waist.

"I laid a wool blanket on the floor in my room, and he's sleeping there," he said. "I thought that would be safest."

"Good thinking. Dede needs to come into the house."

Friedrich wasted no time in helping the young woman indoors, where Lotte instructed her to lie down on the sofa with a cushion beneath her knees.

Dede's eyes closed in exhaustion.

"Will you go out and call an ambulance?" Lotte asked Friedrich. "I'll wait here with the two of them."

He scratched his head. "Are you sure?"

"I know exactly what you're going to say. Don't ask, just do it."

Friedrich threw on a jacket and went. A moment later, she heard the car start.

She turned back to Dede, and saw her looking up through half-closed eyes. "Niam's awake. He's hungry."

Lotte smiled at her instinct—the baby was kicking heartily with his legs. "Can you hold him?"

Dede gestured for her to bring Niam over. She pressed her lips together as her son thrashed about, greedily seeking her nipple.

It felt to Lotte like an eternity before the ambulance arrived. The emergency doctor, a man in his thirties, pointed to Dede.

"Is that the patient?"

"She certainly is." Lotte took Niam from Dede, holding the doctor's gaze firmly.

The doctor kept his bag in his hand. "I don't treat kaffirs. She's obviously not so badly injured. Call a black doctor."

Lotte got up and walked slowly over to the doctor. "I beg your pardon? I hope you're not making a diagnosis without even examining her?"

"Now, you listen to me! There's nothing for me to do here," the doctor hissed and moved to leave.

She stood in his path. "You listen to me, young man. This woman is my maid. She was brutally beaten on my property with wooden batons. I expect you to do your duty." Startled by the sharpness of Lotte's voice, Niam whimpered. "Or do I have to remind you of your oath?"

The doctor's features froze.

As he shifted uncomfortably from foot to foot, Lotte saw from the corner of her eye that Friedrich had turned away to hide his smile.

His features pinched as if he were sucking a lemon, the doctor began his examination. Dede endured his efforts in silence. Lotte could sense how his disparaging words had stung her. Dede probably experienced disrespect from the whites on a daily basis, but Lotte knew from her own experience that that kind of pain didn't go away.

"The injuries to her head are superficial. But the hematoma on her side indicates damage in the area of the spleen. You need an X-ray, girl." The doctor used the informal form of address and avoided looking at the patient as he spoke to her.

"My *naam* is Dede Achebe," she said, clearly and unequivocally. "Aren't I entitled to the same respect as you, Mr. . . . . ?"

The complacency vanished from his face. "Dr. Stuart Richards."

"*Dankie*, Doctor. And I'm Miss Achebe to you."

"What makes you think you can talk to me like this?" the doctor said through gritted teeth. "I'll write you a referral for hospital admission."

He scribbled something on a couple of papers.

"Just a moment." Friedrich drew himself up before him. "Aren't you going to take her to the hospital in your ambulance?"

Richards's scornful look was all the answer he needed. Dede turned away.

Friedrich crossed his arms. "At least inform the police, man! You can see for yourself that Miss Achebe's been attacked."

"I suggest you do that yourself," the doctor said curtly. Without so much as a glance at Friedrich, he tossed his instruments away in his bag and left Lotte's house as quickly as he could.

The next few hours were turbulent. Friedrich offered to take Dede himself, but Lotte wouldn't hear of it. She quickly packed up some essentials for mother and baby, and insisted on carrying the child herself. On the way out, she put up a sign outside the Blue Heart, stating that the center would be closed for the day.

The first hospital they tried refused to admit Dede, making it quite clear that she should go to a hospital for blacks.

Dede's mind was obviously becoming fogged, as she hardly reacted to Lotte's soothing words. Friedrich stopped the car again a little while later. If it weren't for the hand-painted sign, "Clinic for Blacks Only," they would probably have driven right past the dilapidated-looking building. They helped Dede out, her listlessness causing them increasing concern.

They were met at the entrance by a musty smell. A gaunt black doctor in an old white coat eyed the new arrivals critically and called for a nurse with a stretcher. "Is that the patient's baby?"

"Yes. He's called Niam, and he's still being breastfed." Lotte brushed away tears. "What's going to happen to him now?"

The doctor reached his arms out. "Give him to me. We'll take care of him until his mother is feeling better."

"Thank you," she said with relief.

"Please wait outside." The doctor waved a hand brusquely. "We'll let you know when there's any news."

Lotte raised her chin. "Certainly not. Dede's my friend, and we're staying here."

The doctor didn't reply. He handed the baby to a nurse, settled Dede, who was no longer conscious, on the stretcher, and hurried with her through a set of swinging doors.

Lotte sat down on a bench, Friedrich by her side. The paint on the wall opposite was peeling, and the wind blew through the window. A smell of vomit came from one of the patients' rooms.

"What a desolate place," Friedrich murmured with a shake of his head.

Lotte nodded and looked at the clock. The night was almost over, and the hard bench was making her back ache.

The time dragged by. Friedrich paced up and down the corridor while she tried to ignore the horrible smells. After a while, he brought her a paper cup of water he had managed to get from a nurse. She sipped it and made a disgusted face.

"I'm going to the police to lodge a complaint in person. It's disgraceful, forcing Dede to come to this grubby, poverty-stricken clinic for treatment even though there's a modern hospital much closer to us."

Friedrich looked sidelong at her. "I'll come with you. You can rely on my full support."

She raised her eyebrows. "That's all? You're not going to tell me to be careful or reasonable?"

He responded by kissing her brow. Lotte looked at him in confusion.

A door opened, and a doctor came up to them. "Miss Achebe's in the operating theater now. Her spleen's been ruptured, and we need to remove it. We've also confirmed the suspected concussion."

"The poor girl," Lotte whispered.

The doctor's eyes went to Friedrich, then back to Lotte. "It'll be expensive. Who's going to pay?"

"I'll take care of that." Lotte handed him her business card.

"Thank you. You may as well go home now. We'll be in touch."

"We'll wait till she comes out of surgery," Friedrich said, earning a look of gratitude from Lotte.

"As you wish. Please excuse me."

The doctor hurried into one of the patients' rooms. Lotte shuddered and leaned her weary head back against the wall.

"Wait here a moment," she heard Friedrich mutter, and watched with a puzzled frown as he left the building. He returned with a soft blanket from the car, which he laid around her shoulders. "It won't be much longer, I'm sure. Try and relax a little."

He put his arm around her, and she leaned against him.

"We're getting too old for this madness, staying up all night." Friedrich yawned. "We need our beauty sleep."

"I'm so glad you're here. Thank you."

It was getting light by the time the swinging doors finally opened again and a nurse came toward them. Lotte was suddenly wide awake.

"I'm pleased to tell you that Miss Achebe's come through well."

Lotte let out the breath she'd been holding and rose shakily. "Thank you."

Chapter 14

Ceara

Dublin

"Shall I come with you?" Aidan asked, stroking Ceara's silky hair. It was nine in the morning, and he was on call that day but didn't have to go in to the station.

"No, thanks. I have to do this alone. I've waited far too long, and I've got to put an end to it once and for all."

"Good luck. Don't keep me waiting too long—you know how I worry."

His love showed in his eyes, and Ceara couldn't help smiling. "I'll come back as soon as I can."

She paused at the workshop door to hang a "Closed Today" sign. Her nerves were fluttering, and she reminded herself she was a grown woman. People probably showed up at the Red Cross every day to look for lost family members.

Ceara had no sooner boarded the busy bus than she felt as though all the other passengers' eyes were on her. *I'm imagining things already,* she thought, and stared out of the window. Twenty minutes later, she reached her stop and was relieved to walk the last stretch on foot.

When she found herself in front of the old brick building with the white Red Cross flag flying over the entrance, Ceara felt weak at the knees. "It's time to confront your past," Dr. Hamlin had said yesterday at the end of their session, after reading her questionnaire responses carefully. "You need to take action, Mrs. Foley."

She'd wanted to run from the therapist's office there and then, feeling as if he were blaming her for her amnesia. But now, after sleeping on it, she understood. If she wanted to get better, she had to still the demons of her past. Silently encouraging herself, Ceara entered.

A receptionist with a friendly face asked what she had come about. She listened, nodding occasionally, then led Ceara to the woman responsible for the tracing service. When Ceara left the building a short while later, she took a deep breath of the fresh, rain-soaked air and opened her umbrella.

At home, Aidan took her damp jacket from her. "Did you learn anything useful?"

Ceara leaned against his broad shoulders. "They took my application. The woman said she can't promise anything, but they'll do their best."

"That's good." He held her a little away from him and regarded her. "You're afraid, aren't you?"

Ceara released herself, took a few steps onto the covered terrace, and gazed at a group of sparrows bathing in a puddle. "Can I borrow the sheet music from your latest tune?" She hurried into the kitchen to avoid his penetrating gaze.

"Sure. Why do you need it?"

"Oh, I just want to copy the notes to decorate a piece I'm working on."

"Help yourself. It's on the bookshelf in the music room."

"Thanks, darling."

Ceara was peeling potatoes when the familiar howl of the fire siren reached her ears, and she lowered the knife.

"Shit," Aidan said, already slipping into his work gear. "I was hoping for a day off." He kissed her quickly and fastened his jacket.

"Be careful," Ceara called after him, but her husband was already out the door.

She normally liked being alone, but today the prospect made her uneasy. She turned the radio up as she cooked. Then she went into the music room Aidan had set up in the attic, space that other families in the neighborhood used as children's playrooms. As it always did, the space triggered the memory of the moment when she'd been told she would never have children. "It makes no sense to keep brooding over it," Aidan often said, but what did her husband know about the gnawing inside, which made itself felt whenever she saw mothers with prams?

Ceara pulled herself together. She found the folder containing the music and took it to the workshop. She searched rapidly through a box until she found what she was looking for.

With a sheet of tracing paper and an offcut of silver wallpaper under her arm, she went to the office, where she began to sketch out the first notes of the children's melody.

She was half finished when Rhona burst into the workshop looking grim, placed her bag and a bakery box on the table, and sat down without a word.

"What's up?"

"I've brought us a chocolate cake."

Since when did Rhona eat chocolate, especially at lunchtime? With a shake of her head, Ceara tidied her craft materials away on a shelf over the desk and got out plates and forks, all the while watching Rhona out of the corner of her eye. Ceara didn't have much of a sweet tooth herself—if Rhona baked cookies, it was only because she and Aidan had a soft spot for them. Something must have happened. Experience had taught Ceara to wait until her foster mother raised the subject herself; Rhona hated feeling pressured.

So Ceara watched her serve the cake and even cut herself a second piece. This must be serious. Her patience was tested to the limits but eventually, after gulping down her tea, Rhona leaned back in her chair, hardly able to look at her.

"I've got something to tell you, love, but I've no idea how to begin."

"Just spit it out," Ceara said gently. She'd never seen Rhona at such a loss.

She brushed a few cake crumbs from her skirt. "I haven't been able to stop thinking about this business with your family, see. And then I—I—"

Ceara found it hard to keep her impatience in check. "Please, out with it, Mum."

Her foster mother raised her head. "Sorry, but it's so difficult. Right, OK. I went to Limerick, to the Light and Hope offices."

"The adoption agency?" Ceara frowned. "Why didn't you tell me? We could've gone together."

Rhona threw her napkin down on the plate. "You're upset enough as it is, and I didn't want to raise any false hopes that might not come to anything. So, I thought I'd just make a few inquiries, to see if they had any more information about the Doyles."

Ceara's pulse quickened. "And?"

"It was nothing like I'd expected. It turns out the Light and Hope building's been a medical center for years now."

She stared at her foster mother in bewilderment. Her fork clattered to the floor and she bent without thinking to pick it up. "What happened?"

Rhona poured herself another cup of tea. "I asked around in the nearby shops. It seems the adoption organization closed down suddenly in 1946."

Ceara's eyes widened. "Did you ask them why?"

"I couldn't get anything out of them. Some of the shops had only opened recently, and the folks at the established ones didn't want to talk." Rhona sighed. "Don't look at me like that. Do you think it would have been any better if I'd taken you along to Limerick with me?"

"Yes, but it's OK," Ceara said softly. "I know you meant well." She gazed into space. "Do you think the Red Cross will know about this business with Light and Hope?"

Rhona tilted her head to one side. "It's possible, since you were placed through them." She gave a melancholy smile. "I just—I want you to know I'll do anything I can to help you search for your family. Whatever happens, I'm here for you."

Ceara stood and gave her a hug. "I know."

Rhona brushed a tear from the corner of her eye.

Moved, Ceara stroked her cheek. "Don't cry. You'll always be my mother. But I've got to know where I'm from. I'm not going to abandon you, though, you understand?"

"Of course."

"How was your date, anyway?" Ceara asked.

"You mean with Lucas?" Rhona's cheeks took on a rosy glow. "He really is a wonderful cook. We're going to the Abbey Theatre next week."

"Oh, how lovely." Ceara felt a cozy warmth spread through her as well. Was Rhona maybe falling in love with this Lucas? She liked the idea; her mother had been alone for far too long.

Rhona drew away from her embrace. "I have to go, my love. I've got some things to do in town."

"That's fine. I've got a piece I want to work on for a while."

"Is it anything to do with the silver wallpaper and the tracing paper here?" Her foster mother indicated the craft materials on the shelf.

"Yes, that's it. I've used some offcuts to make a box for keeping playing cards in."

"How nice," Rhona said.

Ceara handed her the cake box. "Come to our place for supper tonight. Aidan would love to see you, too."

"I'd love to." Rhona pinched Ceara's cheeks and chuckled when she protested. "See you later, then."

Once Rhona had gone, Ceara's eyes fell on the tracing paper with the musical notes. It was now early afternoon, but she only needed a few minutes for the tracing, and Aidan wasn't home yet.

Ceara lost herself in the lines of music, and as she traced the shapes with a fine pencil, the children's melody echoed through her head. She hardly noticed a dreamy smile twitching at the corners of her mouth as the scene came to life before her eyes. The silvery light of the evening sun looked like it did in her dream. She hummed the melody as though she'd done so a hundred times before, and felt the sweet weight of the tiny child in her arms. The child was crying, very quietly, and the trembling of its rosy lips pierced her to the core. With a cheerful shout, she spun the child around and was delighted to hear the crying stop and see the gray eyes light up. Birds took up the tune with her, and the warm wind made her skirt billow out. All at once, the peace was broken by the shrill sound of a siren. She jumped. Why did it suddenly seem so dark? She looked up. Long shadows gathered in the sky, bringing a deep rumbling with them. The meadow beneath her feet vibrated. Whimpering, she hugged the child to herself and cradled its little head.

Help, she cried silently. *Help!*

As if from a great distance, she realized that someone was shaking her shoulders gently.

"Ceara, love."

The concern in the familiar voice jolted her back to reality.

"Is everything OK?" Aidan's face hovered close above hers, his warm hands on the back of her neck. He was still in his uniform and smelled of smoke.

"Um, sure." Ceara blinked. She felt cold, shivering as if it were the depths of winter. She froze as she became aware of where she was. She was cowering in a corner of the office, her arms thrown protectively over her head. Her heart was racing.

Aidan helped her to her feet and held her tight. He was pale beneath his tan. "What happened?"

"I—I've no idea," Ceara stammered. "I was thinking about the dream and then—then there was a child in my arms."

Aidan whistled through his teeth. "Do you remember what this child looked like? How old they were?"

"It was a baby, a few months old maybe, with dark, downy hair."

He stroked her cheek. "Why were you crouched in the corner? What were you afraid of?"

"I could see planes overhead. The noise was unbearable."

They both stood unmoving for a long while, holding each other close. "Are you feeling better now?" he asked as her trembling subsided.

She nodded into his chest, though she could still feel the shaking underfoot.

Aidan lifted her chin. "Tell me honestly, have you felt like that before? So afraid that you huddled in a corner?"

"No, I can't remember ever doing so," she replied truthfully. "It scares me. Am I going mad?"

He looked at her intently. "Don't ever let me hear you say that again. But I do want you to tell me if you saw anything else."

Ceara told him all she could recall. "I loved the baby and wanted to stop the crying," she finished.

He handed her a notebook that had been lying on the shelf, his expression giving nothing away. "Write it down, love, so you don't forget anything."

"I'll do it soon," Ceara said, amazed at the strange, husky sound of her voice. She looked up at him. "I had a brother or a sister. I can feel it. If they're still alive, I've got to find them."

"And you will," Aidan replied, pressing her into a chair. "Let's recap what we know so far. 'Dolly's Dream and Awakening' is by a German

119

composer. You obviously know it from your earlier life. There's this child in your dream you're comforting when it cries. Not to mention the planes and the shaking earth that scare you so much."

"That's right." The images from the silver dream, as she called it in her mind, flashed once again in front of her eyes. "It feels like a scene from the war, where I'm trying to protect my little brother or sister. Apart from that—" She broke off. "The wailing of the siren was familiar. I wasn't hearing it for the first time."

"What if these things really happened, before you lost your memory? What if you're actually German?"

Ceara frowned. "Don't you think that's stretching it a bit? Musical compositions are played everywhere, not only in the country where the composer was born."

"That's as may be, but I doubt that a little-known piece would be played abroad, especially during the war, when German culture was effectively banned for us."

Aidan's arguments weren't easy to brush aside. She snuggled up to him. It was frustrating—the deeper she delved into the dream, the more mysterious it became.

Chapter 15

Lilian

London

Lilian's nerves had been on edge ever since the meeting with Chief Inspector Lewis. No week had ever seemed longer. The days felt too short, the nights too long, and she was hardly able to think of anything other than the taped witness statements the chief inspector had mentioned. The telephone rang and she jumped up. At last, it was Inspector Wilson's call telling her they were expected at the police station the following day. She breathed a sigh of relief, but spent the night unable to sleep, longing for the morning.

Heavy rain clouds were darkening the sky when Lotte called Lilian and Peter the next day before they left.

"Good grief, why didn't you tell me before about Lewis and those recordings?" Lilian could hear the agitation in her grandmother's voice.

"We didn't want to tell you until we actually had an appointment to hear the tape."

Peter smiled as his mother huffed audibly.

"We've got no idea what to expect, and we're really nervous about it," Lilian added.

"Friedrich and I will keep our fingers crossed that the recording helps you in your search," Lotte said. In the pause that followed, she cleared her throat. "I haven't told you all my news either. It's about Dede."

Peter and Lilian listened intently as Lotte recounted everything that had happened.

"She's on the road to recovery now, but you should have seen the poor thing! It's appalling, what those thugs did to her. We're going to the police tomorrow."

Lilian exchanged a look of horror with her father.

"What are we going to do with you, Mama?" he said. "I suppose your sense of justice won't allow you to stay out of it?"

Lotte laughed. "You've got that right. Those criminals should be behind bars. People will think I'm not right in the head, but let them—I don't care. I'd better go. I'll call again soon."

"Of course, Grandma. We've got to go, too. Speak to you later."

"Good luck, my darlings."

When the three of them arrived at Scotland Yard, Lewis was waiting at the entrance.

"It's kind of you to accompany us," Peter said.

"I wouldn't have it any other way, Mr. Dölling. Follow me."

In his office, Inspector Wilson stood to greet them. "It's good to see you again, Mr. Lewis. Welcome back."

"And the same to you. Thank you for your cooperation." The men shook hands.

"Come with me. We won't be disturbed in here."

Inspector Wilson beckoned the little group into a side room. The plain walls were embellished only by a portrait of the queen, who seemed to be watching the proceedings with an eagle eye. Lilian squinted against the harsh light of the fluorescent tubes.

The police officer indicated a group of seats in the center of the room, gathered around a table on which stood a tape recorder.

Lewis sat down next to Wilson, with Lilian, Peter, and Sam opposite.

Her mouth sandpaper dry, Lilian reached for Sam's hand.

"This recording from 1946 contains some information that may help you," Inspector Wilson explained. After completing the necessary formalities, the three of them watched the inspector wind a reel of tape onto the spool. Peter's face remained stoic, but Lilian could imagine the turmoil he was feeling inside. Her own heart began to beat faster.

"I'll let you listen to the interview uninterrupted," Lewis said. "We can talk about it afterwards. Do you agree, Wilson?"

"Of course," he replied.

"Then let's begin." Lewis flicked the "Start" switch.

They listened, spellbound, to the matter-of-fact voice of the chief inspector stating the date of the interview and the case reference number.

"Lieutenant Arthur Grifford, born in London on January 11, 1908, currently stationed in Germany"—he quoted an address in Hamburg—*"is here in person to make a statement. Are these details correct?"*

"They are."

"You say you know Dr. Ernest Cook?"

"I do indeed. He had a practice in Fulham. I worked as an internist at Hackney Hospital until the beginning of 1941. Dr. Cook and I frequently worked together in emergency admissions, especially during the air raids, when he gave us every possible support."

Grifford's voice was soft and calm, giving Lilian the impression of someone who considered every word before speaking.

"How was your relationship with Cook?" Lewis asked.

"Let's call it distant," the internist replied. *"I don't know anyone who claimed to be close to him. Cook didn't like his actions being questioned, if I may be frank. It often caused difficulties."*

Grifford then gave accounts of patients who had been admitted to the emergency ward with acute complaints after being treated by Cook.

If Grifford asked his colleague about these cases, he was told to mind his own business.

"Sounds like a real charmer, this Cook," Sam whispered, and Lilian had to agree.

The old tape recording crackled with age.

"*Dr. Cook is accused of several cases of illegal abortions being carried out in his practice,*" Lewis continued. "*Can you tell us anything about that?*"

"*I'm sorry. I don't indulge in speculation, as a matter of principle.*"

"*Very well, Lieutenant Grifford. Let's move on to the charges brought against Dr. Cook of nine cases of forging documents. I'm going to read out a few names. If you recognize any of them, please tell me.*"

Lilian and her companions listened intently to the list.

"*. . . and Ceara Doyle, Hack—*"

"*Stop! I recognize that name,*" Grifford interrupted.

"*Tell me more, Lieutenant,*" Lewis's recorded voice said.

"Ceara?" Lilian said, horrified.

Inspector Wilson gave her a look. "Shall I stop the tape for a moment, Miss Morrison?"

"Thank you, but there's no need." She shuddered.

Wilson let the tape play on.

"*Well, in 1940 I was living on Sutton Place in Hackney,*" Grifford resumed.

Lilian froze. *Sutton Place?*

"*In the flat above us were the Jacksons with their foster children. I particularly noticed little Emma Dölling.*" Grifford's voice was suffused with warmth. "*She had come to England about a year previously with the Jewish Kindertransport. A sweet but reserved little girl. She seemed intelligent, but refused to speak English with her foster parents. That was the cause of frequent arguments.*" Grifford coughed. "*I never really liked Jackson; he didn't seem like a caring foster father to me. Whenever I got the opportunity, I'd speak German to Emma, and she radiated happiness when I did. I felt really sorry for her."*

Lilian let out an audible sigh and tried to concentrate on what Grifford was saying. His voice suddenly seemed to be reaching her from a great distance.

Margarethe. Oh my God, Margarethe.

"Please, can you come to the point, Lieutenant," Lewis prompted.

Grifford cleared his throat. *"Very well. At the time of the air raids, we internists were responsible for first aid in the hospital, and the surgeons operated more or less round the clock. On that horrific night in December 1940, Dr. Cook personally brought an emergency case to the clinic. Whatever my opinion of my colleague, I was extremely grateful to him for leaving his practice to help out on the ground. The emergency patient I found myself examining in one of the beds was my little friend Emma."*

Lilian gasped. In her mind's eye, she saw her sister, her face pale on the pillow, her unbound hair falling over her brow and cheeks.

"Oh, my poor little girl," her father said, his voice choked.

The tape recorder whirred.

"Please continue, Lieutenant," Lewis said to the doctor.

"A piece of an iron girder had become embedded in her abdomen," Grifford said. *"The sight was appalling even for us war-hardened doctors. Emma had lost a lot of blood and was clearly fading fast. I tried to stanch the flow of blood and clean the wound as well as I could, and all the while she was crying out in German for her mama and papa. I was choked up, as you can imagine."*

"She called out for her parents?" Lewis asked. *"That doesn't sound like a patient who's barely conscious."*

"On the contrary. The seriously wounded often talk or cry out, even when under anesthetic."

"Thank you for the explanation, Lieutenant. What happened next?"

"As I was preparing Emma for the operation, she opened her eyes, and she was terrified when she saw the piece of metal in her lower belly. 'Ganz

ruhig,' *I said to her in German. 'Steady now.' I kept talking away to the little girl, reminding her of the conversations we'd had in German. 'We're helping you. You're in good hands. Trust me, Emma. Do you recognize me? I'm your neighbor, Arthur Grifford. I work here.' I can still see the questions in her eyes. Her reaction told me she neither recognized nor understood me. As I was talking and working, Cook filled out the papers. They were in the name of Ceara Doyle. I thought the man had either lost his wits or he was completely overworked. I was just about to point out his error when she lost consciousness and her condition worsened dramatically."*

Ceara? Emma? Margarethe?

Lilian jumped up, but Peter pressed her back into her seat. For a moment, the only sound in the quiet room was her heavy breathing and the hiss of the tape.

"Fortunately, we were able to stabilize Emma," Grifford continued. *"When I looked up again, Cook had vanished with the papers before I could clarify the matter or thank him for his efforts. The little girl was fortunate in a way, since none of her vital organs were damaged. We were able to save her with an emergency operation, but her uterus had been seriously damaged and had to be removed."*

Her hands in front of her face, Lilian felt Sam's arm around her shoulders and heard her father let out a sharp breath.

"Shortly after, I asked the nurse in charge to reissue the papers in the correct name. Later, when I asked after Emma, the nurse told me she was doing relatively well under the circumstances and had been transferred to the children's hospital."

"Stop!" Lilian caught the former chief inspector's eye. "Chief Inspector Lewis, Inspector Wilson, please could you—could you wind it back a little?"

Lewis nodded. "Of course."

She listened, stunned, to Grifford's last words. *Doing relatively well under the circumstances . . . transferred to the children's hospital.*

The shock was written on Peter's face. "My daughter didn't die in the air raid?"

"Well, she was transferred to the children's hospital at least, as you've just heard," Lewis replied. "I believe this witness was completely trustworthy."

"The question is"—Sam produced a copy of the death certificate from his jacket pocket and laid it on the table—"why was she officially registered dead?"

Lewis scanned the paper and handed it to Wilson. "We hope we'll be able to find that out with your help." He looked at Lilian, who had been following the conversation numbly. "Shall we continue? Grifford's statement is almost finished."

"Of course," she managed to reply.

Inspector Wilson flicked the "Start" switch.

"Do you know what became of Emma?" Lewis's recorded voice asked.

"I'm afraid I don't have any specific information," Grifford said. *"I spoke to a colleague and friend of mine at the children's hospital here. He told me the girl was making good progress and was to be sent to the country—they weren't sure where at the time. I intended to ask after Emma again before long, but that very evening my wife and I had our own house destroyed and were left fighting to survive. We couldn't think clearly; all we could see were the rows of dead bodies and the incredible suffering. That's what prompted us to volunteer for military service."*

"Thank you very much," Lewis said. *"Would you be prepared to repeat your statement in court?"*

"I'd be grateful if this statement could be the end of the matter," Grifford replied. *"As you know, I've come back from Germany specially to make it."*

"We realize that. But I'm afraid tape recordings alone aren't admissible as evidence in court. Perhaps you'd be prepared to have your statement set out in writing for the hearing, Lieutenant?"

"*Of course,*" he said. "*And I'd be grateful if you could send me a copy of the judgment, Chief Inspector.*"

"*That can be arranged. End of the record of the statement by Lieutenant Arthur Grifford.*"

The tape sputtered to a stop, and silence descended on the room.

Lilian moistened her lips. "Which children's hospital was my sister taken to?"

"We found her name in a hospital on the outskirts of the city. She was taken there as Ceara Doyle."

Lilian stared at Lewis in incomprehension.

Peter ran a hand over his face. "So they never corrected her name."

Sam gave Lilian a questioning glance.

"But—but that's not so bad," Lilian said quickly, having recovered her voice. "I'm sure the mix-up can be cleared up. It says in the hospital records when a patient is transferred to a convalescent home, and which one."

"I'm sorry to say that's not the case here," Lewis said. "The hospital was itself destroyed by a German air raid in 1941. The patients' documents were all lost. We've searched throughout England for Ceara Doyle and Emma Dölling, but we've found nothing. All we know about her transfer to the children's hospital and, later, the convalescent home, is based on what Grifford's colleague told us. Emma's trail ends with her release from Hackney Hospital." He looked at her. "I'm afraid none of the surviving staff at the children's hospital remembered your sister. We also have to consider the possibility that she died in the air raid on the clinic."

"No! I can't believe that," Lilian said, choked by tears.

Sam put an arm around her.

"Mr. Lewis is right," Wilson said. "But we'll look into it. It could take a while, though."

"I'd be really grateful," Lilian said quietly.

Lewis caught her eye. "There's something else. The Jacksons were among the families who didn't want to make a statement in court. We summonsed them to the station in view of Grifford's comments."

"What did you make of them?" Lilian asked.

"Mr. Jackson seemed surly, nervous. And he sweated noticeably when we were questioning him. My colleague and I had the impression that he had something to hide. His wife confirmed his statement that they didn't know Dr. Cook. In any case, the Jacksons refused to come to court to confirm any of it."

"We also got in touch with the Jacksons recently," Peter said.

Sam described their afternoon at the Jacksons' house. "Emma's history left Mr. Jackson cold. His wife at least showed a little empathy, but there was no real affection there either."

"He shut us out when we asked for the names and addresses of any former foster children," Peter continued. "We thought that was strange."

"But then we talked to William Field and Sally Russell," Lilian said. "They were living with the Jacksons at the same time as my sister."

"We tried that, too, in 1946," Lewis said, "but at the time, the older foster children were either not yet of age or refused to be interviewed. And since we had nothing definite against the Jacksons, all we could do was wait until a better opportunity arose. Did you find out anything new from Field or Russell?"

Lilian told Lewis and Wilson about the conversations with William and Sally.

Lewis frowned. "Do you know whether Mrs. Russell actually witnessed Jackson identifying Emma's body with Dr. Cook?"

Lilian shook her head. "I think Sally was still with Mrs. Jackson."

"Yes, he was alone when he was talking to Dr. Cook," Peter said. "But Sally saw them from a distance."

The former chief inspector's expression brightened. "Well, that means we have a new line of investigation, and we can interrogate the Jacksons again."

Inspector Wilson had been making notes as they spoke.

"So, then, Dr. Cook and Jackson conspired to forge my daughter's papers?" Lilian's father spoke aloud what she had been thinking.

Lewis held up his hands. "Let's not speculate too wildly or jump to conclusions. It won't help us. We'll be in touch as soon as there's any news, and together we can discuss what to do next."

The two police officers stood.

"One moment, please," Lilian said. "Please could you get us Grifford's address?"

Wilson blinked. "I'll see what can be done. May I keep the copy of the death certificate?"

Sam handed it to him.

"Is this all, or do you have any other documents relating to Emma?"

"Yes, here you are, Inspector." Sam took an envelope from his jacket pocket. "We've got copies of her orphanage admission documents."

"Excellent. We'll be in touch."

"Thank you very much," Peter said.

Lilian smiled at the officers, but couldn't bring herself to speak. *Margarethe. Oh my God, Margarethe. Are you still alive?*

A short time later, they were sitting in a bistro. Someone pressed a glass of water into Lilian's hand.

"Drink this," Sam said.

As her shock gradually eased, she became aware of her father sitting across the table from her. Lilian gripped her glass without looking up.

"Assuming that the name on the hospital admission papers was never corrected—"

"That doesn't make sense," Sam said.

"Surely Margarethe would have corrected the error herself when she awoke after the operation," Peter said. "Don't forget she was already nine at the time."

She stared at him, then jumped up. Her glass fell to the floor and smashed. "I've got to go." She turned quickly and reached for her purse.

Sam stopped her. "Where are you going?"

"To the Red Cross office. Let me go. If I have to, I'll continue the search for her abroad!"

Sam shook his head. "It's late, love. They must be closed by now. We'll ask tomorrow."

Her heart beating wildly, she looked between them. "It won't wait. Don't you understand? My sister's alive. I know it."

Sam drew her into his arms. "Dashing around blindly isn't going to get you anywhere."

"Sit down before you fall down, girl," her father said.

Sobbing, Lilian tried to break free, but Sam was having none of it and guided her gently back to her seat.

Chapter 16

Lotte

Cape Town

The afternoon sun had sunk low over the rooftops by the time Friedrich and Lotte left the local police station.

"It's outrageous!" Lotte fumed. "Did you notice how the police officer hardly took any notes during my statement? I'll bet my life he tossed them straight in the wastebasket!"

Friedrich glanced sidelong at her. "I'm not surprised by any of it. They don't give a damn about the blacks."

He steered her smoothly toward Green Point Common, which wasn't far from the police station. From afar they heard the cheerful voices of children running around boisterously on the neglected playing fields and soccer pitches. The walk along the Sea Point promenade rewarded them with outstanding views of the sea and Cape Peninsula jutting out into the ocean.

On reaching the park, they sat on a bench, and Lotte looked out to the fixed point in the distance that had drawn her gaze for years.

"Robben Island," she said, feeling the customary unease that rose in her every time she looked at the prison island.

"I know," Friedrich said. "Do you remember that day, soon after I arrived, when you showed me this place?"

"How could I forget?" Lotte replied with a small smile. "Peter, Lilian, and Sam were still asleep. It was such a beautiful morning, and we brought a flask of tea. We sat on this very bench."

Friedrich nodded. "Robben Island was hidden by fog, and we wondered how many prisoners must have tried to escape to the mainland despite the treacherous currents."

"Hardly anyone has succeeded, as far as I know. Most of them drown." Lotte watched a swarm of seabirds circling overhead. She turned and looked into his eyes. "What should I do if the police refuse to pursue the case?"

"Nothing. You've done all you can."

They sat in silence. A few boats swayed on the shimmering Atlantic in the evening light. A group of young white girls wandered past them, laughing. They made Lotte painfully aware that she—indeed, her whole generation—had been denied this lightheartedness. If there was anything Lotte truly wished for, it was to see whites and blacks, Christians and Jews, walking together along the seafront as though it were the most natural thing in the world. As though things had never been any different.

"My tourist visa will expire soon," Friedrich said, rousing her from her thoughts.

She studied his familiar face with its furrowed brow and the large hands that were made for hard work, yet could hold little Niam so tenderly. Her heart grew heavy. "The time's flown by. You must be missing Hamburg, though?"

"Not in the slightest."

She blinked. "What about the Alster? The fresh breeze, the summer rain? You must have many good friends at home."

"I've got acquaintances and neighbors with whom I enjoy the occasional chat. But friends?" He took her hand. "I've put in an application for a permanent residency permit. As a pensioner with a secure income, I think I've got a pretty good chance of getting it."

Lotte shook her head in disbelief. "But—I don't understand. You've got a house in Hamburg."

He waved this away. "Unnecessary clutter."

"What about your furniture, your heirlooms and mementoes?"

"Old junk, the lot of it."

"But, Friedrich, do you think you can give up your homeland just like that? I still remember only too well how difficult—"

"There's no comparison," he interrupted firmly. "I don't have any relatives left, in Hamburg or anywhere else, and I've got no one to worry about but myself." He looked at her. "Everyone I love is in Cape Town."

Lotte blinked again.

"You know, Peter and his family were my first true friends. It was so hard to let them go off into the unknown. It means so much to me to have found Peter again. What would I do without you all in cold, rainy Hamburg where my rheumatism would be back to plague me?"

"You've got rheumatism?" she said. "You never said anything."

"I hardly notice it here in Cape Town. This climate's good for me." He looked at her intently. "I called Hamburg this morning and spoke to the young couple who live across the street. We used to chat all the time. They're expecting their first baby, and they've been looking for a bigger place for months. I've offered them my house. In return, they'll clear it out and renovate it. What do you have to say to that?"

"Skillfully done." Lotte laughed with surprise.

"It was, if I say so myself." Friedrich beamed. "And I've hired an agent to find me an apartment in your neighborhood. I don't need much; one or two rooms and a small balcony will be enough."

"What would you say to a room with a bathroom, sea view, garden access, and family nearby?"

"You mean—?"

She put her arms around him. "Stay. I get lonely in that big house."

He held her tight. "Well, if you're asking—"

"Oh, I am. Please." She suddenly felt young again, and full of joie de vivre. "It would make me so happy."

"How can I refuse the wish of a beautiful woman?" He immediately turned serious. "Once I'm granted the residency permit, I'll have to return to Hamburg briefly to clear up a few formalities. But that won't be for a while yet." Friedrich looked out to sea. "It's getting dark; we ought to be going."

"I'd like to visit Dede. What do you think?"

"I was going to suggest it." He linked arms with her, and they made their way to the hospital.

There, they were met by a nurse who looked them up and down as though they were irritating insects. Even as she directed them to Dede's ward, she made no secret of her disapproval.

"Whites aren't actually allowed in here, in case you hadn't noticed. You're going to get us in trouble."

Lotte chose not to reply. She tried to understand the nurse's position—after all, it wasn't the blacks who made the rules. Yet she never ceased to be dismayed at how deep the chasm between black and white had become, with racial segregation even penetrating the worlds of sickness and death.

"Please keep it brief," the nurse said, leaving before Lotte had a chance to ask about Niam.

Voices could be heard inside, but as she and Friedrich entered, they fell silent abruptly. Dede was on a ward with four women of different ages, who acted as though they hadn't seen the visitors. They were lying on hard beds below frosted-glass windows that let in hardly any light. One of them had clearly just used the bedpan—the stink of excrement took Lotte's breath away.

Dede was in the bed by the window, feeding Niam. Her eyes widened when she saw them. "*Meesteres*, Mr. Fred."

Her affectionate name for Friedrich always made Lotte smile.

"How are you, Dede? And please call me Lotte."

The young woman's right eye was swollen, and her head was bandaged. She was lying feebly on the pillow, but her cheeks had regained a little of their color.

Lotte breathed in sharply.

"My side hurts, but it's OK." Dede paused to help Niam, who had lost his latch, disturbed by their arrival, and was now searching greedily for her nipple. "I didn't think they'd let you in here."

"You obviously don't know me that well, my friend," Lotte replied.

"The doctor says that if my temperature stays down, I'll be able to go home in a few days."

"We hope so," Friedrich said.

"We certainly do. May I sit?" Lotte asked.

Dede patted the bed by way of reply. Niam made sucking noises, and Lotte was unable to resist reaching out and gently stroking his black hair. "May I ask you something?"

"Of course."

"What actually happened? Why were you left lying behind the summerhouse?"

Dede closed her eyes in anguish. When she opened them again, the horror of what she had experienced showed in the bitter lines around her mouth. "Niam was restless in the night with stomach pains. Once I finally got him to sleep, I went to bed as well. I was woken by a noise, a woman calling my name. I thought it was *meesteres*, and something was wrong. Dede Achebe isn't afraid of the dark, no, not at all."

Lotte patted her hand to reassure her. "You're strong and brave, we both know that."

"Thank you." Her eyelids grew heavy. "The woman called again. Then I was scared that something bad had happened to *meesteres*."

"Oh, Dede." Lotte struggled to stay calm. "I'm so sorry." She gazed at Dede thoughtfully. "You're absolutely sure it was a woman's voice?"

"Yes, that's why I went out. Then someone grabbed me and dragged me to the back of the house. There was a second person there. I saw them raise their arm. I was hit on the back of my head, and I lost consciousness."

"And you have no idea who they were or why they'd do that?"

"None. I am willing to take risks for my cause, but they came in the night—they could have hurt my baby."

"This mustn't happen again." Lotte sensed the surreptitious looks that passed among the other patients behind her back.

"I've got an idea," Friedrich said. "What do you think about swapping rooms, Dede? I'll move into the summerhouse; you'll be safe in the main house." He narrowed his eyes to slits. "If the bastards dare to return, they'll get the shock of their lives."

Dede's eyes went from one to the other. "*Dankie*, but I am going to move out."

Lotte leaned closer. "Alone, with a little baby, out on the street? Why would you want to risk that?"

"I don't want *meesteres* to be caught up in trouble on my behalf." Niam started to hiccup; Dede lifted him up and patted him on the back. "I'd never forgive myself if anything happened to you or Mr. Fred."

"I understand that. But are we really supposed to give up without a fight?"

"They will be watching us."

"Fine. Let them. We've got nothing to hide."

Dede was silent.

Friedrich nodded grimly. "Please don't misunderstand, but we're reluctant to let you go when those people could still be after you." He lowered his voice. "Or don't you like living and working with Lotte?"

"I do, very much." Dede's lips thinned. "But Mr. Fred, are you not afraid of the authorities and the people who beat me up?"

"Of course we are," Lotte said. "But I won't let anyone dictate who can live in my house or work for me."

"Please stay at least until those people lose interest in you." Friedrich gestured to Lotte. "We'll leave you in peace now. Just think about our offer."

Dede looked down in embarrassment.

"Get well soon," Lotte said. "We'll come back to see you tomorrow."

They were just turning to go when Dede whispered, "Please wait a moment."

Friedrich and Lotte moved closer.

"Could I have a room at the Blue Heart?" Dede whispered softly enough that the other patients on the ward couldn't hear. "I am afraid they would find me again in your house."

"It's no less dangerous at the Blue Heart," Friedrich observed.

"But they are less likely to look for me there. And this way, I will not endanger you." Dede looked at them pleadingly. "Please, could I have the room at the back, so no one can see me from the street? There's a path leading straight to *meesteres's* house from there. The bushes are as tall as trees; no one would see me."

Lotte nodded. "Very well, Dede. But you must promise me you'll be careful."

"Yes, I promise. Thank you."

Friedrich smiled and put his arm around Lotte. "We ought to go before that nurse throws us out."

Darkness had fallen over the city. But Lotte was pleased to be away from the ward. She drew her wrap tighter around her body. "It smelled awful in there. I'm disgusted by the conditions in that clinic."

"We'll bring Dede and the baby home as soon as we can," Friedrich promised. "Let's go now. You know how dangerous the streets of Cape Town can be at night."

Fortunately, they didn't have far to go, and Lotte was soon relieved to be sitting on the terrace with a blanket over her knees, a glass of good Shiraz in her hand. Friedrich had put on the record of Yiddish songs she loved to listen to. Lotte was constantly amazed by the way he judged her moods so well. The old melodies she'd known since childhood soothed her as always.

They sat together peacefully, each lost in their own thoughts. Lotte stole a glance at Friedrich. She didn't want to imagine how the last few days would have been without him.

"I'll make Dede's new room a little cozier tomorrow," he said after fetching a little snack. "Let's just hope she doesn't pick up an infection in that pigsty."

"Thank you, love. I feel sorry for the doctors and the staff, having to care for patients under those conditions. It must be so frustrating."

"I'm sure."

"Dede said there was a woman among her attackers. I can't understand that. What could Dede have done to make a woman get involved in such a brutal act?"

"I wish I knew. They must have been whites—nothing else would make sense."

Lotte shuddered.

He drained his glass and stood. "Will you be opening the Blue Heart again tomorrow?"

"Definitely."

"I'll come with you. I can get Dede's room ready while I'm there. We have to be careful at the moment."

Lotte yawned behind her hand. "Yes. I'm going to bed now. I'll see you tomorrow."

He kissed her on the cheek. "We deserve a good night's sleep. Goodnight, my angel."

She frowned. "Can you believe that's what my parents used to call me when I was a little girl?"

He grinned like the Cheshire cat, and a warmth came to his eyes. "It slipped out. You mean so much to me, and I can never find the right words."

Lotte found herself tongue-tied at the confession. She looked at him a moment without moving. "Thank you," she managed. "Sleep well."

He followed her with his eyes as she went into the house and closed her bedroom door behind her.

Chapter 17

Ceara

Dublin

Ceara always closed the workshop at noon on Tuesdays, to spend the afternoon doing the accounts. But this afternoon she had an appointment she wasn't looking forward to at all. Before leaving the office, the telephone caught her eye, and she called the Red Cross.

"Yes, hello? My name is Ceara Foley. I need to know if anyone has news about my application. It's only been a few days, but—"

"We're open until six, Mrs. Foley," the woman said. "You're welcome to come in. Shall I make you an appointment?"

After agreeing to go later that afternoon, Ceara hung up and stared at the phone, her agitation growing.

An hour later she was sitting in a very different sort of room, hands folded in her lap, staring darkly at the sofa with its colorful cushions as she waited for Dr. Hamlin. Rays of sunlight shone through the window and lit up a piece of rock crystal as big as her hand. The butterflies in her stomach fluttered as the therapist strode in.

"Please make yourself comfortable on the couch and close your eyes."

Ceara obeyed. The couch was more comfortable than it looked. She heard a bicycle bell ringing outside. Her hands were sweaty.

"Tell me what you're thinking," Dr. Hamlin said.

Hesitantly at first, she told him the latest version of her silver dream.

"That's interesting, very interesting. Your impressions seem to be getting more vivid."

"I've contacted the Red Cross," she continued. "I'm going over there later."

"I wish you luck. I'm glad about your decision to look for possible brothers or sisters. How do you feel after telling me about your dream?"

"I'm all unsettled and I feel helpless. There's nothing I'd like more than to run away."

"That's understandable, Mrs. Foley. Is there anything that would help to make you feel better?"

"Music. I like the children's song from my dream."

"Very well. Imagine it's playing, and let's see if you can enter into the dream right here and now. You'll talk me through it as it happens, and you'll be perfectly safe."

Ceara concentrated, and as though it had been waiting in the wings, "Dolly's Dream and Awakening" popped into her mind. The quiet, gentle piano notes had their characteristic soothing effect on her.

"What feelings does the piece trigger in you?"

Ceara thought about it. "Security. Warmth." Before she knew what was happening, a sob rose in her throat.

"Very good. Where are you?"

At first she could still feel the soft couch she was lying on, aware of the street sounds from outside. But then the sights and sounds blurred, and she found herself in another place. "I'm standing in a meadow. Birds are twittering overhead. The air smells of summer flowers." The feel of the sun on her skin was intoxicating.

"Can you feel the wet grass under your feet?"

Ceara watched the green blades waving in the gentle breeze, tickling her toes. "Yes."

"What time of day is it?"

"The sun's low in the sky, so it's late afternoon. There are tiny droplets shimmering in the air. The melody's being carried on the wind, and the child in my arms is making happy sounds." She smiled.

"Fine. Describe your surroundings."

"There are a few old trees in front of me. The light's so beautiful—shimmering silver."

"How old are you, Mrs. Foley?"

"Nine," she replied, amazed at how readily the answer came to her.

"Look down. What are you wearing?"

Ceara felt soft fabric against her skin. There were large buttons at her cuffs. "A dress with a white belt and a red coat. It's my favorite coat. It's got two big pockets, and I want to wear it all the time." She looked at the tiny baby in her arms. "The little one's fussing. Must be hungry."

"Can you still hear the melody?"

"Yes, but it's very quiet."

"Will you take a look around, please? Where's the boy with the conductor's baton? Can you describe him?"

Ceara hugged the wriggling bundle close and looked across the meadow, searching for the fallen log, but couldn't see it anywhere. She suddenly felt a lump in her throat. "The boy—he's gone. He's—he's not under the tree or anywhere else in the meadow." She was aware of her heart thumping loudly. Her voice turned shrill. "Where's he gone? I can't see him anymore!"

She felt a hand on her arm. "Breathe deeply, Mrs. Foley. Everything's all right." Dr. Hamlin waited until she had calmed down. "What are you feeling now?"

"The birds are joining in the melody." Ceara listened, enchanted. "The music's getting louder. The birds are singing so beautifully."

"Good. What do you want to do now?"

142

"I want to dance and spin round in a circle."

"Then dance, if it makes you happy."

In her mind, Ceara turned faster, shouting for joy. She began to feel dizzy, but couldn't stop. She wanted to feel her skirt billowing out, to hear the child in her arms stop crying. The child should be happy and laughing like she was in that silver moment. *I'd better not spin so fast, or the baby will be frightened.*

She came to a stop, looked down at her arms, and cried out.

"Steady, Mrs. Foley. What are you afraid of?"

"The baby! The baby's vanished. Oh God, it—it can't be happening!" There was a catch in Ceara's voice. She covered her face with her hands and shuddered. She suddenly felt cold all over, as she looked around, panic-stricken. *Where are you, little one?* It was as though her insides had turned to ice.

"You're only dreaming, lying here on my couch," the doctor said soothingly. "Nothing can happen to you. You're safe."

But Dr. Hamlin's voice sounded a long way away, as did the music. Then it fell silent, along with the birds, and the wind subsided.

"How do you feel?"

"I'm freezing." She shivered. "It's so quiet. I'm scared. Where's the baby? I've got to look after the baby."

"You'll warm up soon." She sensed the doctor placing a soft blanket over her. "I'm here with you. You're not alone."

My name is Emma, an inner voice whispered desperately. *Only Emma. I want to go home. Please can I go home?*

"You can open your eyes now if you want to," Dr. Hamlin said.

As Ceara did so, she realized her face was wet and her limbs were heavy as lead.

"Well done, Mrs. Foley. How do you feel?"

"As if I've just run a marathon." She moved to stand, but the doctor indicated that she should stay lying down.

"It shouldn't feel like that," he said with a shake of his head. "It's probably because you brought yourself back to the present too suddenly."

Her vision cleared, and she studied his face. "Did I?"

"You said, loud and clear, 'My name is Emma. Only Emma. I want to go home.'"

"I don't remember that." *Emma?*

"Why don't you rest there for a while, and then we'll discuss what you experienced."

Shaken to the core, Ceara stared out of the window.

The doctor left her in peace and concentrated on writing his notes. After a few minutes, he raised his head. "How do you feel now?"

"The dream's changing. It's upsetting me," Ceara replied quietly.

"I see this as a good sign. You're clearly more open to allowing the memories in." He put on his reading glasses. "Mrs. Foley, you say your most recent dreams have happened spontaneously and have been markedly different from the earlier dreams you had at night. Is that right?"

"Yes, it is."

He tapped his fountain pen on the desktop. "It makes me wonder what could be triggering them. Is it when you feel a certain way, see something in particular, when you're in a particular place?"

Ceara thought hard, but only felt more confused. "It's nothing to do with where I am. It's happened both when I was in company and when I was alone. When I've been dancing or working." She stared at the crystal. The sun had gone behind a cloud, and the rock looked colorless and insignificant without the sunlight reflecting off it. All at once she was hit by a realization like a bolt of lightning. "Something's just occurred to me, though I've no idea how it's relevant," she said in a faltering voice. "It all began with a piece I was making." She described the little box. "Since I began working on it, the dream started coming in the daytime, too, and always with that specific piece of music."

Ceara looked down at the doctor's feet; he was wearing sandals with white socks—some clichés were based in reality. She looked up. "I can't get the tune out of my mind. That was also the trigger—" She stopped.

"The trigger for what?" the doctor pressed.

This was the moment she had been wanting to avoid, but Dr. Hamlin wasn't going to let her off the hook now. "Last time, when the dream had ended, I was huddled in a corner, trembling and terrified of foreign planes above me."

Dr. Hamlin nodded. "How long were you like that?"

"I don't know. It felt like an eternity, but it was probably just a couple of minutes." She could tell from his expression that he was comparing symptoms and diagnoses from a reference book only he could see.

"Very good, Mrs. Foley. Please, can you write down what you see and feel? And if fear overtakes you again, think of the meadow and how happy the dancing made you feel. Hold on to those feelings. We'll meet again next week."

She felt hot and cold. "Will you ask me to go into the dream again?"

"But of course. It's the key to unlocking your subconscious."

"No," Ceara declared. "I don't mean any offense, Doctor. But I don't want to go through that again. You have no idea what it was like, how dreadful I felt when the baby—when I was alone."

"It's a new, difficult experience, Mrs. Foley. But I'm begging you not to make a hasty decision."

She got up. "I . . . Thank you. Goodbye." She grabbed her handbag and strode out of the building, followed by the bewildered gaze of the secretary.

Once outside, she stopped and leaned against the wall. *My name is Emma. Only Emma.*

Across the road, she saw a small park with a pond. She sat down on a bench beneath a row of birch trees. Children rode past on bicycles without taking the slightest notice of her. An old woman hobbled by, cursing her disobedient dog.

Near Ceara, a squirrel dashed up one of the trees and vanished from sight.

What had happened to the baby, and why had she called herself Emma? She felt a jolt through her body. Was that the name she was born with? Why did she feel the loss of the child like a smoldering fire inside her even though she didn't actually know if they were related? Could blood ties be strong enough to survive the passage of time?

Ceara looked at her watch and was horrified to see how late it was. She hurried to the Red Cross offices.

The kindly caseworker, a neatly dressed woman in her forties, greeted her with a firm handshake. "Please take a seat. I've had a quick look at your file. I assume you're wanting to find out if there have been any developments?"

"I am, but I've also found out something else in the search for my family." Ceara told her about Rhona's trip to Limerick. "It seems Light and Hope was closed shortly after the war. Do you know what happened?"

The caseworker raised an eyebrow. "There were quite a few rumors, but the organization looked respectable enough. We never had any problems with them."

Ceara took a deep breath of the fresh air coming in through the window. "Was everything done correctly in my particular case?"

The caseworker looked at her sympathetically. "That's what we're trying to determine, Mrs. Foley. I'm afraid we haven't yet found clues in any of the hospitals, convalescent homes, or children's homes in Ireland. We've therefore asked the International Committee for assistance. We're just waiting for their reply. We've made a start by forwarding your documents with your parents' names and details to the relevant people. I've added a note for them to check for any possible brothers or sisters. Sometimes you come across useful information when you're looking for something else."

Ceara felt as though someone had deleted her past at the moment of the air raid as if it had never happened. But that was simply impossible. What about her parents' identity papers, or at least their death certificates? What about her school reports? Ceara nodded. "Good idea. Thanks very much."

"You're welcome. I'll call you as soon as we have any news."

Ceara was lost in thought on the way home. Rhona was weeding in the front garden and gave her a cheery wave as she approached.

"Hello, love. I'm glad you're back. I've made a strawberry punch. Do you want some?" Rhona stood with her hands on her hips. "Or are you going to creep back into your dusty workshop despite this gorgeous weather?"

Nothing could have been further from Ceara's mind, and in any case, she didn't feel like touching the little box again that day. "Thank you, a glass of punch would be lovely."

Chapter 18

Lilian

London

It was still early in the morning when Lilian heard the door close. Her father had probably gone out jogging. He had been running much more frequently recently—to clear his head, he said. Lilian rolled onto her side and looked at Sam. His mouth was slightly open as he slept, his features relaxed. Her eyes went to the desk, to the little red box in which she'd kept her music box since dropping it on the ground. She pressed her lips together.

In her dreams the night before, she had been with Emma, holding hands and running through fields and meadows. They had been singing and laughing, hopping in rhythm with each other as carefree children did. It felt as though the dream would never end.

Emma, Lilly, Charlotte, and Peter Dölling.

Those names felt more familiar to Lilian than their birth names: Margarethe, Gesa, Clara, and Paul Blumenthal. But the real names had a much deeper meaning for her father—they represented a chance to reclaim his identity, to acknowledge his roots to the world.

Would her sister's birth name have meant so much to her?

Are you still alive, Emma? Margarethe?

Lilian peered at the clock. The Red Cross office opened at nine. After that, she would be meeting the buyers of her flat to go through the legal formalities. She slipped silently out of bed and crept from the bedroom. *It'll be time to pack before long,* she thought as she pulled on a skirt and blouse and applied her makeup. After suppressing a sigh, she made breakfast, then woke Sam.

"Have you been up long?" he murmured drowsily, reaching out to stroke her hair.

"Yes, and I'm pleased to say I slept really well."

A little later, over a plate of bacon and eggs, he looked deep into her eyes. "How about we go on a little shopping expedition later, to look for souvenirs for Lotte and Friedrich? I'd like to spend a few hours alone with my future wife."

Lilian smiled. "How can I resist?"

Her father soon returned, and they told him their plans as he joined them for breakfast.

"You cook an amazing fried breakfast, my girl." Peter ate heartily. "I don't mind at all if you two want to go off on your own—make the most of the lovely weather. I've got a few things I need to do myself."

"It's not far to the Red Cross office by Tube." Sam made an exaggerated bow. "Let me take your arm, Madame."

"You're too kind, sir," she said with a chuckle.

Peter looked up at her and squeezed her hand. "You're freezing."

Sam winked. "She always gets like that when she's nervous. See you later."

It wasn't long before they reached the big gray building.

How could Lilian have known that, just a day before, another young woman with reddish-brown hair had stood in front of a similar door some three hundred and sixty miles away, looking at that iconic flag fluttering above it?

She and Sam stepped resolutely into the inviting reception area. Lilian found herself waiting in line once again, but as there were a number of people looking after clients, it took only a few minutes for them to reach the counter. Sam squeezed Lilian's hand as they outlined their inquiry to the woman behind the desk.

"Would you follow me, please, Miss Morrison?" The receptionist led them briskly along a corridor and showed them to a couple of seats. "Please wait here until you're called."

If anything was guaranteed to set Lilian's nerves on edge, it was the tedious waiting and uncertainty that dogged her every step.

Sam had picked up a car magazine and was idly leafing through it. Lilian watched the second hand of the clock on the opposite wall.

Are you still alive, Emma?

Eventually, a dark-skinned, stout woman in her fifties opened the door and called her name.

"I'm sorry you've had to wait. My name is Amba Rai. Please come in." She gestured for them to sit. The walls of the simply furnished office were covered with colorful photos of laughing families from all over the world, giving it a cheerful atmosphere.

Mrs. Rai smoothed her sari before sitting and asking Lilian's full name and contact information. She then squinted thoughtfully and took a file from a cabinet behind her.

"I'm looking for information about my older sister, Emma Dölling," Lilian said. "But we have reason to believe she could be going by the name Ceara Doyle." She laid copies of official documents on the table. "A local search didn't turn up anything, which is why I've come to you in the international section, to ask you to expand the search."

Why was Mrs. Rai paying no attention to her documents, leafing through the file instead? Lilian tried to conceal her consternation.

"I'm glad you've come today," Mrs. Rai said without looking up. "I would have contacted you soon in any case."

"I don't understand."

"No, I wouldn't expect you to." Mrs. Rai put on her reading glasses and smiled. "It seems someone's looking for you, too."

Lilian gasped in surprise. "My sister?" Stunned, she watched Mrs. Rai turn a page in the file. "What's that file? Is it mine? But that doesn't make sense. This is the first time I've come in."

Mrs. Rai tapped a stapled notebook. "True, but you called us and described your situation. It was my colleagues in Ireland who sent me these documents. You're being asked to get in touch with the Irish branch of the Red Cross."

"The Irish branch?" Lilian echoed. "What have they told you? Is there a clue about Emma?"

Mrs. Rai snapped the file shut. "Yes. It would be best if you spoke to my colleagues about it all." She handed Lilian a card. "The contact details are all here. I've made a note of the file reference number for you."

The colorful photos on the wall suddenly blurred, and Lilian heard a roaring in her ears. *Emma,* she sang out silently. *My Emma.* She stood, her cheeks wet with tears.

She wanted to reply, but was unable to make a sound.

Sam quickly came to her rescue. "Thank you very much."

Mrs. Rai shook his hand. "Do come back if there's anything else you want to ask." She turned to Lilian. "And please keep me posted. You have no idea how often our searches come to nothing, so we love to hear all the good news we can."

"Of course," Lilian replied quietly.

A little later, she and Sam left the building hand in hand. Taking no notice of the curious stares of passersby, he drew her into his arms, and she laid her head on his shoulder. "I want to get back as soon as we can, to tell Papa everything. And then—then I'll call them."

"OK, let's go." He tapped her on the nose. "You're pale as a ghost. The first thing I'm going to do when we get home is make you some strong coffee."

"Ugh! You know what I think about coffee!" She hugged him. "Oh, Sam, someone's looking for me. I still can't believe it."

"Me neither."

On the way back to Sam's apartment, Lilian was hardly aware of her surroundings. It wasn't until they stepped inside that she came to her senses again. Two men's voices drifted toward them from the living room.

She immediately recognized the retired chief inspector. He jumped up from the sofa and hurried over.

"I'm glad you're here. We've been waiting impatiently, haven't we, Mr. Dölling?"

Peter hugged his daughter, and Lilian looked in confusion between them. "Mr. Lewis. This is a surprise."

He smiled, and Sam gestured for him to sit back down.

"You won't believe this, Papa," she said. "We've been given some information that might lead us to Emma!"

"I know, my love," her father said gently. "Mr. Lewis has been kind enough to come here in person to let us know. You look worn out. Come and sit down."

"I'll make the coffee. Does anyone want a nip of whiskey in it, in honor of the occasion?" Sam picked up a bottle from a side table next to the sofa.

Lilian declined. Sam quickly made the coffee and poured a dash of Irish whiskey into three of the cups.

"Cheers!"

Lewis accepted his with a grin. "Retirement has its advantages." He turned to Lilian. "Inspector Wilson called me. I assume you've been told that the Irish Red Cross wants to speak to you?"

Lilian raised her eyebrows. "I have. So, you know, too?"

"Yes, Inspector Wilson told me. They got in touch with local authorities here. Have you called Dublin yet?"

"No, I was going to do it when we got back here."

"First, let's drink to the good news." Sam raised his glass and clinked it against the others'.

Lilian shuddered as she sipped her coffee. It was far too strong for her taste, but it did help to clear her mind. *What does the Irish Red Cross have to do with us? What happened to you, Emma?*

Her pulse rose to new levels. "Please, will you excuse me a moment. I—I have to make that call."

"Quickly now," Sam said. "We can't stand the tension for much longer."

Lilian went to the desk in the bedroom, and Peter followed. With clammy hands, she dialed the number on the card and asked to speak to the relevant caseworker.

"Miss Morrison! Thank you for getting back to us so quickly. My name is Rory Sanders."

"Hello." Her father was watching her intently. "What have you found?"

"My colleague and I are working on the case of a client who came to live with a foster family when she was nine and is now looking for her birth family. Light and Hope, the organization that handled the case in 1941, was closed down a few years later. As it turns out, the description you gave our British colleagues of your sister's height, age, and distinguishing features match those of our client and the personal details from Light and Hope. And, as you guessed, the girl was brought here under the name Ceara Doyle. She must have married since. For a few years now, she's been Ceara Foley."

Lilian's legs wavered, and she sank into the chair. "Emma."

Peter leaned in close, trying to listen in.

"Are you still there, Miss Morrison?"

"Y-yes, I'm here."

"My colleague and I wanted to tell you immediately. Please remember that nothing's absolutely certain yet, but we have high hopes."

"Of course. I don't know what to say." Lilian's gaze fell on the little case containing the music box.

If you're still alive, Emma, I'm going to find you.

153

"It's a lot to take in. We'll be in touch when we know more, Miss Morrison."

"Thank you, Mr. Sanders."

Lilian lowered the receiver and stared at the little case. Was it possible that the silver music box, which had given her father and grandfather so much comfort, could bring her even more luck and happiness than it had already? That its net of invisible threads could draw her family back together?

She had no idea how long she sat there, unmoving, before Peter ran a hand over her hair. His face was pale. "Come on, love. Tell me all about it."

Lilian threw her arms around him. "Oh, Papa. They think she's called Ceara Foley now. She might be in Ireland! Alive!"

Her father didn't reply, but she felt him trembling.

Back in the living room, Sam and Lewis listened expectantly to Lilian's account.

"My God," Sam said. "I'm so happy for you both."

"It would be amazing if they're right," Lewis said.

"They are. Everything about her description matches." Warmth flowed through Lilian. She looked at Sam and then her father, who she noticed was having great difficulty sitting still. Her eyes then came to rest on the former chief inspector. "It's very kind of you to have come specially."

"Well, there are one or two more minor details." He placed a piece of paper on the table. "You asked us for Lieutenant Grifford's address. I doubt it's still current, so I've given you his date of birth as well. That should help you trace him."

"That's marvelous," Peter said. "Thank you."

"You're welcome. I also called Sally Russell and William Field yesterday. Inspector Wilson has an appointment with both of them tomorrow afternoon at the station. He wants them to make a statement about the day of the air raid."

"The Jacksons can't stop them anymore," Lilian said quietly. "They're adults now."

Lewis nodded. "Precisely. And we need all the details we can get to move this case forward. Fortunately, Sally and William weren't that young in December 1940, so we're hoping they'll remember the day well." Lewis stood. "Please excuse me now. I've arranged to meet my wife for lunch." He smiled. "Give yourselves time to take in the news. We'll talk again tomorrow morning."

"Of course. I'll see you out." Lilian swayed slightly as she said good-bye to the retired chief inspector at the door. "I can't thank you enough."

"We're in the same boat, Miss Morrison. I've wanted to make progress on this case for a very long time. I wish you good day."

She watched him, his hands thrust casually into his pockets, as he strode out of the building.

Chapter 19

Lotte

Cape Town

The day was drawing to an end, the shadows of the trees that lined Clifford Road growing longer. Lotte closed the Blue Heart and hurried home. She paused on the way to exchange a few words with neighbors, but her thoughts kept drifting to Dede. Before opening the Blue Heart for the day, she and Friedrich had gone to fetch Dede and Niam from the hospital and take them to their new accommodations. Dede's gratitude had been heartwarming, and Lotte was now looking forward to a relaxing evening.

Friedrich met her at the door with a smile. "How was your day?"

"A bit nerve-racking. I kept catching myself listening for Dede or Niam."

"It's lucky their room's set apart from the others." He hung her shawl up in the hallway. "Anyway, it'll only be for a little while, until she's well enough to start working with you again. Then she'll only be at the Blue Heart at night. Was anyone in any of the other rooms today?"

"No, they're empty." She looked at him intently. "You don't think she'll up and leave, do you?"

"Dede's a smart woman. She won't do anything that would put Niam in danger. Trust me." He brushed his fingers against her cheek. "You look tired. Are you hungry? I've made us some sandwiches."

"No, thanks. But a glass of cold lemonade would be lovely. I'll just go and freshen up."

Lotte washed, slipped into her favorite colorful kaftan, and flung open the door that led to the sandy garden path. She froze. On the doorstep was the bloody corpse of a rat, its severed head lying next to it.

She shuddered violently. Shaken to the core, she couldn't take her eyes from it. She stood paralyzed, her thoughts a jumble. This could only be a warning. A warning to stop protecting Dede?

Lotte closed her eyes and tried to calm down. The senders of this silent message clearly knew where she slept. The thought sent her blood racing through her veins.

Once she had regained control, she gingerly wrapped the rat in an old dishcloth, then buried it beneath an umbrella thorn that marked the boundary between her garden and the neighbors'.

Lotte scrubbed her hands with a brush until they were red, patted her cheeks to bring some color back, and went to find her friend. He was in the kitchen.

He'd lit a candle and set out a plate of appetizing savories and diced fruit, with a glass of lemonade for her. Her stomach turned at the thought of eating.

She pushed the plate aside, drank deeply, and picked up the daily paper. She normally loved starting the evening with a leisurely hour's reading. Friedrich usually sat opposite her, his head bent over a magazine or a book. But that evening, the words swam in front of her eyes, and she put the newspaper back down on the table.

Friedrich looked at her through his rimless glasses. "Is everything OK?"

"No. I need to get out." The house suddenly seemed too small, suffocating her. "Are you coming with me?"

The lines on his forehead deepened. "Of course."

Without another word, she helped him up, grabbed her shawl as she passed, and marched outside.

Friedrich followed her in confusion. "Where do you want to go?"

"To the promenade. I need the sea air."

He didn't ask her anything more, and they turned onto St. John's Road in the direction of the ocean.

Halfway there, Lotte guided him into a restaurant. In the pretty rear courtyard with a well in the middle, she ordered white wine spritzers.

"What's this about? We've got perfectly good wine at home, and—"

"I need to talk to you, in a place where the walls don't have ears."

He frowned, his thick brows almost meeting. "Who would be listening in on us at home?"

She waited until the waitress had brought their drinks, before reaching across the table for his hand. Trying to keep her composure, she told him about the rat with the severed head.

Friedrich's expression darkened. "Was there a note?"

She shook her head.

He squeezed her hand. "I don't like this at all. Maybe it would be better for you to go back to the police and ask them to drop the case."

"That would mean them getting what they want. It wouldn't be right or fair."

"Of course it wouldn't. But you and I aren't going to conquer racial hatred on our own. Are we supposed to put ourselves in further danger?"

"They wanted to scare me, and I hate to say it, but they've succeeded. That's what bothers me the most."

"We're going back to the police tomorrow," he said firmly. "Please, Lotte. They were at your bedroom door."

What kind of a world is this, where the color of your skin counts more than justice?

Lotte sighed. "I guess you're right. Safety comes first. I'm just glad that Dede isn't living in the summerhouse anymore. If they'd found her there—"

He placed a finger on her lips. "She's in a safe place, provided she isn't seen." He nodded toward her glass. "Don't let your wine get warm."

They spent a good hour in that peaceful courtyard, then strolled to the promenade. Friedrich took her hand, and Lotte let him. His presence did her good. A few minutes later they reached the road along the sea front. Lotte breathed in the gentle breeze and took in the sight of the colorful fishing boats rocking in the harbor beyond the lights of the cafés and restaurants. A handful of Jewish men with brightly patterned yarmulkes on their heads walked past.

On the way back, they passed a synagogue on Arthur's Road, and Lotte decided she would visit the mikvah before opening the Blue Heart the following morning. It had been weeks since she had visited the ritual baths. The ancient rite always helped her when she was plagued with worries or her spirit was uneasy, and she sometimes even found answers to questions that had been bothering her. Maybe a solution would occur to her this time, too, and she would find a way of protecting Dede from the white wolves and safeguarding her own home without betraying her principles.

"Did you hear a word I said?" Friedrich asked with feigned indignation.

Lotte had been nodding absently every now and then as he told her enthusiastically about a lovely garden he'd been reading about in the paper. Nothing could have interested her less right then than garden design.

"It would be easier to care for," he was saying. "Think about it, at least. We're not getting any younger, after all."

A piercing siren sounded behind them, interrupting his monologue. Friedrich and Lotte turned, and a few moments later, a red fire engine raced past them. They had only gone a few steps more when they saw thick columns of smoke rising above the rooftops.

They exchanged looks of alarm and hastened their steps. The fire seemed to be coming from Clifford Road. *God almighty!*

Lotte's worst fears were confirmed as they saw a young neighbor running toward them.

"Mrs. Kuipers, the Blue Heart's on fire!"

Lotte ran without knowing where she found the strength. The acrid smoke took her breath away. A row of police cars, ambulances, and fire engines stood before them like a wall. Officers from the emergency services barricaded the street, holding back residents from the nearby houses.

"Dede! Where's Dede?" Lotte cried. Friedrich followed her as she dashed up to a fireman.

He grabbed her sleeve. "Stop! You can't go any farther. There's a risk of explosion!"

But Lotte was not to be deflected. "Have you—have you seen a young black woman? She's got a little baby!"

The fireman shook his head. "Get back to safety immediately."

Oh my God, the gas pipes! The thought made Lotte's head hurt. "That—that's my center! Please, you've got to get them out of there!"

"The emergency services are doing what they can. Get back. There's nothing you can do here."

But Lotte wasn't listening. All she could see were the blazing roof timbers and the dazzling flames flickering inside the house. She pushed past the fireman and dashed toward an ambulance parked by the road barrier. Friedrich's shouts were lost in the general commotion. Someone barred her way, but she managed to evade him.

The ambulance crew were just getting out.

Lotte bent over, clutching her side. "A young woman," she managed to say between gasps. "She's in my house with her little son—he's a baby."

The doctor sat her down on a folding chair and strapped an oxygen mask to her face. "You're staying here, lady. The emergency services are doing all they possibly can."

Friedrich had caught up.

"Your wife's being rather reckless," the doctor said severely. "Once she's caught her breath, please will you take her to safety?"

"That's why I'm here." He knelt by Lotte. "Are you feeling OK now?"

"I'm not moving from here," she protested hoarsely. "I can't."

"You must," he said firmly, and he led Lotte, still protesting, from the danger zone.

A dozen people had gathered at the corner of a nearby building, from where they had a good view of the Blue Heart. They greeted Lotte, and some whispered behind their hands.

"Ignore them. It'll be OK."

But Friedrich's words passed over her with the wind. *Dede. Niam.*

Suddenly, a massive explosion shook the ground. Lotte screamed. A rain of thick timbers, shards of glass, broken furniture, and roof tiles flew through the air. People dropped to the ground in terror.

A ghostly silence descended.

Her eyes wide with horror, Lotte watched the frantic activity of the emergency services. The unreal scene played out as if in slow motion before her eyes.

Please let them be unharmed!

A big, strong man emerged from the smoke. To judge from the tag on his lapel, he was an emergency doctor. He was supporting a thin figure in pajamas, a woolen blanket draped over her shoulders.

Lotte and Friedrich hurried over to the swaying, listless apparition, dodging a couple who were watching in tears.

"Thank God!" She hugged Dede, but the young woman remained strangely stiff, hardly raising her head. Lotte wondered if she recognized her.

"Oh, little Niam!" Lotte looked at the little boy in her arms. "Is he all right?"

When Dede still didn't reply, Lotte shook her by the shoulders.

The emergency doctor beckoned her aside and lowered his voice. "The baby didn't make it. Smoke inhalation. He must have suffocated in his sleep. But she won't hand him over. We've tried everything, but she bites and scratches if we get too close."

"Thank you for bringing my friend out." Lotte tried to grasp the situation. "I'll talk to her. Please give us a moment."

The man looked at her skeptically before moving a respectful distance away.

Lotte stared in horror at the heap of debris that had once been her beloved center. She laid a hand on Dede's back. Like a marionette with broken strings, the young woman let her. The hairs on the nape of Lotte's neck stood on end as she once more became aware of the little bundle Dede clung to like a drowning woman.

"I'm here, sweetheart," she whispered, her voice threatening to give out on her. Friedrich laid his jacket around her and stepped unobtrusively behind her. Instinctively, Lotte cupped her hands around the young woman's face. "Can you hear me? You're not alone. I'm here with you."

Dede's empty eyes sent a jolt of pain through her. But the young woman still made no move to release herself from Lotte's embrace.

Lotte tried again. "Dede. It's me, Lotte Kuipers. You know—" She racked her brain for the right words. "Both of us have lost more this evening than we can bear." She forced Dede to look at her. "But together we can get through it." Lotte hardly felt the tears streaming down her cheeks, leaving light tracks down her soot-blackened skin. "Poor little Niam."

Dede's eyes cleared for the briefest moment.

"May I touch him for a moment, darling? I—I want so much to say goodbye to him."

The young woman didn't reply, but allowed Lotte to run her fingers down Niam's pale cheeks.

Lotte's voice became more intent. "Of course, I understand you don't want to let go of him. But your little Niam has gone up to the stars, and we need to wash him and prepare him for burial. Do you understand?" Lotte closed the baby's eyes. *Adonai, don't leave me.*

Dede's lips quivered. It seemed as though Lotte's words had finally reached her. Lotte reached out carefully for the baby, but the young woman refused to budge.

"Dede carries her son and—also wants to bury him."

"Of course." Lotte rocked the woman and her baby in her arms and felt relief as her tears mingled with Dede's.

"If only—Dede had stayed in the summerhouse." The young woman's face was masklike. "Niam would still be alive."

"No, my love. You only wanted to protect him." Something in Lotte seemed to turn to dust, quietly and irretrievably. "The fault is all mine."

There was silence between them for a few moments, then Dede gave a barely perceptible nod of resignation.

Friedrich put his arms around the two women. "Come on, my darlings. Let's go home."

Chapter 20

Lilian

London

Lilian, Sam, and Peter crowded around the telephone as Friedrich gave them the dreadful news about the fire.

"How's Mama? Tell me the truth, Friedrich!" Peter snapped into the phone.

"Your mother's getting over the shock, but Dede . . . her little son died in the fire."

Lilian gasped. "Oh my God! So they were nearby when the fire broke out."

"It's much worse than that," Friedrich replied after a brief pause. "They were sleeping in the back room of the Blue Heart. Dede asked your grandma for a room there after the recent attack. And now she's blaming herself for what happened. Lotte feels like she should have seen it coming, too."

"Grandma couldn't possibly have known," Lilian countered.

"Well, there was one thing." Friedrich told them about the headless rat. "Lotte says she should have taken the warning more seriously."

Peter was weeping silently. Lilian ran a hand down his back as she spoke. "If only we could be with you right now."

"There's nothing we can do at the moment anyway." Friedrich's voice quivered with anxiety. "She doesn't want to see anyone. Until the moment we got Dede into the house, Lotte seemed in control. But then she broke down. She goes through the motions, and she's talking to the police. But most of the time, it's as if she's far away. She avoids all attempts at conversation."

Peter shook his head. "Everything she built lying in rubble and ash! I'm so glad she didn't get hurt, at least."

"Do they know how it could have happened?" Sam asked.

"The investigation's still underway. But I'm convinced it's arson." Friedrich sighed. "The question is how I can keep Lotte and Dede safe. I'm scared."

"As long as Dede's living with you, you're putting yourselves at risk—and she's not safe there either," Sam said.

"He's right," Lilian said. "You'd all be safer if Dede went someplace no one would think to look for her."

Friedrich laughed bitterly. "Do you really think I could convince Lotte to let her go? She feels responsible for the girl—now more than ever."

Lilian pictured the drop-in center and the loving attention to detail with which Lotte had created such a welcoming space in the simply furnished rooms. The building was always full of life, offering a true refuge for young women and their children—they were given attention, encouragement, and support there. It hurt to even think about it now.

"We know very well what Grandma's like, Friedrich." She fought to retain her composure. "But we have to work together to find a solution. Are you going to tell the police to drop the case?"

"We already have. Hopefully the attackers will leave Lotte and Dede in peace now. I don't mind telling you, I feel like I'm sitting on a powder keg."

"I can believe it. Thank you from the bottom of my heart for all you're doing for the two of them," Peter said.

"Don't talk nonsense. Your mother's a wonderful person, and she means the world to me."

Lilian snuffled. "I want to tell you how happy we are that you've decided to stay with Grandma. It's a comfort to know she's not alone. But what's going to happen next? The Blue Heart was Grandma's pride and joy. Her work means everything to her."

"It burned to the ground, Lilian. Rebuilding the center would be a massive feat, and I don't even know if Lotte would want to. Right now, I'm just happy if I can get her to eat anything."

Peter exchanged a look with his daughter. "Is it that bad?"

"Lotte moves through the house like a ghost. She spends most of the night out in the garden." Friedrich sighed. "But what about you? Do you have any news for us?"

Peter motioned them to stay silent. "We're following a couple of leads, but there's nothing specific to report. Please give Mama a big hug and tell her we all send our love. We'll be back home as soon as we can."

After hanging up, he turned to meet Lilian's look of incomprehension.

"Why didn't you tell him about Ceara? Grandma needs some happy news right now. Our latest discoveries could have been just the thing to pull her out of her depression."

"Our latest *guesses*," her father corrected her gently. "I'd rather wait until we know for certain. It'll also give your grandma more time to come to terms with the tragedy there. It's still too fresh."

"You're right, Papa."

She couldn't begin to imagine what her grandmother was going through, much less the young mother, what it meant for a few hooligans to destroy your dreams and kill an innocent child. Lost in thought, she placed her glass of cold juice on the table.

"Grandma's strong, Papa. She'll be back to herself before too long."

Peter stared into space. "I'm not so sure."

Lilian turned the glass around with her hand. *How much can one person bear?* She kissed her father's cheek and looked to Sam. "Can I leave you for a while? I need to stretch my legs and get a bit of fresh air before we go meet Wilson. It's all been a bit much for me."

The inspector had called early that morning and asked them to come to the station at two o'clock, without revealing the reason for the meeting.

"Off you go," Sam replied.

Lilian put on a cardigan and left the apartment. The possibility of being reunited with her sister had dominated her thoughts and turned her life upside down once again. But at the same time, she felt a strong urge to be by her grandmother's side in this dark hour. It was terrible not to be able to hug and comfort her. Deep in thought, she wandered through the park, tossed back and forth by her emotions like a boat on a stormy sea. She returned to Sam's apartment just in time for a bite to eat before they had to leave.

On the way, they all put forward their theories about the reason for Inspector Wilson's summons, but could think of nothing concrete.

"It must be important, in any case," Lilian said, "or else he'd have told us over the phone."

A surprise awaited them at the police station, as they saw two familiar figures with Lewis and Wilson.

"Sally, William!" Lilian exclaimed. "How lovely to see you!"

"You, too," Sally replied. "Any news?"

Lilian told them both about Ceara.

"A lead, at last." Sally smiled.

"Fingers crossed for you," William added.

Lewis gestured to them. "Let's find somewhere quiet where we can talk." He waved across the station at police officers hammering on their typewriters, cigarettes at the corners of their mouths. "Follow me."

He took them to the back room they had used before.

"Do you want to go first?" Wilson asked Sally.

"Gladly." She looked at William, who had sat down next to her. "We both gave statements about the night of the air raid, and we agree on what happened. Uncle Alfred and Dr. Cook talked together alone. Neither of us saw Emma's body or overheard any of the men's conversation."

"So there aren't actually any witnesses," Lilian muttered.

"And for that reason," Wilson continued, "we've called the Jacksons in for questioning. We thought you'd also be interested."

Peter's eyes widened. "They're here now?"

"That's right." Lewis pointed behind him. "Behind this door is the room from where we observe interrogations unseen. Once I've opened it, please be quiet so the Jacksons don't hear you. You'll listen from there while I conduct the interrogation."

The dimly lit room had just enough space for them. A one-way mirror took up half of the wall opposite them.

Lilian looked, spellbound, at the elderly couple sitting at the table. Alfred Jackson glanced at the clock and loosened his untidy tie. Daisy, wearing a neatly starched blouse with an old-fashioned skirt, was sitting stiff as a ramrod. She reminded Lilian of a schoolgirl being scolded by her teacher.

"What does it feel like to see your foster parents in an interrogation room?" she whispered to William.

"It's hard to describe. On the one hand, I feel obliged to them, but I also think they deserve this."

She was amazed by his forthrightness. "Do you believe they're capable of committing a crime?"

"I wouldn't have, once," he said. "But since I've become a father myself, I see a lot of things differently. There's no doubt that the Jacksons treated Sally and Emma badly."

There were a few more questions Lilian wanted to ask, but William pointed to the couple. "Uncle Alfred's acting like a lout, don't you think?"

She nodded in silent agreement.

Alfred Jackson was loudly drumming his fingertips on the wooden table. His wife nudged him in the ribs.

"Don't do that."

"How much longer are they going to leave us to stew?" he said angrily. "We've been waiting almost an hour already. As if we didn't have better things to be doing!"

"Calm down, Alfred. Someone's coming." Daisy Jackson indicated the big mirror. "And I'm sure the police can hear us."

"And what if they can?"

Lilian stared at the couple. *Do I believe they're capable of committing a crime?* They may not always have been loving foster parents, but that didn't make them criminals.

"I'll go and sound them out a little now," Wilson said. "Wish me luck."

Lewis came to stand by Peter. "Our friends clearly don't like being questioned again."

"Mr. Jackson looks furious," Peter agreed.

Lewis folded his arms. "Let's see what he has to say for himself."

Inspector Wilson had by now entered the interview room and sat across from the couple. "Let's go back to the night of the air raid in December 1940, when young Emma Dölling died. I'd like you to describe what happened from the moment you began to look for the girl. Why don't you begin, Mrs. Jackson?"

Sally, Lilian, and the others listened to her account, which more or less aligned with what they had already heard.

"And did you know Ceara Doyle?" Wilson asked.

Mrs. Jackson folded her hands in her lap. "Ceara? Wasn't that our neighbors' girl, Alfred?"

His lips were thin. "No idea. Too long ago."

The police officer leaned his elbows on the table and stared at the man. "You know exactly who I'm talking about."

"What makes you think that?"

"He's fuming," Sally murmured to Lilian. "Whenever he used to look at us like that, we'd make ourselves scarce."

Wilson didn't take his eyes from the man. "I'm also certain that when you met Dr. Cook that day, it wasn't for the first time."

"Are you implying I've been lying to you?" Mr. Jackson countered icily.

"Answer me!"

"I can't remember, damn it!"

Wilson glared at him, unmoved. "But you remembered Cook's name, despite your memory lapses."

He certainly knows what he's doing, Lilian thought.

"Which leads me to my next question," Wilson continued. "You and Cook identified Emma. What injuries did you see on her body?"

Mr. Jackson ran a hand over his face. "Her leg was torn apart, and she had a wound on the back of her head."

"Oh, really?" The police officer leaned farther across the table. "Listen to me. We have evidence that Emma Dölling survived the air raid."

Mrs. Jackson turned pale. "That's—there must be some mistake!"

Her husband remained stubbornly silent.

"The good Dr. Cook even took her to the clinic himself."

"What's that got to do with us?" Mr. Jackson growled.

"You tell me!" Wilson frowned. "Did you and Dr. Cook swap the girl for someone else, perhaps?"

Jackson lurched to his feet, sending his chair clattering to the floor. "Of course we didn't! What good would that have done me?"

"So how do you explain the fact that Emma Dölling was admitted to hospital with completely different injuries from the ones you describe? Whose body did you identify, Mr. Jackson?"

"I'm not putting up with these allegations a moment longer, Inspector. Don't say another word, Daisy. We're getting a solicitor."

"You're perfectly within your rights to do so. But I'm forbidding you from leaving the city," Wilson said calmly. "If you do, there'll be consequences."

Looking at him darkly, Jackson took his wife's arm and swept her out.

Peter stood. "Stop them! I don't believe a word that man said!"

"We don't have a motive yet," Lewis explained calmly. "We can't arrest them without more evidence. They're nervous now, though. He's lied several times, but since we're not in a position to question Cook, we'll have to wait for the report about the former director of the Light and Hope adoption agency." Lewis looked from Peter to Lilian. "But don't worry—if the Jacksons did conspire with Cook, we'll get them."

Chapter 21

Ceara

Dublin

With a trained eye, Ceara examined the ornamentation on the wooden lid of the little box before picking up her burin again. The grain of the wood was preventing the image of the child from standing out distinctly enough. As she concentrated on her piece, she recalled a fragmented scene from her dream the previous night. She had been pushing an old-fashioned baby carriage, a small, gleaming box tucked inside her coat. Gurgling cheerfully, the baby kicked its legs beneath a crocheted blanket.

Ceara shook her head pensively. The little box in her dream was different from the one on the workbench before her, but she couldn't remember exactly what it had looked like.

The boy in her carving looked too serious. Ceara worked on his smile and gave him a few wild locks of hair, all the while whistling along to a tune on the radio she had just switched on.

She put the little box on the shelf in her office, gripped by an inexplicable sense of regret.

She turned next to the rosewood bookshelf she was making for Stewart O'Brien's home library, which was going to cost him a small fortune. O'Brien was a city council member, so she would do well to concentrate on her work.

Ceara sawed and planed and wiped the sweat from her brow, the stuffy air hanging over the workshop like a blanket of smog. Aidan was on an early shift and had left the house at four that morning. Rhona was meeting her admirer in town for breakfast. Ceara could work in peace until the time came to open to the public.

She was studying her plans, a mug of tea in her hand, when the bell over the door rang out, announcing the arrival of Sean Simmons. The postman, with golden hair and prominent ears, tipped his hat.

"Morning, Mrs. Foley. Mail for you." He handed her a stack of letters and was out of the door before he'd finished wishing her good day.

Ceara's attention was drawn to an official-looking envelope. Pearse Street Garda Station, Dublin 2. She held it in her hand and gazed at it for a moment before opening the envelope and unfolding the letter.

You are asked to come to the station on Tuesday, 24th September, 1963 at 9 am, in connection with the case of Owen Fitzpatrick, former managing director of the company Light and Hope.

It was signed by one Inspector Liam Keane.

Ceara stared at the writing until the letters blurred before her eyes. Tomorrow—so soon! She felt butterflies in her stomach. She was still pondering it sometime later when Buzz O'Reilly rapped on the window. He must have rung the bell, but she was miles away.

"Everything OK, girl?" The old man put a hand on her shoulder. "You look like you've got a fever."

Ceara came to herself and touched her flushed cheeks. "No, I'm fine, Mr. O'Reilly. What can I do for you?"

He scratched his neck, looking slightly embarrassed. "Well, I'm looking for a present for my youngest grandchild, Erin. She'll be three at the end of December, and I'd like to give her something she'll be able to enjoy for a good few years. I was thinking of a little chair with a fairy-tale scene, brightly painted."

Ceara peered through the window. What was keeping Rhona? She was dying to tell her about the letter. "I'll gladly make you something," she told the old man. "But don't you think a plastic chair would be more suitable for a little whirlwind like your Erin?"

"I won't have anything as newfangled as that through my door," O'Reilly said indignantly.

Ceara grinned. "As you wish. What fairy-tale image were you thinking of?"

As they discussed the details, the old man couldn't take his eyes away from the shelf. He pointed to the carved wooden box. "Well now, that's a pretty thing!"

"Ah, that. It's not finished yet, Mr. O'Reilly."

"I don't mind, sure—could I have a look anyway?"

She laid it hesitantly in his hand and watched him examining the piece from all angles.

"Very imaginative. My compliments, Mrs. Foley," he murmured at last. "Did someone commission it?"

"In a manner of speaking," she replied quickly and breathed more freely once it was safely back on the shelf.

"What are you going to charge when it's finished? It's so lovely. I've got to have it."

She avoided his eye. "It's not really for sale. But maybe I could make you something similar? We can talk about it when it's finished, OK?"

Buzz seemed satisfied with that. They chatted for a while longer, until a customer came to fetch a stool that Ceara had fitted with replacement feet.

Her customers had no sooner left than Rhona appeared, her apron flapping and slippers on her feet.

"Hello, lass." She was fiddling with an envelope. "Look what I received in today's mail."

A brief glance was enough—her foster mother had received the same letter.

Ceara showed Rhona her own envelope. "I've no idea why they're asking us to come, Mum. But it must be important. I suppose something's come to light."

Rhona's expression brightened. "That must be it." She hugged her daughter. "Things are moving forward. I'm so pleased for you." She looked at Ceara with mock severity. "You've been very quiet about your recent therapy session with Dr. Hamlin. You did go, didn't you?"

"Yes, I did," she murmured.

So much for her hope that Rhona wouldn't broach the subject. Ceara didn't want to think about the session, which had gone so differently from what she'd expected. She had been arming herself mentally for days in anticipation of dealing with the silver dream again. Instead of that, the memory of the long, lumpy scar on her lower belly and the pain it caused had crept into her thoughts. She would never forget the first time she'd looked in the mirror after the operation. Her body had been covered in wounds, some small and deep, others more superficial. A narrow cut snaked up the inside of her left upper arm from her elbow. Even her face showed traces of shrapnel cuts. Sections of her scalp had been singed. A doctor had assured her that her hair would soon grow back, that the cuts on her face would heal without leaving scars, and that the one on her arm would hardly be noticeable in time. She had stared blankly at her deformed stomach. How ugly it looked, how repulsive.

Ceara still sometimes traced the scar with her fingers. It was now faded and less obtrusive, but was still clear to see. Her emotional scars were much worse, though.

Whenever Aidan caught her looking in the mirror, he would always say how pretty he found her feminine curves and lovely skin. He didn't understand that she found her body useless—unfit to bear a child.

"Penny for your thoughts." Rhona brought her back to reality.

"Nothing that matters, Mum." The doorbell rang, and Ceara took a deep breath. "More customers. Shall we go together tomorrow?"

"Yes, let's," Rhona called after her as Ceara turned to the couple who were waiting by the door.

For the rest of the day she felt as though the workshop clock had stopped. She took another order and repaired the door of a kitchen cupboard. When Aidan appeared later that afternoon, she was painting the last few notes onto the inside of her little box. She flew into his arms.

"I could get used to passionate homecomings like this," he murmured with a grin between kisses. "Is there any special reason for it?"

She handed him the letter. "Mum's received a similar one."

"The police certainly haven't wasted any time," Aidan said. "How exciting! I wish I could come with you tomorrow, but I'm on duty."

"There's no need."

"We've got a rehearsal soon at Padraig's. I'll cook dinner after that, OK? I saw some wonderful steaks in Mitch's window—couldn't resist them."

Ceara smiled and nudged him. "I'm sure I won't be able to either. But stop distracting me from my work now, or I won't be finished on time."

Aidan winked and left the office.

They spent a quiet evening together. After dinner, Aidan got out his banjo and played her a few new tunes they wanted to introduce at their next gig. Despite the catchy melodies, Ceara found it hard to concentrate.

That night in bed, Aidan soon fell into a deep sleep. She got up quietly and spent most of the night outside in the garden. Her limbs were leaden with weariness, but she knew that thoughts about her sister and fear of the silver dream would keep her awake. She might as well watch the moon make its way across the sky.

Ceara and Rhona arrived at the Garda station half an hour early and sat in the waiting area. Ceara tapped her feet restlessly. Why was it taking so long? Apart from a receptionist, there was no one to be seen.

Finally, a slim man in his forties approached. With his protruding eyes, sparse hair, and distinctively shaped nose, he looked to Ceara like a molting bird.

"Mrs. Foley. Mrs. Ward. I'm Inspector Liam Keane. Would you like to come with me?"

In his office, the inspector opened a file. "Thank you for coming on such short notice."

"Why are you thanking us? After all, you summoned us," Ceara replied. "I don't understand. What does this Fitzpatrick case have to do with me? And why was my mother called, too?"

"One thing at a time." Inspector Keane gave her a friendly smile. "Do you agree to me recording this?"

"Of course," Rhona replied.

"Thank you." He switched on a tape recorder, then in measured tones began to outline the findings to date about the Light and Hope organization.

Rhona and Ceara listened with growing dismay.

"Now, I don't want to jump the gun," the inspector continued, "but Fitzpatrick is suspected, along with a couple of accomplices, of having falsely substituted children between 1941 and 1946, and in the last couple of years, passing them off as war orphans in order to make money from them." He cleared his throat. "It looks as though you were one of the children in question, Mrs. Foley."

Ceara gasped to relieve the pressure that suddenly weighed on her chest. "I was sold?" She felt sick.

Substituted. Passed off as a war orphan.

"For God's sake!" All the color had drained from Rhona's face. "I can assure you that we didn't know a thing about it! My husband and I would never have gone along with anything like that."

The inspector turned to her, his expression serious. "Really, Mrs. Ward? I've learned that you and your husband suffered from childlessness for many years. Tell me, how far might a despairing couple like you have gone to satisfy your longing for a child?"

Rhona sat up straight in her chair. "Children aren't goods for trading, Inspector. I know there are couples who would go to any lengths, but not us!"

Ceara could tell how difficult she was finding it to stay calm.

Keane picked up a pen. "Please will you tell us how you came to be foster parents?"

Rhona looked at her shoes as she spoke. "We were on various adoption lists for years, but they were always looking for younger or wealthier people. We'd almost given up when we received a letter from Light and Hope, asking whether we'd be prepared to give a new home to a war orphan."

Keane made notes. "Did you know this organization?"

"No, but we'd heard of it."

"What did you pay to Light and Hope?"

Rhona named a high, four-figure sum. "The agency fee took up every bit of our savings, but we were told the fee was especially high due to all the medical care war orphans needed, and we accepted that. I've kept the invoice, in case you need it."

"That would be helpful, yes. Send it in to us, please. Would you be prepared to repeat your statement in court, Mrs. Ward?"

"Of course."

"Thank you for answering my questions."

Ceara stroked Rhona's hand in silent support.

"There's one thing I don't understand," Rhona said. "Why would the criminals do this to a nine-year-old rather than a younger child? They must have worried that Ceara would remember her real name and family."

"We're also very interested in that question, Mrs. Ward. But Fitzpatrick, the agency director at the time, is still refusing to talk to us."

No one said a word for a few heartbeats.

"So that means the real Ceara Doyle was declared dead under my name." She looked up, her eyes moist.

"That's what we're assuming at the moment."

Rhona muttered sadly under her breath.

Ceara's heart leapt to her throat. "So—who am I?"

Inspector Keane looked at her reassuringly. "It's rather complicated, and the situation hasn't yet been fully clarified, so I'd like to ask you to get in touch with the Red Cross. They'll be able to tell you the latest developments. Right now, it's important for you to know that we're doing all we can to find the guilty parties and bring them to justice." He closed his file. "I wish you good luck, Mrs. Foley. Mrs. Ward, you'll be hearing from me."

Ceara didn't know how she found the strength to stand. She thanked the inspector mechanically. Her feet moved as if by remote control. The only thing she was aware of on the way to the bus stop was Rhona's hand firmly in hers.

Substituted. Passed off as a war orphan.

"Are you OK, love?" Rhona asked as they sat on the bus.

"Yes, but I just—I just don't understand how people could do that kind of thing." Ceara gazed out of the window, knowing if she looked at her foster mother she wouldn't be able to hold back the tears.

"I'll make us a nice cup of tea as soon as we get home," Rhona said gently.

"That's kind of you, Mum, but I need a bit of time alone before I open the workshop."

"No problem." Rhona forced a smile. "But if you change your mind and want company, you know where I am."

Ceara kissed her on the cheek by way of reply.

Ceara used the peace and quiet of the workshop to put the finishing touches on the little card box. She painted the remaining notes neatly and then sat back to examine her work. Once the paint had dried, all it needed was a coat of varnish.

Aidan's words drifted into her mind. *What if these are actual memories from before you lost your memory? What if you're actually German?*

She had dismissed his suggestion, but maybe he wasn't as far from the mark as she had thought.

I'm called Emma. Only Emma.

Yesterday she had leafed through a dictionary of names. The name Emma had a long tradition in Germany, and had become popular by the late nineteenth century.

She saw herself in a beloved red coat with the precious little box in her pocket. She could almost feel the fabric beneath her fingers. The little box fitted perfectly in her hands as though it had been made for her. The baby in the carriage was wearing a little knitted hat and slept peacefully, the chubby little cheeks reddened by the cold. Mama used to tell her not to take her favorite toy outside. At this thought, her lips formed a stubborn pout. On the outside of the box, she could feel the little heart patterns she loved so much. *Papa promised to engrave my name on it. He always looks so sad now that Mama's not here anymore.* She carefully drew the box from her coat and lightly kissed the lid that gleamed in the winter sunshine.

Ceara jumped. She shook her head as if she could rid herself of the echo of the emotions she had been feeling just a split second before. It had happened again—the little box she was making seemed to be a kind of gateway to her past. She had actually felt grief for the mother she couldn't remember, concern for the father, and the cold breath of some other place's winter wind on her face. All these tiny scraps of memory were somehow connected to the little wooden box. She quickly put it back on the shelf; she couldn't bear to think of it slipping from her fingers in a careless moment. Ceara reached for the telephone, put the receiver back down, and began to pace up and down the office. Life was crazy, and hers more than anyone's! She'd started out doing all she could to retrace her roots—and now that she was finally about to find out about her childhood, she was creeping around the telephone like a cat on hot bricks. Ceara splashed cold water on her face and wet the back of her neck. It was time to look reality firmly in the eye. The years of hiding were over.

"Red Cross. Rory Sanders speaking. How can I help you?"

"Hello. It's Ceara Foley here."

"Mrs. Foley! I've actually got your file out. I'd like to make an appointment so we can talk without being disturbed."

Chapter 22

Lilian

London

Lilian had spent the days since the Jacksons' interrogation in a state of feverish anxiety. If only there was something she could do to speed up the investigations, but the police and the Red Cross had asked her to be patient. In order to keep herself occupied, she spent the time packing up things she no longer needed. They intended to donate the furniture that the new tenants didn't want to a charity shop. Sam had even sold his lovely old bureau. Lilian looked around. Her worldly goods were due to be collected tomorrow, and then she, Sam, and Peter would fly to Cape Town with only the barest essentials.

One morning, she sat gazing at the silver menorah Sam had bought her at an antiques market. Lilian had framed the old photo of Margarethe and set it down on the desk next to the candelabrum and the case containing the music box. What would her sister look like now? Was she happy in Ireland? Did she think about her birth family, or had she long since left the past behind? These and similar questions thrummed in her head.

For a few days, Lilian had been working on a new job—a short story for a forthcoming anthology of work by a well-known German author, which was to be published that December on the hundredth anniversary of his death. She was almost finished. It felt good to have something to concentrate on. She took her silver treasure from its protective case and looked at it pensively. Suddenly, she jumped up as if stung by a wasp and hurried into the living room.

Her father was writing a letter, probably to August. Sam had just come back from helping the new owner of his desk to carry the piece to their car.

"Is something up, love?" he asked, frowning.

She didn't reply, but stood turning the music box in her hands. "What? How?"

Peter and Sam exchanged a charged look.

Her father came over to her and drew her into his arms. "We've been wondering when you'd notice it's been repaired."

"But we agreed it shouldn't leave our hands."

Peter nodded, trying to keep a straight face. "And we kept our word, didn't we, Sam?"

"Absolutely," he confirmed.

Smiling at the confusion on her face, Peter lifted her chin. "You must have noticed the jeweler's shop near the Tube station?"

Lilian murmured agreement.

"I've looked in there a few times to get a bit of inspiration for our future collections," her father continued. "The designs of the jewelry and silverware in their displays are truly wonderful. They even make some of them themselves. Last week, the manager came over to chat—he must have been able to tell I had a professional interest—and we talked shop for a while. I told him about the music box, and he offered to let me repair it in his workshop."

Lilian brushed a tear from the corner of her eye. "It doesn't look like it's ever been broken. You've got a magic touch. Thank you so much, Papa."

"It was my pleasure." Peter stepped back. "By the way, I talked to Friedrich on the phone earlier. Your grandma's feeling a little better. It seems we have Dede to thank for that—the girl insists your grandma isn't at all to blame for Niam's death. The arsonists could just as easily have targeted the house as the center. The two of them are spending a lot of time together at the moment, Friedrich says."

"Oh, I'm so relieved to hear it." Lilian frowned with concern. Her father didn't talk much about his own worries, but the last few days had left their mark on him, and he was showing his age. "Does that mean they confirmed that it was arson?"

"I'm sorry to say they have. But that's not the most important thing right now. I'm worried because your grandma still doesn't want to talk to anyone much. I've been wondering whether I ought to get the next flight to Cape Town."

"Lotte wants to be left alone for a while. We should respect that." Sam put an arm around each of them. "The last few days must have been a nightmare. Give her a little time."

"You're so wise." Lilian kissed Sam. "I'd best get back to work."

Sitting at the desk in the bedroom, she traced the engravings on the music box with her finger. Would Margarethe even remember it? As Lilian studied every detail of her grandfather's skillful silversmithing, she felt a sense of melancholy. Johann had made it at a time when he, his wife, and his son had been relatively observant Jews. After Lilian's family fled from the Nazis, the music box was a constant reminder that love and family unity were what counted, representing values that could never be taken away from them. Not even death had succeeded in separating them. But times had changed, and her family was now scattered throughout the world. Apart from her grandma, none of them really thought of themselves as particularly Jewish.

Lilian lowered the music box. Her father had told her that, even though she had just recently learned about her background, she herself was counted a Jew by the simple fact that she was born to a Jewish mother. She suddenly wondered how she could preserve the values embodied in the music box and pass on to future generations what it signified to her family. The heirloom would only live on if it was more than a relic from earlier terrible times. It needed a future. And it would only have one if her children and Margarethe's added their own stories to the old ones. Children's hands needed to hide it under their own coats. Secrets needed to be stowed away in the hidden compartment. They would surreptitiously trigger the little lever and shout for joy when the little black bird sprang from the lid. The music box could accompany tomorrow's children and comfort them when they first encountered lovesickness. She dared to hope for it all.

With a smile, Lilian set the music box down by her typewriter and turned her attention to the text she was translating. The sun climbed higher. She found the story enchanting and wanted to take the best possible care to ensure that the English translation captured exactly the right tone to convey the atmosphere. Since Lilian had become aware of her German roots, her work had taken on new significance.

At lunchtime, she covered the typewriter and returned to the living room.

Her eyes fell on a white envelope lying on the table. "The Dublin police! Why didn't you tell me?" she asked Sam and her father, who were sitting peacefully on the sofa, reading the papers.

"Maybe because we knew full well that, if we did, you'd never be able to concentrate on your work," Sam replied cheerfully. "Sit down, love."

Lilian did as he suggested. Her fingers trembled as she opened the letter. Sam and Peter looked over her shoulder as she read.

> *Dear Miss Morrison,*
> *We wish to inform you that, after a protracted hearing, Owen Fitzpatrick has made a detailed confession. He admits he is guilty of colluding with Dr. Ernest Cook to*

substitute emigrant children for the victims of an air raid
over London in 1940, to abduct them and send them
abroad. We are currently trying to trace any other affected
persons. Fitzpatrick further states that he shared the
agency fees with Cook and obtained money fraudulently
through the Light and Hope organization. Fitzpatrick
moved on to new circles, in which he continued his crimi-
nal activities involving young victims of war. But this
time, he was careless and was exposed during a tax inves-
tigation. He was brought before the magistrates' court,
and it is now a matter for the judiciary to decide the
extent to which the early cases can be brought against
him. Please find enclosed a copy of the record.

    Yours sincerely,
    Inspector Liam Keane

Lilian shuddered, read the letter again, scanned the record, then handed both to her father. "He really did conspire with Cook."

Peter gazed into space. "But why would Cook do it? As a registered doctor, he had a secure living. There was absolutely no need for him to have committed such awful crimes."

"True," Lilian said. "How on earth could he have destroyed people's lives like that?"

"The man must have had some other reason," Sam said, shaking his head. "Maybe Lewis knows more."

"You're probably right, Sam." Lilian closed her eyes in anguish. *How will Margarethe feel when she finds out?* She couldn't imagine the turmoil the revelation would trigger. Not only had her mother been murdered, not only she been separated from her family, but her identity had been stolen from her a second time. The crooks had thrust her into a life that wasn't hers. *How wretched, how underhanded.*

"You know, I can't stop thinking about the false name," she continued. "At the time Cook recorded Ceara's details, Margarethe must have been suffering from memory loss, maybe head trauma. And when she asked questions later, they must have fed her false information."

"That's far too complicated," her father said. "To do that, Cook and Fitzpatrick would have needed accomplices. But the more people who knew about their plan, the riskier it would have been."

Sam nodded. "I think it's improbable, too."

Lilian said nothing. There was something here they were all overlooking. "I need to get out. What do you think of going for a jog?"

The two men declined, so Lilian went alone to Hyde Park and began to run. Just a few months ago, she would only have done any athletic activity because of Sam. Now she found that running was the best way of clearing her head.

Back home, as she came out of the shower, Peter tapped his watch. "If we want to make sure we're on time, we should be making tracks."

They had arranged to see Sally and William in town.

"But not a word about Cook or the Jacksons," Sally had said, laughing, on the telephone. "Let's just do something nice for once. We'll be back to racking our brains again soon enough."

Lilian was looking forward to getting to know them both better, but she wouldn't be able to abide by Sally's prohibition. She was dying to tell them the news about Fitzpatrick's confession.

The five of them met in a restaurant near a big cinema. William and Sally listened attentively.

"Emma didn't deserve that," William said in bewilderment.

Sally narrowed her eyes. "I bet the Jacksons knew about it. And Uncle Alfred's going to let the cat out of the bag sooner or later. That day can't come soon enough!"

The strength of her reaction disturbed Lilian. Sally had been estranged from the Jacksons for many years, but the pain of her loveless childhood was obviously still fresh.

But the new movie starring Elizabeth Taylor and Richard Burton soon drew them in, helping them to forget reality long enough to enjoy a happy evening. Afterward, they all strolled along the Thames for a few miles before parting warmly.

That night, Lilian enjoyed a deep, dreamless sleep in Sam's arms.

Chapter 23

Ceara

Dublin

Although it wasn't like her at all, Ceara had made herself a pot of strong coffee. But instead of driving the weariness from her bones, it only set her nerves on edge. She picked up the freshly varnished wooden box and marveled once again at how often she felt moved to touch it, and the feelings it triggered in her every time. As she finished it, it had become part of her. In an hour, she would be sitting in the Red Cross office. Maybe the box would bring her luck. She wrapped it carefully in a silk scarf and tucked it into her bag.

Ceara's restless fingers knocked over a glass of water, half of which spilled over her two-piece suit. Cursing softly, she dabbed at the water with a napkin. She could still hear Sanders's serious voice in her ear. She gazed out into the October sunshine and the colorful carpet of leaves Rhona was sweeping from the driveway.

Sanders probably wanted to tell her as kindly as possible that they were giving up the search for her family. She told herself she'd get over it somehow and carry on as though the last few weeks had never happened; those weeks when she had hoped so fervently that she would finally discover the truth.

Ceara picked up her purse and almost forgot her keys as she left.

"Let me know how you get on," Rhona called after her.

Aidan had offered to go with her, as this was one of his days off, but Ceara had asked him and Rhona to wait for her at home.

She sat on the bus, staring at her boots and trying to ignore a young couple who were arguing loudly.

All the seats were taken in the Red Cross waiting room. She wouldn't have been able to keep her feet still in any case. The minute hand of her watch moved agonizingly slowly around the dial, and she found little of interest in the glossy women's magazines.

When Mr. Sanders called her into his office, she was astonished to see a second man sitting there. It was the police officer who had questioned her and Rhona.

"I hope you don't mind that I've invited Inspector Keane to our meeting?"

"Of course not."

Sanders showed her to a seat as a young woman set a jug of water and a plate of cookies on the table.

The serious expressions on the two men's faces made Ceara's stomach tighten. There was a file next to the sugar bowl.

Sanders spoke first. "Mrs. Foley, as we looked into your case, my colleagues here at the Red Cross and I worked closely with Inspector Keane." He indicated the file. "We've invited you here today to tell you the outcome of our investigations." He paused for a moment. "We've traced your past, Mrs. Foley."

The scene played out in slow motion before her, every detail unnaturally clear. The potted plant on the windowsill that hadn't seen a drop of water for weeks. The mole on the police officer's brow. The large framed bulletin board with family photos and thank-you cards. Ceara gripped her purse, feeling the outline of the wooden box inside. "Who am I?"

Sanders gave her a hint of a smile. "Your name at birth was Margarethe Blumenthal. You were born in Altona, near Hamburg . . ."

Although Ceara listened intently, his words seemed to expand to a storm of sound that threatened to engulf her.

"Before your family fled, your Jewish parents gave you the name Emma Dölling."

I'm called Emma. Only Emma. She'd had no idea where the words came from and why they haunted her so.

A German-Jewish family. Kindertransport. A stay in a children's home. Foster parents. The words sparked like little flashes of lightning in her mind, leaving a flurry of burning questions.

"I know we're bombarding you with information here, Mrs. Foley. But take a look at this." Sanders gestured to Keane, who laid two photos on the table.

"This is you, when you were admitted to the children's home," Keane explained.

Ceara stared at the little girl's face, at her own defiant expression, her face shadowed with suffering and sadness. Seeing it threatened her composure.

"We've got more news for you," the inspector continued, and slid an envelope across the table. "This is a record of Fitzpatrick's last statement. Read it when you've got a quiet moment."

Ceara felt the artery in her neck throbbing.

Sanders offered her a cookie, but her fingers were trembling too much, and she declined. "You had a sister who was around one at the time. Her name at birth was Gesa Blumenthal, but she was later called Lilly Dölling."

Ceara shuddered as the silver dream slid into her mind. Once again, she felt the sweet weight of a tiny child in her arms. The child was crying, very quietly, but the trembling of the rosy lips pierced her to the core.

He placed another photo on the table, this one showing two people. "Look, Mrs. Foley. This is your sister, Lilian, today, and the man with her is your father."

An attractive young woman was leaning her head on an older man's shoulder. She had the same hair as Ceara and the same sweep to her eyebrows. The way the man smiled easily into the camera felt profoundly familiar. Ceara couldn't take her eyes away from the picture. She brushed tears from her cheeks hastily. "They're alive? Where—where are they?"

"Yes, they're well, and they've been looking for you for months."

Ceara reluctantly tore her eyes from the photo. "How did they find me?"

"We'll leave them to tell you all about it. They've come from Cape Town especially, and they're staying in London at the moment. Your sister's dying to hear from you."

Sanders passed her a card. "If you'd like to agree to a meeting, of course we'll support you in every way we can. We've got an excellent team of psychologists who specialize in family reunions. You'd be welcome to meet at our premises."

"Thank you so much," Ceara managed to say.

"Get in touch any time if you need any more details." Inspector Keane looked at her closely. "Is someone coming to collect you?"

"No, I've come by bus. It's not far."

"The way you're feeling right now, I don't think it's a good idea. I'll call a cab."

A little later, Ceara found herself in a taxi. She stared at the photo again and again, oblivious to the traffic and the music from the car radio. Grateful that the driver wasn't talkative, she laid the photo in her little box and closed the lid carefully.

Aidan saw the taxi arrive and hurried out to meet her.

He made a face. "About time. Rhona's driving me crazy, fluttering around like a mad thing. She's baking scones, talking to herself the whole time."

Ceara smiled. "Yes, I can see it's high time I was back at home."

"You're beaming, love. Have you got some good news?"

She winked. "You're no calmer than Mum. But I'm looking forward to those scones, I can tell you that."

Inside, Rhona rushed to greet her, her face flushed. A tempting smell filled the kitchen as Ceara braced herself for her family's questions. She didn't have to wait long.

"Well, girl, if you don't want me to burst with anticipation," Rhona began as she opened the oven a crack to check on the scones before coming to sit by her, "tell us what you know. Out with it."

The tension on their faces brought home the importance of this moment. Today marked the beginning of a new chapter in her life, and nothing would ever be the same again.

"I'm Margarethe Blumenthal." How strange the name sounded, yet she found it important to pronounce it properly. "A German Jew who was taken to England on the Kindertransport under the assumed name of Emma Dölling when I was seven." Ceara's voice trembled as she placed the photo on the table. "This is my sister, Gesa, and my father, Paul, though they're now known as Lilian and Peter—it's a long story; I'll explain later."

Rhona's hands flew to her mouth, and she stared in silence.

Aidan picked up the photo. "There's a definite family resemblance. Do they live nearby?"

"No, in Cape Town, but they're in London at the moment. I—I've got their telephone number."

"Oh goodness, the scones!" Rhona jumped up and hurried over to the stove.

Ceara noticed her surreptitiously wiping her eyes.

Aidan was playing with her hair as he thought. "Are you going to call them?"

"I can't wait." She leaned her head on his shoulder. "I'm happy and confused at the same time." She looked up at him. "It feels like a door's opening, which is good in one sense, but I don't know what's behind it."

"I'm sure the two of them feel the same way," he said gently.

Ceara was watching Rhona.

He followed her gaze. "I know what's going through your mind, love," he said quietly. "You're not so worried for yourself as for Rhona and how she's taking the news. Am I right?"

"I understand how she must feel, Aidan. But whatever the future brings, nothing's going to change between us."

"I know." He nudged her gently. "The scones smell divine. Come on."

While Aidan set the table, Ceara took the plate from her foster mother and hugged her.

"Are you pleased for me, Mum?"

Rhona sniffed noisily. "Of course I am; very much, little one. As long as you keep a place in your heart for me, that's all I ask."

"Now, just you listen to me!" Ceara said indignantly. "Dad and you were at my bedside whenever I was ill. You did everything you could to help me get over my fears and self-doubt. I turned to you with all my heartaches." She kissed Rhona's cheek. "How could I ever forget all that?"

"Do you remember your big argument with your father?" Rhona smiled. "When Brady tried to tell you it was such a waste for a clever girl like you not to go to university?"

"Like yesterday. Things got really heated between us. But Dad was glad in the end that I was there to take over the workshop."

"Stop it, or I'll get all sentimental." Rhona gestured to the table. "Scones are at their best while they're still warm. Don't let them go cold."

As they ate, Aidan chatted with Rhona, leaving Ceara free to think about Lilian. Her feelings hadn't deceived her. That sweet little sister she had spun around in circles was just as real as the photo on the table—as was her father, about whom she hardly knew a thing.

Papa promised to engrave my name on it. He always looks so sad now that Mama's not here anymore. What had happened to her birth mother?

And then there was the shiny toy in the pocket of her red coat. It was the varnish that made her little wooden box shine, but she now realized she had unconsciously modeled this box on the one from her dream.

Aidan cut a scone in two, spread it generously with butter and jam, and set it on her plate.

"Inspector Keane gave me a copy of Fitzpatrick's last statement," Ceara said.

Aidan looked at her. "Have you read it yet?"

Ceara shook her head.

Rhona sniffed. "I wouldn't touch that report if you paid me, Aidan. That man's sick! Which means I don't need to know anything else about him. What do you think, Ceara?"

"No, I suppose it's not going to tell us much new." Ceara glanced at the clock. Would her sister be in now? Her pulse quickened as she imagined making the call. She knew that the longer she delayed, the more excuses she would find to put the conversation off until another day. She stood.

"Excuse me for a few moments. I—I'll be in the office." Ceara moved to go to the door, but Aidan stepped into her path and cupped her face in his hands.

"Good luck, my darling. Everything's going to be fine."

Ceara nodded and hurried into the workshop, hoping her courage wouldn't desert her. She threw the office door shut behind her, glad the workshop was closed that day. With everything going on, she couldn't possibly have carried on with her work without breaking something.

She dried her clammy hands on a towel and picked up the phone, silently praying she would find the right words.

Ceara sat down and dialed, feeling slightly dizzy. The phone rang several times, then she heard a young man's voice on the line.

"Sam Flynt speaking."

"Ceara Foley. Sorry, I must have the wrong number."

"Ceara?" he said slowly. "No, no, this is the right number. I'm Sam, Lilian's fiancé."

"Oh. Oh, I see." She hesitated, running her hand over the wooden box.

"Wait a moment. I'll just fetch her."

"Thank you, Sam."

All the words Ceara had been carefully practicing since leaving Sanders's office had suddenly vanished.

"Hello? Lilian Morrison here."

Her sister's voice went straight to her heart. She struggled to breathe. "It's me, Ceara. Margarethe."

"Margarethe! Is that really you?" Lilian sobbed.

They were both speechless, crying and listening to the other's erratic breaths. It seemed like an eternity went by as the two women tried to grasp the fact that they had actually found each other again.

"The man at the Red Cross gave me your number."

"We're so grateful to him," Lilian replied. "Where are you?"

"At home in Dublin." Ceara gave her address mechanically.

"I can't believe we've found you. It's a miracle. You're alive!"

Ceara wanted to reply, but she couldn't say a word—it was all too incredible, too wonderful, too emotional.

"Papa and I would so love to see you before we return to Cape Town." Lilian's voice shook with excitement.

Ceara stared at the little box with its childhood scene, searching for the words, but there were none that could even come close to conveying how she felt. It would all be so much easier if the damned tears would stop. "Me too . . . But I've got a workshop to run. I . . ."

"It's not a problem. We can come to see you this weekend. Would that be OK for you?"

"Of course. You could stay with us."

There was a heartbeat's silence between them.

"Papa," she heard Lilian saying. "We're going to visit Ceara this weekend. Can you believe it?" She said to Ceara, "I'll put him on."

Papa. She was whisked back in time. She knew what his voice sounded like, how she loved hearing him say her name. She pictured his narrow, expressive face, his smile that always looked a little sad. She felt his hands as he gently stroked her back when they parted. Another man had come and taken her to the station. She heard the conductor's shrill whistle in her ears. *All aboard!* Then she was sitting in a compartment, hugging her wailing baby sister tightly to her, watching the man on the platform gradually getting smaller until he finally vanished from view.

"Margarethe. My little girl. We've got you back."

"Yes, Papa," she replied, amazed at how naturally the word came out. "I've got so many questions and—and I still can't really believe it."

"Neither can I. But we've got all the time in the world to get to know each other again. In the meantime, we'll make travel arrangements right away." His voice sounded husky. "I can't wait to see you, my darling, darling little Margarethe."

Chapter 24

Lotte

Cape Town

Her hands thrust deep into her cardigan pockets, Lotte stood watching the site being cleared. Almost a week had gone by since the devastating fire, but she still thought she could detect a hint of smoke hanging over the scene. A crane roved like the limb of some prehistoric animal over the rubble of her building, while a digger loaded charred timber into a dumpster. Lotte felt as though every load took a part of her with it.

Early that morning, Dede had buried her little Niam according to Zulu customs. Ewa had arranged it. *May Adonai look after her.* Like Lotte, her friend of many years refused to shun her black neighbors. As often as time allowed, she went to see a Zulu family who had been driven into poverty by apartheid and brought them food. When Ewa asked if they could arrange an appropriate burial for Niam, they agreed immediately, taking care of everything. Burials usually took place on Zulu soil, and were led by a headman. Lotte knew how much it meant to Dede. The most painful aspect for Lotte was that she herself couldn't be there.

Dede bore her grief with amazing dignity. Lotte heard her crying at night, but she insisted on going back to work, toiling from morning till night without a word of complaint. Maybe the young mother took strength from the Zulu belief that the body was of little importance. They honored the souls of their dead, regularly bringing them offerings to keep their memories alive.

Lotte could feel the sympathetic looks of her neighbors as she turned away from the hectic activity of the salvage workers among the ruins and set off for home.

Friedrich was mowing the lawn; he waved as she approached. Dede was kneeling in the living room scrubbing the floor, her face expressionless. Lotte resisted the impulse to talk to her and went to sit outside. Dark clouds crossed the sky and gathered over the summit of Table Mountain. A flock of crows flew, cawing, over the house.

When Friedrich had finished, he came to sit with her and followed her gaze. "I told Dede again that she should rest for a few more days, but she won't listen to me. Her wounds are still raw, but instead of giving herself time to recover, she insists on scrubbing away as if the devil were driving her. We've got to do something."

Lotte shook her head. "No, leave her be." She knew from her own experience all about the rage that followed the initial pain. When her beloved Johann had been taken, she had cursed fate, but also her husband himself for leaving her alone. In moments like that, it was good to work off such feelings in ways that couldn't inflict damage. Sometimes that could even mean obsessively scrubbing floors. "Will you join me in a glass of wine?"

"No, thanks."

Lotte came back out to the terrace with a glass of white wine and downed half in a single gulp.

Friedrich watched her every move. "I've got some savings. The money could help towards rebuilding the Blue Heart."

Lotte straightened. "Thank you, but that's not what I want. The Blue Heart is history. In the past."

"You don't really mean that," Friedrich said gently.

"I do. Will you get that into your head once and for all? I'm too old to start over again."

"You? Too old?" He laughed softly. "You have the heart of a lioness, Lotte."

"But not the strength. Not anymore."

He moved to take her hands, but she drew away. "Are you putting yourself out to pasture?" he pressed. "That's just not you."

"You know, I think it sounds like heaven." Lotte drained her glass.

"Ah, so you want to spend the autumn of your life in the garden, watching the plants grow, and playing cards with ladies of your own age."

"What's wrong with that?" she replied stiffly. "You asked me recently why I didn't hand my work over to younger people. You were right, Friedrich."

He stood, clasped his hands behind his back, and paced up and down the garden path. Then he stopped abruptly in front of her. "Listen. You're leaving those homeless young women to their fates."

"That's not fair!"

"Maybe not, but that's what it looks like." He took hold of her shoulders. "Listen to me a moment, whether you want to or not. And don't you dare tell me it's not my place."

Lotte wanted to argue, but the words wouldn't come.

"It's understandable that you want to close that chapter." He held her eyes. "But you're locking yourself away in your grief without sparing a thought for those you've taken under your wing because it hurts too much to think about them. Am I right?"

"I don't deserve your accusations." Lotte tried to stand, but Friedrich gently pressed her back down into the garden chair.

"Someone has to tell you the truth, my love." His face gave nothing away. "If you really do want to give up, first you must accept the consequences so you can continue to look yourself in the eye."

Lotte had to fight to keep sitting still.

"Think of Anike, who can't find work because she used to be a drug addict. You helped her to go back to school and get a chance at a better life." Friedrich leaned down toward her. "Or shy Daniele, who was thrown out of her home by her father because of her illegitimate child and steals in order to feed little Grace."

"Stop it!" Lotte hardly recognized her own voice. "You don't have to remind me. I'm not senile yet!"

"But I do have to remind you, damn it." Friedrich's face was a mixture of concern and impatience. "Fate has been cruel to you, but that doesn't for a minute mean you should put your head in the sand."

"Clever words." She laughed bitterly. "I really can't wait to hear the solution you've worked out for me."

He drew up a chair and sat next to her. "You told me you know all the corners where the girls usually hang out. Go and tell them your decision in person. That's what I'd want if I were them; it's the least you can do."

Lotte swallowed. In her mind's eye, she saw the women and girls who came to the Blue Heart regularly for support, their young, emaciated faces.

Friedrich nodded. "And once you've done that, you can talk to Dede."

"Dede?" she said. "What's she got to do with it?"

He made a despairing face. "Think about it, Lotte. You'd worked out a plan to help her live an independent life."

I'm going to give her practical experience in keeping accounts and looking after young mothers and their children, as well as pass on what I've learned over the years.

Lotte looked across to the summerhouse, a dark silhouette against the sky. "I know."

"She needs you, especially now that her little boy's died."

Lotte said nothing, the images of the last few weeks playing in her mind's eye. Dede with Niam in her arms, appearing for the first time at the Blue Heart. Like an echo, Lotte could hear her own voice, offering help. The hope lighting up Dede's young features. Her motionless figure behind the summerhouse. The never-ending hours in the drafty hospital corridor.

His voice softened. "Tell her you won't be able to train her. She deserves an honest explanation. Don't you agree?"

His words shook the wall Lotte had built around herself. Her vision blurred into a monotone gray, as though all the color had drained from her life. "I—I can't. What would become of her?" A sob rose to her throat. She stood.

Friedrich held her tight. "There's a solution for every problem. I'm sure you'll find a way."

They glanced inside. Dede had put the chairs back in place and was looking for her next task.

Lotte leaned on Friedrich, watching the grieving woman's grim activity. "You're right. I mustn't blind myself to reality a moment longer."

"It would never stop eating you up inside. Take some time to think about it. I hope you won't take what I've said the wrong way."

"No. You're the only one I'd allow to talk to me like that." She met his eyes. "I'm so tired."

"Go out to the garden and rest." He kissed her brow and went into the house.

Following his advice, Lotte stretched out with a throw over her legs and closed her eyes. She realized she must have nodded off when she felt Friedrich shaking her shoulder.

"There's a telegram from London." He handed her an envelope.

Heavy with sleep, Lotte opened it.

Dear Mama. Our Margarethe's alive. We're meeting
her next weekend. Call us. With love, Peter.

The letter fell from her hands and landed on the grass. Friedrich picked it up and read it quickly.

A few moments passed in stunned silence. Then Lotte jumped to her feet, her weariness suddenly gone. Without bothering to put on her slippers, she hurried barefoot into the house. "Lord almighty, our little Margarethe," she repeated again and again. In a flash, she changed into a dress, then fumbled for a shawl and bag.

Friedrich was waiting for her in his hat and jacket. Their eyes met in silence.

They strode quickly to the post office. Lotte didn't notice the bewildered looks her neighbors gave her as she hurried past without a word of greeting.

Out of breath, they reached the building. There were five customers waiting before them. A blond man in a suit seemed like he would go on talking forever, and refused to allow Friedrich's indignant grumbling to abridge his conversation.

Lotte went up to him. "For heaven's sake, could you hurry up? I've got a very important call to make!"

But the man just waved her away, so she and Friedrich sat on a bench to wait. The people at the post office counter glanced sidelong at them from time to time. Someone asked whether Lotte was ill and needed a doctor. How could they know she was crying for joy, that her trembling was not a sign of weakness, but was because every word of Peter's message was sending new energy through her veins?

The day had turned out to be the best one she had experienced for a long time.

Adonai, you heard my prayer.

Lotte suddenly remembered the words she had once used to send her son on his way. *You never get anything in life without having to give something else up.*

Her warning might be turning out to be true—in the most wonderful way. A building, however stuffed with beloved memories, was ultimately only a thing, roof and walls made of stone, concrete, mortar. And if fate decreed that she had to lose the Blue Heart but had been given the chance to know her granddaughter instead, she was not going to shed any more tears over the building on her own account. It seemed to Lotte as though the last pieces of the puzzle needed to complete her happiness were falling into place. She couldn't hope for more from life than to be there on that glorious morning in a stuffy post office with all its hectic noise and the feel of Friedrich's hand in hers.

When they reached the front of the line, it only took the man behind the counter two attempts to connect them.

"Mama." Peter's voice sounded far away, yet more full of life than ever. "You got my telegram?"

"Yes, it's just arrived, my son. We came to the post office as fast as we could. I'm so excited."

As she listed to Peter's story, she alternated between holding her breath and letting out sounds of surprise.

"Isn't it wonderful, Mama? She's alive, and she called us the very day she found out about us." He paused. "Are you still there, Mama?"

"Yes. My—our greatest wish has been granted. Thanks be to God. Oh, I'll spend all weekend thinking about you. Please can you give Margarethe—Ceara—my love?"

"There's nothing I'd like more."

"Tell her," Lotte hesitated, "that I love her, even though I never had the chance to know her. There's nothing I want more than to see her soon."

Friedrich and Lotte headed home soon afterward. Dede had withdrawn to the guest room. On the kitchen table there was a plate of *koesisters* with a glass jug of syrup to accompany them.

"I can't believe the way Dede's still taking care of us," Friedrich murmured, taking a bite of one of the doughnuts. "We're going to have to take care of her, too, aren't we, Lotte? No matter what."

"We are." She smiled. For the first time since Niam's death, she felt hungry again.

After they'd eaten, Friedrich leaned back on the kitchen chair and watched the shrubs around their terrace rustling in the wind. The telegram had obviously also moved him. "You know," he said, "your granddaughter was always really special to me."

"Tell me about her. What was she like?"

"I've never met a six-year-old who was so serious, strong-willed, and clever, but at the same time so sensitive. Her behavior was more like that of an older child. I think she worked a lot of things out for herself. In that respect, she was like her father. During the months that she and her parents lived with me, she was the one I was most concerned about."

Lotte tilted her head. "Why?"

"It goes without saying that being on the run was hardest for the little one. She was too young to fully grasp what was happening. She always carried the music box with her, even in their most dangerous moment." He broke off, his brows meeting as he frowned.

"When was that?"

"When the SS men stormed into the farmhouse, the family hid in the crawl space. The little one must have panicked, because at the very moment the thugs were standing above them in the storeroom, she dropped the music box, and the little bird jumped out and sang."

"Oh my God." Lotte clapped her hands over her eyes. "That could have cost them their lives."

He nodded. "The poor child was horribly upset with herself. But my instincts told me that something else lay behind it all. When I pressed Peter and he told me about their false identities, her behavior suddenly made sense to me. She sensed her parents were keeping things from her to protect her. But I'm sure that what most tormented her was that she could no longer be Margarethe, daughter of a Jewish silversmith from Altona."

"If only they'd emigrated with us. But they felt responsible for my brother-in-law Max and Dr. Fisch," Lotte said. "I'm so glad she got to grow up with a foster family and not in an orphanage."

"And from what your son said, it seems the Wards truly loved and cared for her," Friedrich added. "Nothing like those Jackson people in London. That's a huge blessing."

"You're right," she said. "It remains to be seen how great the gulf is between Peter and Lilian and Ma—Ceara." She rolled her eyes. "I've got to get used to not saying Margarethe."

"You will." Friedrich smiled. "Well, I think we should celebrate this wonderful day. Don't you agree?"

"Celebrate—two old folks like us?"

"But of course. Wait a moment."

Lotte watched, frowning in confusion, as he walked nimbly over to the summerhouse and returned almost immediately with flushed cheeks.

"I don't think there'll be a better time, Lotte."

Why's he suddenly as awkward as a schoolboy?

He fished something from his pocket and placed a broad silver bracelet around her wrist.

She blinked. *The most valuable part of a friendship is the love it awakens* was engraved around it in flowing script.

"You've enriched my life," he declared. "I want to thank you with this little gift."

"As you have mine," she said with increasing bewilderment. "It's beautiful. Thank you. That's a saying from the Talmud. But why?"

"I looked it up especially for you." He drew her into his arms. "If— if I don't say it now, I never will. I love you, Lotte. You're my sunshine, my best friend, the person I want to spend the rest of my life with." He grinned. "Even if there's not so much of it left. Are you at least a little bit fond of me?"

Stunned, she looked up at him, then leaned into his broad shoulder. She needed time to compose herself sufficiently to formulate the words that would never have passed her lips but for his confession. "I love you very much, you crazy man."

Chapter 25

Ceara/Lilian

Dublin

Clouds were towering above Ballygall, only reluctantly giving way to the afternoon sun. The previous night's rainfall had left little puddles on the asphalt of Collins Row. Leaves swirled up on the strong wind, dancing in the air before gliding noiselessly to the ground. When the sun peeped through, the trees were lit up for a few moments in their most beautiful autumn colors. Behind them, the gray house looked plain but for the bright red wooden door that caught the eye of everyone who passed. A bus slowed to walking speed, then drew up to the stop and spat out a gaggle of uniformed schoolchildren. A taxi driver, about to set off, swore as Buzz O'Reilly ran across the street to catch the bus at the last second. A man in a single-breasted jacket dragged his little son past the house. The boy tore himself free from his father's hand to jump into one puddle after another with whoops of joy, his brightly colored backpack bouncing up and down with every step. It was Friday, and the residents of Ballygall were hurrying home, looking forward to the weekend. Nothing betrayed how extraordinary this ordinary afternoon was going to be for one family.

Lilian and Sam were sitting in the back of a taxi. Up front, Peter tapped his foot impatiently. The car came to a halt on Collins Row.

"There they are!" Lilian nodded toward the two people waiting outside the house with the red door. "Oh my God. What—what shall I say?"

Peter gave her a crooked smile before turning to pay the driver. "Just be yourself."

Lilian's eyes were drawn by the slim woman in comfortable overalls, chestnut hair falling softly over her shoulders. A powerfully built man had his arm around her.

Incapable of speaking, Lilian approached her sister, who stood stock-still, her trembling lips the only sign of movement. She would never forget for the rest of her life the moment their eyes met. The world seemed to stop turning as the sunlight broke through and caught Ceara's features, which resembled her own so closely it was almost painful. Lilian studied in amazement the serious mouth, the wavy hair a few shades darker than her own. A gust of wind moved a lock to reveal faint scars on Ceara's neck.

"You must be Aidan. I'm Sam."

The two men embraced warmly.

"My little girl," she heard Peter say huskily.

Ceara reached out her hands to him. "Papa—I remember you."

Peter hugged her to him as she sobbed.

When he released her, the young man called Aidan smiled, and Lilian moved closer. All at once it seemed easy to bridge the distance between herself and her sister.

The two women looked at each other through tears, and Lilian took Ceara in her arms. "My darling big sister," she murmured in Ceara's ear. "I've got you back."

Her sister wiped her eyes. "You look so much like me." She released herself and smiled. "This is my husband."

"I'm delighted to meet you," Aidan said warmly. "Come in, all of you. The wind's cold today."

Lilian reached out and touched her father's pale but radiant face. "Let's go in, Papa."

She immediately felt at home in the simple house with its warm colors.

Aidan carried their bags in and showed them to the living room. A fire was crackling in the fireplace.

Lilian ran her fingers over the fine marquetry of the table.

"It's a one-of-a-kind original. Ceara made the furniture herself. She's a brilliant carpenter."

Lilian was amazed. "Really? I can't even bang a nail straight into a wall."

Aidan grinned. "Make yourselves at home."

Ceara's hands were shaking as she served drinks before taking her place next to her sister on the sofa. Lilian could sense her shyness as Ceara looked at them each in turn. "How did you find me?" Ceara asked.

Lilian took a deep breath. "It's a long story."

"I want to hear it all."

Her gentle smile reached deep into Lilian's heart. "It was only this year that I found Grandma and Papa."

Ceara widened her eyes. "You—you didn't grow up with them either?"

"No. I didn't even know about them." Lilian told her briefly about her life with the Morrisons.

"We thought you were dead," Sam said. "But your sister insisted on finding out all about your time in London. It was something she had to do before she could emigrate to Cape Town and marry me," he added. "My chances have increased massively now."

Ceara's and Aidan's laughter rang out, helping to alleviate the tension in the room.

Peter took up the thread and told her of the many stages in their search—about the Jacksons, Dr. Cook, and retired chief inspector Lewis, who had taken up the case as a personal mission, up to the moment when they discovered that Ceara was still alive.

Pain shone on Ceara's face as a momentary silence fell.

"I don't think I remember the Jacksons or that horrible doctor who stole my identity. I've been suffering from amnesia since the air raid in 1940." Ceara was gazing into space. "My first conscious memory is in the hospital, when I came to and saw Rhona sitting by my bed."

"Oh, you poor thing!" Lilian exclaimed. "I'm so sorry. Papa and I will tell you everything we know."

"You've got the whole weekend for that," Aidan said gently but firmly. "I've arranged to go over to our regular pub this afternoon. My friends and I have a rehearsal there for our session tomorrow, which you're all invited to, of course. Do you fancy coming with me now, Sam?"

"Yes, good idea." Sam kissed Lilian and stood. "I'm sure the three of you have a lot to catch up on."

Ceara accompanied the two men to the door. "I'll show you where you'll be sleeping," she said once she returned.

"Thanks," Peter said. "I'd love to see your house."

They followed Ceara, who had set up a guest room for Lilian and Sam in the attic. Her father would be spending the night in the adjacent office.

As Ceara showed them around, Lilian struggled to contain the many questions burning to get out. Ceara gave the outward impression of a woman with her feet firmly on the ground, but when their eyes met, Lilian saw a deep sadness and anxiety.

They had no sooner sat back down together than there was a knock at the door.

"Mum! Come in."

Ceara introduced Rhona.

"Don't let me disturb you," she said, tucking a gray-flecked lock of hair behind her ear.

"On the contrary." Peter reached out his hands to her. "I'm delighted to meet you. And I want to thank you from the bottom of my heart for loving and caring for Ceara all these years."

"She's been everything to us, Mr. Dölling." Rhona turned to her daughter. "I've made something for you." She hurried out, returned with a full soup tureen and a basket overflowing with bread, then moved to leave with the empty tray.

"Thank you, Mum. Why don't you sit down and eat with us?"

"Not today, love. I'll see you tomorrow." She wished them a pleasant evening and darted out.

Ceara watched her go.

She looks lost. It's a lot for her to take in. Lilian shuffled a little closer.

"Listen," her father said softly. "I know we're turning your life upside down. We want you to know we've come here without any expectations whatsoever. Just to see you here with a loving husband and mother is enough to make us very happy."

Ceara nodded. "Thank you. I appreciate you saying that."

Lilian felt how hard it was for her sister to put her thoughts into words.

"To be honest, for a long time I completely resisted confronting my past. But now here you are with me and it all feels so familiar, even though I don't know the first thing about you."

Lilian squeezed her hand. "We'll get to know each other over time. Everything else can take care of itself."

Ceara's smile didn't reach her eyes. "You know, when Mum and Dad brought me back into the world of the living, I was offered every conceivable kind of treatment. I'm still struggling to this day with fears and nightmares, but things are gradually getting better. Rhona's my mother, and nothing's going to change that."

"She always will be," Peter replied. "Rhona's a part of our family now, too."

"Thank you, Papa."

Lilian could hear the relief in her voice.

"Did you love your adoptive mother, Lilian?"

How wonderful it was to hear Ceara speak her name. "Yes, but not like you love Rhona. We had so little in common."

"That's a pity." Ceara turned to her father. "Can I ask you something?"

"Of course."

"I have this dream where I'm a little girl. In it, I sometimes hear your voice and think how you're sad now that Mama's no longer there. What was my mother like? What happened to her? You don't have to answer right now if it's too painful."

The red glow from the fire accentuated Peter's features. "My poor little girl. Please don't worry about asking. The images of that dreadful night have been with me for many years, and they'll be there to the end of my life." He paused. "Your mother? To me, she was the prettiest, most wonderful woman in the world. She wanted to be a kindergarten teacher more than anything, but the Nazis' racial segregation laws made it a profession for Aryan women only. She refused to give up her dream, though, so we converted to Christianity. My Clara followed her dreams, loved her family, and was an adoring mother to you both."

Lilian watched her father's words conjure a dreamy expression on Ceara's face.

"But to answer your second question," her father continued, "we'd changed our names, fled Altona, and made it as far as Bremen. It happened on Kristallnacht, a few days before your seventh birthday. We'd managed to get hold of tickets for the ocean voyage to Cape Town, where your grandmother Lotte, my mother, had emigrated in 1930.

Then the shopkeeper we worked for betrayed us to the SS. We hid the two of you in an underground shelter, but the thugs spotted us on our way there and shouted at us to stop. Afraid that they might find you—the SS didn't mind killing children—we ran. They shot at us. Your mother died on the spot," he said in a hollow voice. He attempted a smile. "But that's enough sadness for one day."

Ceara, who had been listening with her lips pressed together, reached for his hand.

The sisters' eyes met, and Lilian felt a bond between them already, a bond that with time would grow unbreakable. As long as they lived and breathed, they would never truly be parted again.

"So, do you have your own workshop, Ceara?" Peter said, tearing Lilian from her thoughts. "I saw the sign as we came in."

Her face brightened. "Yes. I took it over from my—from Dad. Do you want to see it?"

"Do we!" Lilian replied. "I so admire people like you and Papa. I only have to look at something, and I drop it. I'm as clumsy as they come."

Peter grinned. "You've got other talents to make up for it."

Ceara looked up at him. "Are you an artist?"

"I wouldn't quite say that. I'm a silversmith, and I run a jewelry business in Cape Town."

Her eyes shone in the firelight. "You're a craftsman like me."

Peter kissed her brow by way of reply.

As the two of them talked, the hints of Afrikaans in her father's English blended with her sister's Irish accent like music to Lilian's London ears.

The workshop was a scene of activity and chaos, and the thought of her sister handling such specialized tools filled Lilian with awe. Ceara made a pot of tea in the office, while Lilian and Peter looked around the workshop.

"Do you run the business alone?" Peter asked later as they sat around the desk in the office with tea and fruitcake.

The two of them were soon engrossed in a conversation about their work, leaving Lilian to look around. An object on the shelf caught her eye. "Is that something you're working on, Ceara?"

"The wooden box? It's more or less finished, actually. A regular customer's offered me a good price for it, but it's not for sale. It—it's come to have personal significance for me."

"Can I have a closer look?" Was Lilian imagining it, or did Ceara hesitate briefly?

"Why not?"

As she looked at the image of the little boy on the lid, Lilian froze.

"What's the matter? Don't you like it?"

Lilian stared as if spellbound at the little boy with the conductor's baton in his hand. There it was—the book on his lap and the birds singing a melody. Without a word, she handed the little box to Peter.

"How is this possible?" Her father's voice sounded strange.

"I don't understand. Is something wrong?"

Lilian wanted to stand, take her sister in her arms, and explain what was going on, but she felt rooted to the spot.

"There's nothing wrong, darling. That picture. The similarity's stunning." Their father hesitated.

The hairs on Lilian's arms were standing on end. She reached for her bag, took out the silver music box, and set it down next to the little wooden one. Tears were flowing down her cheeks. "Where did you find this image?"

Ceara reached out her arms to both of them. "I saw it in my dreams. How come these scenes are almost identical? I don't understand."

"Your grandfather made this music box in 1914," her father explained. "You loved it more than anything. When you were separated from your sister, you gave it to her as a parting gift." He leaned toward her. "Do you remember the music box?"

Ceara took hold of the two little boxes and sank heavily onto a chair. "You wrapped your little arms around my neck," she murmured, her eyes closing, "and you—you didn't want to let go. The shiny little box in the pocket of my red coat. Oh my God!"

Breathless with emotion, Lilian watched her sister, whose gaze was fixed somewhere in the distance.

"Will you tell us more about your dream?" Peter asked.

Ceara took a deep breath, then began to describe the meadow with the silvery light, the baby she was holding, and the melody that played while they danced with wild abandon. About the planes and the way the ground shook before exploding beneath her feet. "The dream has been with me for as long as I can remember. But since I chose the scenes for the lid of this little box, it's been changing."

"In what way?" Lilian asked.

"There are new details, like an old-fashioned baby carriage. My therapist believes that memories and dreams get mixed up together."

"You liked to take your sister out walking," Peter said. "And the red coat was real. You cried bitterly when we had to get rid of it."

Stunned, the three of them looked at one another.

"Grandfather's music box was what started it all," Lilian whispered at last. "It's what brought us back together."

Her father's expression softened. "That's right, and it will always be with us."

"When are you going back?" Ceara asked, her voice shaky.

"On Monday," her father replied. "We want to visit Dr. Grifford in Hamburg, to thank him for saving you at the hospital and testifying to the police about Cook misidentifying you. Without that, we'd never have found you. From there, we're going on to visit my old friend August in Regensburg. Then we have to return to Cape Town. Your grandmother needs us."

Ceara was horrified when Peter told her about the fire at the Blue Heart.

"You must get back to her as soon as possible," she said as if to her-self. "I'd so much love to meet her. My God." She paced up and down the office, fighting tears.

"I've been asked to give you your grandmother's love. She's over-joyed that you're alive," Peter said. "This year, her birthday's at the start of Hanukkah. She'll be seventy-six."

Ceara looked at them both. "So we don't have much time."

She was a few steps ahead of Lilian, who wondered whether Ceara was referring to their stay in Ballygall or their grandmother's age.

That night, the two sisters sat up talking into the small hours. As dawn broke, Ceara told Lilian she felt as though she'd only brushed the surface of her family's story. Neither of them felt tired in the slightest, but overflowed with joy. The two of them would soon be half a world away from one another, though. When would they see each other again?

The next day, Ceara took her family to see Dublin Castle; they vis-ited Christ Church Cathedral, explored Temple Bar with its little theaters and pubs, and marveled at the numerous street artists. They finished off the evening at the Shamrock. With her family around her, Ceara found it easier to relax despite the hubbub of voices around her. Seeing her older sister laughing with Rhona, Papa, and Sam, and watching Aidan playing the banjo, warmed Lilian's heart.

The atmosphere was cheerful as they gathered the following morn-ing for breakfast. She and Ceara listened with amusement as the men chatted about sports and music. She caught a fleeting sadness in Ceara's eyes. They only had a day left: on Monday morning, she, her father, and Sam would be flying to Hamburg.

Lilian sat beside her sister on the sofa. "Could you try to come to Sea Point for Grandma's birthday?"

Ceara shrugged. "I don't know. I've never closed the workshop for longer than a couple of days."

Aidan came over. "Go with them, love. We've been saving for years and never touched a penny. Make the most of the opportunity. You don't have any urgent orders, and any deadlines you do have can be postponed. Rhona can answer the phone for you."

Ceara broke into a relieved smile and nodded, tears gleaming in her eyes.

"What a wonderful idea!" Her father beamed. "Nothing would make us happier, Ceara!"

Chapter 26

Ceara

Altona, Hamburg and Regensburg

And so it happened that Ceara, with clammy hands, boarded a plane for the very first time. She had been assigned a seat apart from her newfound family, which suited her, since they could have no idea what this step meant for her, how much it cost her to overcome her fears. Silently counting the minutes, she avoided looking at the view from the window. Only when they landed in Hamburg did her heart stop racing.

They checked into the same hotel where Lilian and Sam had stayed a few months before and spent the evening in the hotel bar.

"Have you read Fitzpatrick's statement?" her father asked.

"No, but I've brought it with me. I guess it's time." Ceara took the letter from her bag, read it, and threw it onto the table as if it had burned her fingers.

Peter read aloud. "The accused states as follows for the record: Dr. Cook and I agreed that we wanted to give these pitiable Jewish children the chance of an untainted life by giving them respectable identities and placing them with Aryan families, where all Jewish thoughts would be driven out of them. We did it for the good of the children."

Four pairs of eyes met in utter dismay.

"They made money from the suffering of others!" Lilian's eyes blazed.

"The good of the children?" Ceara's cheeks were glowing fiercely. "We were nothing to them but Jewish scum."

"Scum they trafficked to make a packet of money," Sam added with unmistakable sarcasm. "To think that you wondered at one point in the search whether Cook might have secretly been Jewish! A secret Nazi sympathizer, more like."

"Disgusting." Her father seemed to be gradually regaining his composure. "Not a hint of regret. Those crooks ripped families apart."

"It's probably too late to prosecute Fitzpatrick for his crimes from the war years," Sam said. "I suppose they can only call him to account for his more recent offenses."

Peter put an arm around Ceara. "Let's leave it to the court to judge him. Hate poisons people's hearts; I know from experience." He looked at his family. "We're together. That's what counts."

"You're right, Papa," Ceara said.

At Peter's request, they went to Altona early the next morning. The sky was cloudless, but an icy wind was blowing. Lost in thought, her father strode before them through the familiar streets, pausing to look at the shops around the Altona marketplace. When they finally came to his parents' house on Königstrasse, he stood before it in silence. The building was one of the few that had survived the war intact. The ground floor, which had formerly housed the Altona Market Jewelers, was now papered with posters of glamorous models—a hairdresser's salon. Ceara moved close to him.

"We lived up there on the second floor," her father said, and she could hear how the ghosts of the past were very much alive in his voice. "They've put new windows in now, and even central heating, I imagine."

Taking care not to rush him, Ceara and Lilian each put an arm through his and stood for a long time in respectful silence while he cried for the worlds that had been lost. When he was ready, they walked together to look up Dr. Grifford.

It turned out that he now practiced cardiology at a clinic in the district of Eimsbüttel.

It was late morning when they reached Weidenstieg. The street was lined with small shops like a string of pearls. The welcoming yellow brick building stood out among the turn-of-the-century houses.

"He's on the ground floor." Sam indicated the doorbell.

"Is it possible for us to see Dr. Grifford?" Lilian asked the receptionist. "It's a personal matter, and it won't take long. Please tell him it's about"—she gave her sister a smile—"about Emma Dölling."

They had clearly come at a good time, because there was only one bored-looking patient in the waiting room, leafing through a magazine. When they were called, Lilian and Ceara followed the receptionist to a room at the back while the two men waited.

Ceara immediately noticed the fine workmanship of the antique desk. A tray of old scalpels and stethoscopes and a framed family photo gave the room a personal touch. A slim doctor in a white coat arrived a moment later.

"I'm Dr. Grifford," he said in perfect German, his English accent only faintly discernible to a keen listener. "What can I do for you?"

"My sister's German is a little rusty," Lilian said. "Do you mind if we speak English?"

"No problem." Dr. Grifford offered them both a seat and peered at Ceara keenly. "You look familiar—you've been to my clinic before, haven't you?"

She smiled. "Not exactly, Dr. Grifford. You treated me many years ago at Hackney Hospital. I'm Emma Dölling, and this is my sister, Lilian Morrison."

"Little Emma Dölling from Sutton Place!" He stroked his chin. Like most people of his generation, his whole countenance changed when talk turned to the war years.

"That's me," Ceara said warmly. "We've come to thank you from the bottom of our hearts. Not only did you save my life, but with your statement to the police, you helped me find my family again."

"I only did what anyone would have done. But I'm glad you've come to see me. I've often wondered what became of you. That business with Cook forging documents, the implications . . ." He fought back tears.

Ceara suddenly felt sorry she couldn't remember the kindly doctor to whom she owed so much.

He asked, and she told him, about her life. As she finished, she ventured a question that made her nervous. "What was I like then, at the Jacksons'?"

"Stubborn, frightened, and unhappy," he replied after considering it for a moment. "Though you and I got along well. You know, I even considered asking the Jacksons to let you come and live with us, but my personal situation was rather complicated."

"That's incredibly generous," Lilian said. "Thank you for taking care of her like you did."

"I didn't get half as much opportunity as I would have liked." Dr. Grifford turned to Ceara. "The first time I heard you laugh was when the Jacksons brought a puppy home. Have you made contact with them?"

Ceara shook her head. "And after everything I've heard, I'm not going to either."

"I understand. And have the courts passed judgment on Dr. Cook?"

Lilian told him about Cook's suicide and about Owen Fitzpatrick's statement.

The doctor listened, shaking his head sadly. "Cook must have been destroyed by guilt, but this Fitzpatrick is still pretending it was all for the good of others. I hope he'll be put behind bars."

"We trust he will." Ceara tilted her head. "May I ask how you, a London internist, ended up moving to Germany?"

"Like so many others, we'd lost everything. Our house was razed to the ground, and London lay in ruins. The sight of thousands of mutilated corpses and the suffering of the starving homeless stirred up hatred in me for the Germans. I was so angry with them that I volunteered to go to the front with the medical corps. In 1942, under challenging conditions in El Alamein, I met two German doctors who made a profound impression on me." He smiled at the memory. "After the war, I was an officer with the occupying forces in Hamburg and met the two of them again. At the time, my wife had just left me, and those two gave me exactly the friendship and consolation I needed. We're still friends to this day. We opened this clinic together in 1950, and I married my current wife. She runs the gynecological clinic on the second floor." He turned a framed photo around. "We've got two children. I ended up specializing in cardiology—and here I am."

Ceara smiled. "I'm so glad your story has a happy ending, too." She stood. "But we don't want to keep you any longer. I'll never forget what you did for me. Thank you so much, Dr. Grifford."

"Keep in touch." The doctor shook her outstretched hand. "All the best to you, too," he said to Lilian.

As they left the clinic, it seemed to Ceara as though the circle was complete.

Each of them lost in their own thoughts, Lilian, Sam, and Peter sat at a table in a nearby café while Ceara went to find a telephone box.

"Hello, darling," Aidan said. Fortunately, the connection was good. After she had told him her news, he said, "Buzz sends you his love and says that it's high time you had a holiday. He's asked if you can make him a box for playing cards just like yours."

Ceara laughed. "We'll talk about it when I get home."

"There's something else—a letter from the police for you."

She paused. "Will you open it, please?"

Paper rustled. "The Jacksons are in detention awaiting trial. Alfred confessed to instructing Cook to make you disappear."

"Why?" was all Ceara could say.

"He said they'd had nothing but trouble with you."

The reply momentarily took her breath away. "God, I hope I won't be called to testify. How could they look me in the eye?"

"I bet you won't. And don't upset yourself. They're not worth it. Let's change the subject—when are you going to Regensburg?"

"Tomorrow! And I'm glad to say that this time we're going by train." His deep laugh sent a wave of warmth through her body. "I'll let you know when we arrive. Say hello to Mum for me. I love you both."

"And we love you. Enjoy your travels and give Sam, Peter, and Lilian my love, too."

"I will."

The others were pleased to hear about the Jacksons' fate, although Ceara was relieved they didn't ask her any more questions. Why rub salt into the wound? The subject nevertheless dominated their thoughts for the rest of the day.

Later, they went for a walk by the Alster, but a fine drizzle drove them back to the hotel, where they enjoyed a good dinner and talked late into the night.

When they boarded the train the next day, it was still dark, and the fog was so thick they could hardly see their hands in front of their faces. Her father took the seat next to her. Smiling, they watched Lilian grow drowsy with the rattling of the train and the warm air from the heating ducts, until she drifted off with her head on Sam's shoulder. He tucked a cushion under her head and settled down to read the paper.

Ceara's father stroked her cheek. "You must be confused by all the names. I'm trying hard not to call you Margarethe, because I'm not sure whether you'd like it."

"That's very considerate. I love the name Margarethe, but—"

"No buts; it's fine. I think Ceara's a beautiful name. Let's leave it at that."

"Thank you, Papa."

They arrived in Regensburg early that afternoon. Ceara immediately noticed the wiry old man leaning on a stick and waving a handkerchief energetically.

"Uncle August!" Peter called out to him, his eyes shining with tears of joy.

August raised his peaked cap. "How lovely to see you, my boy!" Heedless of the stream of passengers flowing from the train, he took Peter in his arms. Behind him was a dark-haired woman with fashionably short hair. "My daughter, Friedel."

She welcomed them warmly.

Lilian and Sam greeted their father's old friend. Lilian had told her sister the day before about their emotional reunion with August a few months ago.

Then Ceara found herself standing before August, who had fought alongside her grandfather, Johann, in the First World War, and owed his life to him. The story of how Johann had carried his comrade through enemy territory to the field hospital had made an impression on Ceara. It was all the more tragic since August's rescue had meant Johann's death. August had stayed close to the family ever since. Ceara stood patiently as he studied her. Despite his age, he was very alert, but his left leg seemed stiff.

"Our little Margarethe. Thank God! There you are, so lovely and rosy before my eyes—it's a miracle! Come here." August kissed her gently on the cheek.

His reaction brought a smile to her lips.

He took Ceara's suitcase, brooking no argument. "So, my friends. Let me show you our new home."

It didn't take long to reach Friedel and Rudolf Schlichtinger's neat townhouse on Birkenstrasse, which August enjoyed telling them he had helped to build. He showed them to the guest rooms and introduced them to the rest of the family.

What Ceara would have missed if she'd stayed at home! She would never have met the sprightly pensioner with his dry sense of humor, or been taken to his heart as though she had never been away.

While Lilian and Sam played in the garden with his granddaughters, Uschy and Monika, she stayed with August and her father as they reminisced and exchanged news around the kitchen table.

"We haven't heard from Lotte for a while," August said, his expression one of concern as he stretched out his lame leg. "Friedrich said she's a little better, but we all know how much the women's center meant to her. It must have been such a blow. I'm glad you'll be back in Cape Town soon."

Peter nodded. "If you call her, please don't say a word about Ceara."

"I want to surprise her," Ceara said.

"I'd love to see your grandmother's face." August chuckled. "She'll fall off her chair."

He entertained them over a fruit schnapps with tales of the times they'd lived through together, until the conversation eventually turned to Ceara. "Well, my girl, you could be a stubborn little minx when you were small." He was beginning to sound a little fuzzy after the second schnapps.

"In what way?"

August clinked glasses with his friend. "Now, young man, don't you think it's time you told Margarethe how she came to have your precious music box at the tender age of four?"

"You reminded me," her father said with a grin, "that I'd been the same age when my father gave it to me, and insisted you'd take good care of it. You were very convincing."

"In truth you had us all wrapped around your little finger," August said. "But let's not dwell on the past for too long. We're much better off living our lives and gaining new experiences to amuse our children and grandchildren. Am I right?"

Ceara laughed. "I like that idea very much."

Chapter 27

Lotte

Cape Town

Lotte found one of her regulars on Voortrekker Road between a hotel and a restaurant. Behind the commercial zone were the houses of the upper-middle classes, who every now and then tossed the tramps a few coins. The blonde girl was sitting cross-legged on a step, begging, a blanket wrapped around the baby in her arms. Her surprise showed in her eyes.

"Mrs. Kuipers!"

"Good morning, Daniele." Lotte gave her two bread rolls with cheese. "Eat these. When you've done, there's something we need to talk about."

A good hour later, Lotte was satisfied and made her way home, stopping at the market for fresh fruit and vegetables. She frowned as she entered the house. Friedrich usually came to meet her at the door. She stopped abruptly as she heard voices coming from the kitchen and nearly dropped her shopping basket.

"Surprise!" Lilian appeared in the doorway, beaming and holding out her arms.

How pretty she looks. Lotte drew her close. "Oh, my girl! Where did you pop up from so suddenly? What a wonderful surprise!"

"It's lovely to see you," Lilian said, turning to Sam and pinching his cheek.

Then Lotte became aware of Peter, and behind him Friedrich, watching the scene with a look of satisfaction on his face.

"You need to eat more, Mama," Peter said after hugging her.

"I'm finding it hard right now, my son."

His eyes met hers, sending warmth through her. "I think I've discovered a tonic for complaints of that kind."

Lotte raised her index finger in warning. "I doubt that. Can you turn back time a few weeks? You shouldn't tease your old mother."

"I wouldn't dream of it, Mama. Do you want to see my medicine?"

He stepped aside to reveal a young woman in pants and a sweater, a little taller than Lilian. She had tied her red-brown curls up in a ponytail, and her gently curving mouth reminded Lotte of her own. Stunned, Lotte closed her eyes. She was seeing ghosts! The image didn't fade.

"Margarethe," she whispered, her voice catching in her throat. "You—you're here?"

The young woman took a hesitant step toward her. "Yes, it's me."

Sobbing, Lotte laid her head on her granddaughter's shoulder. *Oh Lord, you have blessed me and my loved ones.* She didn't know how long she remained motionless in Ceara's embrace before reluctantly releasing herself. "I'm so happy to see you."

"Me too, Grandma," Ceara said hoarsely.

Friedrich put his arm around Lotte's waist. "Come through to the living room, darling."

Lotte saw Peter's eyes widen at the endearment.

"I've surprised you, too, haven't I?" Friedrich laughed. "This pretty lady and I are courting."

Her family's joy was a balm to Lotte. She looked around at them all. "Now we need to think about where you're all going to sleep."

Friedrich's laughter lines deepened. "Don't you worry about that—it's all sorted. They arrived last night and stayed in the guesthouse over at the end of the street."

"I wondered where your bags were," Lotte said.

Friedrich nodded. "Lilian, Peter, and Sam have taken rooms there since Dede is in the summerhouse. I've made up the guest room for Ceara. I hope that's all OK with you?"

Lotte placed her hands on her hips. "Tell me, how long have you known they were coming?"

"Don't give poor old Friedrich a hard time," Peter said with a wink. "We sent him a telegram from Regensburg, hoping it'd arrive in time."

Without waiting for Lotte's reply, Lilian led her to see the splendidly laid kitchen table. Yellow roses in a vase gave off a gentle scent. Candles bathed her family's faces in a soft light. Lotte smiled as her granddaughter offered to prepare the food and drinks, insisting she join the others in the living room to catch up on all that had been happening.

"August sends his love," Ceara said. "I'll always remember the two days I spent with him. He went the extra mile to show us around Regensburg."

Lotte raised an eyebrow. "Even with his leg?"

"Oh yes," Peter said. "He rode in front of us on his adapted bicycle. No one seemed surprised—they must all be used to the sight by now."

Lotte was always moved when she thought of August. "That dear, crazy man. We must visit him next year. Who knows how much longer we all have?"

Lotte listened to Ceara's account of her life. When she laid the wooden card box in her hand, its design so amazingly like that of the music box, Lotte was as fascinated as the others had been.

"Fate couldn't take away your memory of your favorite toy. Part of you has always been with us." Lotte patted Ceara's arm. "It's a pity your Aidan isn't here. I'm dying to meet him, after all I've heard."

"You'll see him soon enough, Grandma." Her granddaughter took a photo from her wallet of Aidan in his fireman's uniform.

"I can see why you fell in love with him," Lotte said. "A man with a solid exterior and a soft heart."

"You're a good judge of people." Ceara turned serious. "I'm so sorry about what happened to your center. What are you going to do now?"

Lotte's attention was caught by something outside. Dede approached the terrace, her expression distant. "I've spoken to a few women today who used to be regular visitors to the Blue Heart. It brought home to me that I can't let them down. It would be a betrayal of my work and all my convictions. Take Daniele—she's living on the street with her baby. Lilian and I gave her private lessons, since she can't afford school. In a year's time, she might have made enough progress to complete her formal education." Her eyes gleamed as she looked at Ceara. "I'm sure there are premises nearby that I can use for lessons and free lunches." She was charmed by her granddaughter's easy smile.

Ceara indicated the garden. "Then there's Dede. Lilian said you wanted to give her some training and experience."

"Yes, in the care of mothers and babies—the kind of work I was doing at the Blue Heart." Lotte sighed deeply. "But I'm sure that'll be the last thing she wants to do after what happened."

"Maybe she won't for now," Ceara said softly. "But life goes on, and she's too young to give up on a better future."

"That's true." Dede must have sensed she was being watched, and waved across to Lotte. "You'll meet her later over dinner. She's being very brave."

Lilian came over to the sofa and stood behind Ceara, placing her arms around her neck. "You're talking about Dede and the other women, aren't you?"

Lotte patted the seat next to her. Lilian obeyed and gestured dismissively toward the men.

"I'll leave them to it. I don't feel like talking about politics, anyway." She leaned toward her grandmother. "Listen, we talked over a lot of things during the flight. Sam and I need to find somewhere to live and suitable jobs. He can apply for a teaching post at the international schools easily enough. It could take me a while longer to get established as a translator—if that's what I decide to do."

"Good translators are in demand everywhere," Lotte said.

"Maybe, but I've been thinking, and I'm not sure it's enough for me."

"Do you have something else in mind?" Lotte asked.

"We want to live near you. It gave us an idea." Lilian exchanged looks with her sister. "I heard you saying earlier that you're planning to rent some rooms to continue your Blue Heart work. Why don't we rebuild the drop-in center?"

Lotte shook her head. "I'm seventy-five."

"We know that," Ceara said. "Just listen to what Lilian's saying."

"We were wondering why we hadn't thought of it sooner," she continued calmly. "As a teacher, Sam's perfectly suited to giving your women and girls lessons, and I could help them with reading and writing in my spare time. You can lead the playgroups, and the guest rooms can be looked after by whoever happens to be free and on the spot." Lilian hugged her. "Don't you see? Sam and I will rebuild the Blue Heart for you. It also means I can respect my adoptive parents' last wishes and build myself a house. We'd run the drop-in center together, as a family."

Lotte sat as if struck by lightning, gazing into the joyful faces of her two granddaughters.

"We're so keen to see your work for the poor women of Cape Town continue," Ceara said. "But only if you agree, of course."

Lotte was at a loss for words. The sisters smiled.

"We know you need something to keep you busy, just like we do." Ceara put on a stern expression. "You're not the type to let yourself be beaten by a few crazy idiots."

"How do you know that?" Lotte asked tonelessly. "We've only just met."

"Because everyone in our family has been brought up to believe we shouldn't ever give up without a fight," she said softly. "Starting with your generation. Otherwise we wouldn't be here."

"You should've seen Ceara," Lilian said. "She's scared to death of flying, yet she came halfway around the world to see you. I've never seen anyone battling their fears with such determination."

Lotte tilted her head. "I think your idea's wonderful. Nothing would make me happier than to continue the Blue Heart with you." She looked into Lilian's eyes. "But there's one small thing I have to insist on."

"What's that, Grandma?"

Lotte's heart felt full. "That you'll come and live with us here until the new center, including your home, is finished."

Lilian nodded. The three of them sat, holding hands, in silence, until Friedrich turned to them with a frown. "Have I missed something, love?"

"You certainly have."

After getting Sam and Peter's attention, too, they announced their decision. Peter hugged his mother and his two daughters, then Sam and Friedrich followed suit.

"Grandma," Lilian said a little while later as they sat at the table making plans, "the package of Grandpa Fisch's notes is still lying there unopened on the sideboard."

Friedrich clapped her on the shoulder. "You're right. I don't think we'll find a better moment to read his diaries."

With her family looking on intently, Lotte opened the package. She revealed a bundle wrapped in old newspaper and tied up with string, with an envelope taped to it.

"Is that Grandpa Fisch's writing?" Lilian asked breathlessly.

"There's no indication of the sender on it." Lotte carefully opened the letter, which consisted of several pages covered in clumsy handwriting. She put on her reading glasses. "It's from Janusz Wiczorek."

Friedrich picked up the letter from Dr. Fisch's nephew, Herzel, and skimmed it. "You remember? Janusz was a fellow prisoner. Read it out, Lotte love."

> *To family of Dr. Nathan Fisch.*
> *I introduce myself. My name is Janusz Wiczorek from Katowice, Poland. Nathan and I are together in Jungfernhof concentration camp, twenty men in room. I nineteen, he more than fifty. We clear snow all day. No one can believe so many dreadful things. Many people freeze to death working, can't bury them because ground hard like stone. If we too slow they beat us with sticks. Latvian police watch over us day and night. Evenings in barracks Nathan always read from Torah. We happy, great comfort for all. He often talk about brother and granddaughter. Once he talk about Paul, Clara, and Margarethe, how much he loves them, that they are escaping, and he begs Lord to save them.*
> *Why do you tell me? I ask. It's dangerous if I know. I not leave here, Nathan said. Give notebooks to brother if you can. At end only four in dormitory. They shoot sixteen-year-old Imre from Hungary because he use latrine at five minutes before seven in the morning. We only allowed at seven. Then three from us sick, typhus. Nathan tells camp leader, we need medicine. He bring, but only very little. Too late for Simeon, Nathan says. He too weak. Only medicine for one man. You take, you young and I old and tired. I say no, but he says I must live, start family and be happy. He has many memories,*

I not. I take medicine. After few days they shoot Nathan. He stand upright, although very sick. I cry. Later they shoot all sick men. I lucky, one of one hundred and forty-eight survivors. But lose a friend.

Nathan write nothing important here because inspections always. That is why I tell you everything.

Greetings from grateful Janusz Wiczorek

October 1945, Katowice

Lotte lowered the letter to the table. "Poor Nathan. That good man's life ended too soon. Yet he remained the man I knew to the bitter end—a doctor in body and soul, to whom the health of his patients was more important than his own."

Lilian had turned pale. "It must have been unbearable for him to be a doctor but unable to help."

"Indeed." Peter's eyes shone with tears as he stroked Ceara's arm. "You've got goose bumps."

"I feel devastated, even though I never really knew Grandpa Fisch," she said, and looked from one to the other of them. "We can only hope those times are never repeated. We lost our mother; Papa lost his wife; Grandma, our grandpa; our mother, her father. But that letter lets us know that Grandpa Fisch's thoughts were with you right to the end. They couldn't break him."

The others nodded thoughtfully and agreed to pass the notebooks around, as none of them felt capable of reading them out loud.

Doctor Nathan Israel Fisch, October 20, 1942. It's bitterly cold. I remember a warm summer evening with my darling wife and daughter. I hope they're safe.

October 25, 1942. Emil went to exchange something and didn't come back. It's snowing. It snowed on my family's last Shabbat together, too.

"Oh yes, I remember," Lotte said to her son. "We invited Dr. Fisch to our house. You know, the evening when Clara told us she wanted to convert to Christianity."

Peter smiled thinly. "Yes, I recall it as though it were yesterday."

October 27, 1942. Janusz isn't eating. I'm worried about him. I remember making waffles with my granddaughter. I can see the sweet little girl before my eyes. She was better than me at puzzles.

Peter turned to Ceara. "He loved playing with you. Your grandpa hated losing, but he never let it show."

"I wish I could see something like this from Mama," Ceara said in a shaky voice.

"Don't worry, my love," her father said. "We'll tell you all about her."

The diary entries ended in late 1942, and the sun was low in the sky by the time they had finished reading them.

"He didn't mention us by name once," Peter murmured. "He wanted to protect us."

"I'm sure," Lilian said. "But have you noticed that in almost every entry Grandpa Fisch mentioned a memory?"

"Yes." Ceara's eyes glistened. "He was gathering them for us."

"So that we never forget them—or him," Lilian said softly.

"We won't," Peter said gently. "His words are full of hope for a better future for us."

"Yes. And here we are," Ceara said. "Grandpa Fisch's wishes have come true."

"You're so right, little one," Lotte said softly, tucking the packet away.

Ceara's words broke the tension the diaries had created in them. They made plans for the building and talked about Lilian and Sam's wedding, to be held the following spring in Cape Town.

Ceara clapped her hands. "Aidan and I will be here, of course. We wouldn't miss it for the world!"

Lotte thought Ceara seemed transformed. *Her voice sounds just like Clara's did when she was excited.*

Dede came in. She wanted to creep past the family, but Lotte stopped her and placed her arm around her.

"Let me introduce my Dede to you. She's our good spirit. We couldn't do without her now."

She shook her head with the beautifully wound turban. "I'm getting better, *meesteres*. It's all right for me to be here?"

Instead of replying, they each went up to the young woman in turn and greeted her. She lowered her eyes, but Lotte could see her silent joy.

"I'll go and make supper for you," she said quietly and darted into the kitchen.

"That woman should be working for Mandela's release and raising her son, not making us dinner," Lotte said quietly.

Friedrich went up to Lotte. "We've got a lot of work to do, darling. But I hope apartheid will soon be a thing of the past."

"I hope so too, so much. Until then, we can only do our best," Lotte replied, then kissed him.

Chapter 28

Daniel

Dublin and Cape Town, 1995

Many years had gone by since the day the family celebrated their reunion in Cape Town. When the silver of the music box tarnished, Ceara restored it to its former shine with potash. When the violence between Protestants and Catholics escalated in Northern Ireland in the late 1960s, she laid out her little wooden box and the music box side by side, and gazed at them with concern. Thinking of the conflict on her doorstep took her back to the war, when she was still called Margarethe Blumenthal and later Emma Dölling. Only the weapons had changed. Most of her memories of the years before the air raid never returned, and the silver dream had faded, eventually losing its terror, until it vanished completely. Ceara accepted it all and filled her life with new, unforgettable moments.

At around the same time, on a sunny autumn day, there was a little girl with pretty blonde braids sitting on Ceara's knee. Paula listened to her adoptive mother telling her how Great-Grandfather had once made the music box for Grandpa. The little girl pouted, too small to grasp why she wasn't allowed to play with the shiny little box when her parents weren't around. But that meant her pleasure was that much greater when Ceara gave her the music box for her eighth birthday, warning her to take good care of it. She made the little girl promise that one day she would hand over the heirloom to her cousin Daniel in Cape Town as a gift for his bar mitzvah.

Rhona, who never married Lucas, lived in her own house until she died in 1975. Ceara missed her horribly. In 1978, Paula gave the silver music box to her cousin after the ceremony in the synagogue, bravely swallowing her tears as she saw Daniel's cheeks glow with pride.

They were watched by his sister, Megan, three years younger, who snuggled into the arms of her father, Sam Flynt. She would have liked the silver music box for herself, but unlike Daniel, she felt a stranger to the Jewish faith, and believed the heirloom belonged with him.

The following year, Lotte died peacefully in her sleep, followed a few months later by Friedrich.

Megan, who even as a little girl showed a penchant for jewelry, learned the silversmith's craft from her grandfather Peter, and took over the Cape Town Jewelers business in the late 1980s.

Her brother, on the other hand, followed in the footsteps of Nathan Fisch and studied medicine.

After Lotte's death, Lilian and Dede continued to run the rebuilt Blue Heart. By that time, Sam was head of an international school, but in his spare time he still gave lessons at the center.

When Nelson Mandela was released in 1990 after almost thirty years in prison and was rapturously received outside Cape Town City Hall by a crowd of tens of thousands of people, Ceara phoned her family in South Africa. Dede in particular was weeping for joy as she followed the events on TV together with Lilian, Sam, and the children. They were all filled with new hope that Mandela—by now old and gray—would one day bring an end to racial segregation. Lilian and Dede fell into each other's arms, radiant with happiness, as Peter opened a celebratory bottle of champagne. Their hopes were fulfilled soon afterward, and the rest of the world was ecstatic to see how this sad chapter had finally been consigned to the past, thanks to Mandela and State President de Klerk.

During the years that followed, the silver music box stood in a specially made glass case in Daniel's living room, surrounded by family photos, his yarmulke, and the menorah his grandfather had made him. In quiet moments, Daniel would pick up the music box and think with love and respect of the family members who had owned it before him and whose lives had been changed by it.

One November evening in 1995, the thirty-year-old doctor picked up his backpack and wished Nurse Jala at the Groote Schuur Hospital a good evening. Only five years ago, it would have been unthinkable for blacks and whites to work side by side, whether they were Boers or Zulus, members of the Christian, Jewish, or African traditional faiths. And Jala was justifiably proud to be the first Zulu to work in the renowned clinic. There were still patients who had trouble getting used to the new laws, but they were soon disarmed by the young woman's smile.

Daniel had only returned a few weeks before from his first deployment for Médecins Sans Frontières in the Congo, where he had participated in a wide-ranging immunization campaign against measles and cholera. He and a number of colleagues also made regular house visits to patients who were too weak to come to them.

Deep in thought, Daniel crossed the street and brushed his thick dark hair from his brow. Although it was already past seven and the South African summer sun was low in the sky, beads of sweat stood out on his brow.

His apartment was on Milner Road, not far from the Blue Heart. It was sparsely furnished; he didn't need much and enjoyed being on the move and traveling light.

On his return from the Congo, he had spent a few days' leave with his family. Lilian had looked after the silver music box for him during his absence. Unlike his apartment, his great-grandmother's house, which his parents had moved into after her death, was protected by an alarm system.

Once home, he enjoyed a long shower. He became increasingly excited as the time approached eight. He had news for his family, and he knew it would trigger a storm of emotions. He could hardly wait.

He had begun his preparations before leaving for the Congo and had waited impatiently for a reply. When the message he'd been longing for had arrived two weeks ago, he had been over the moon with joy and relief.

Daniel smiled and buttoned his light-colored shirt. It was such a shame that Great-Grandma Lotte and Friedrich weren't there to share in this memorable day. Since their deaths, not a day had gone by without Daniel thinking of them. He and Megan had looked up to their single-minded, purposeful great-grandma and loved playing with her. Friedrich had taught them how to ride bicycles, helped with their homework, and secretly sneaked them a lollipop every now and then.

Daniel put down his comb as the doorbell rang three times in quick succession.

Megan was at the door, wearing an impish smile and a blue-gray trouser suit that flattered her delicate figure. With her short, red-brown curls and gentle features, she was the image of her mother. When he thought of how she handled the demands of the jewelry business with charm and calm decisiveness, he knew she had found her calling.

His sister kissed him on the cheek. "Have you got the documents ready?"

He pointed to the briefcase by the table.

She clapped her hands. "Oh, Danny, I can't wait to see Grandpa's face. I wonder what they'll have to say about this."

"We'll soon see. Isn't Henry with you?"

Henry was the manager of Cape Town Jewelers and Megan's fiancé of several months. Daniel had taken to him immediately—a man of his own age who enjoyed playing sports in his free time, and whose mother was of Indian descent. He was lively, well read, skilled as a negotiator, and he loved Megan with all his heart.

"No, I'm afraid Henry has a business meeting he couldn't get out of."

Megan lived in the spacious apartment above the Cape Town Jewelers shop in Sea Point, about half an hour's drive from his apartment and their parents' house.

With a shake of her head, she watched him put on his embroidered yarmulke and turn to gaze at the silver music box in its glass case. "Tear your eyes away from it, Daniel." She put on a severe expression. "Have you seen the time? Come on, we ought to get going."

They walked the short distance to the Blue Heart. When they arrived, Daniel couldn't help remembering happy afternoons spent playing with his great-grandma after school. Those were the afternoons when he'd learned how to respond to awkward questions, since he'd decided to wear his yarmulke outside of synagogue. The fact that the Blue Heart was in the heart of the Jewish quarter, and the significance of that, was something the visiting children were not always aware of. Ewa and his great-grandma had gently suggested he only wear the yarmulke within the neighborhood, but he refused to obey—after all, their black neighbors also stood out from the crowd with their brightly colored kaftans and extravagant headgear. Whether it was the self-confidence with which he wore the symbol or some other reason, the yarmulke earned him little more than a few inquisitive glances. Daniel nevertheless understood his great-grandma's concern. Her own painful experiences had taught her to be careful.

"You remember how Uncle Friedrich and Grandpa built the tree house in the garden for us?" Megan said as they approached their parents' house.

"I certainly do," Daniel replied with a grin. The construction project had been at least as much fun for the two old friends as playing in the house was for the children.

He looked at his sister. "Are we ready?"

Megan nodded.

He soon found himself in a gentle embrace. He was always happy to lose himself in his mother's loving smile. She was still very pretty, he thought, her laughter lines a little deeper and her hair a few shades lighter than before.

"Come in, my darlings." Lilian kissed her daughter.

Sam followed suit.

Their grandfather came to meet them, arms spread wide. He moved more slowly, and walked with a stick since his fall the year before. Though he wore glasses for his farsightedness, the same warmth still shone from his eyes. "It's lovely to see you both. How was your day's work, my boy?"

"Relatively quiet, until a car accident over in Durbanville. Nothing I couldn't handle."

Peter clapped him on the shoulder. He then hugged Megan and asked after her day. "I've opened a bottle of excellent Chardonnay, if you fancy it."

The family took their usual places around the big dining table and sat chatting. Stout candles created a cozy atmosphere, and African music played from the radio.

Sam and Lilian served delicious snacks seasoned with saffron and curry, bread, fruit chunks, and drinks.

His mother cooked kosher when they all got together, without making an issue of it. Daniel found it remarkable that he was the only practicing Jew in the family, although he could tell that his grandfather also enjoyed the kosher food. Although he had converted to Christianity with his wife during the Nazi period, he had never lost his connection to Jewish customs.

Peter winked as he handed him a bowl of grilled vegetables, maybe guessing at his thoughts.

Daniel looked at his family, one after the other. How his mother held a hand over her mouth as she giggled like a young girl at one of his father's jokes. How his sister gesticulated wildly as she talked about the jewelry collection she and Grandpa were planning for the coming year. Their grandfather's wistful smile as he suggested reviving some designs from the 1930s, since nostalgia was all the rage.

If Daniel could have wound back time like a film, he would have seen a similar scene in his family's history. In 1914, it had been his great-grandfather Johann sitting at a large dining table at his brother Max's house, wondering anxiously how they would take his news. Johann's decision to enlist had shaped the family's destiny. But Daniel's great-grandfather's news had ultimately meant his end, whereas Daniel was convinced that what he was about to announce would herald a new beginning for him and those he loved. What a pity that Ceara, Aidan, and Paula couldn't be there to share this moment. They hadn't been able to take time off on such short notice, so all Daniel could do was telephone Dublin later.

As his father poured the Chardonnay and silence descended on the kitchen, Daniel stood and raised his glass.

"Today is a day that Megan and I have been eagerly awaiting for some time. I have something to tell you."

His grandfather raised his hand. "You've finally found a wife," he guessed. "It's high time you started a family."

"Sorry, Grandpa. The woman who has my heart—apart from those around this table—is Paula. But she only has eyes for her books."

His adoptive cousin was studying architecture. The lovely young blonde, for whom he had harbored a soft spot for some time, probably even took her books to bed with her.

Daniel grinned. "Anyone else care to hazard a guess?"

"You've completed your doctorate," his father suggested.

"No way, Sam," his mother said. "My son would never have kept that to himself for so long."

244

He and Megan exchanged a smile. They all looked at him in expectation.

"Wrong." Daniel reached down to the briefcase at his feet, took out a letter, and cleared his throat. "The history of our family and that of the music box is close to all our hearts. Mine in particular, because after several generations, I'm now the last Jew. I know"—he scratched his chin awkwardly—"I've often tried to downplay what the fate of Great-Grandma Lotte and all the others triggered in me. It was almost embarrassing at times for a boy in this day and age."

The only sound in the room was the ticking of the clock.

"When Grandpa gave me his father-in-law's diaries to read after my bar mitzvah," Daniel continued, "it put an idea in my head that simply refused to go away. As the last in the family to uphold the Jewish tradition, I want to pass it on and see to it that the names and histories of our dead are not forgotten."

His grandfather shook his head. "That really isn't necessary. We honor their memory by recalling their lives and talking about them."

"That's not enough for me." Daniel looked around the surprised faces. "One day, there'll be no one left to keep those memories alive. I've found another way. Do you remember that newspaper article I showed you last year? The one about the brass memorial stones set into the pavement outside the houses of victims of Nazi persecution?"

His grandfather thumped the table. "Oh yes, I remember it well. We were really impressed with the artist who initiated the project. What were the stones called again?"

"Stolpersteine," Lilian said. "Stumbling blocks—they're meant to halt people on the street and draw their attention to the victims."

"That's right, Mum." Daniel looked into their eyes in turn. "I got in touch with the artist, Mr. Gunter Demnig. Listen to this." He held up the letter and read aloud.

After looking into the background closely, I have decided to begin by laying Stolpersteine in the Altona district of Hamburg, outside the former homes of your relatives Lotte Kuipers, formerly Blumenthal, and Dr. Nathan Fisch and his daughter Clara Blumenthal, née Fisch, in their memory. I'm planning a further stone for Max Blumenthal in Holstenstrasse in Lübeck, hopefully on the following day. Unfortunately it won't be possible to recognize Johann Blumenthal in this way, since the Stolpersteine are intended to be in remembrance of those who were persecuted, murdered, deported, expelled, or driven to suicide by the National Socialists. Your relative had fallen in the First World War.

Please contact me to arrange dates and times for laying the stones.

Chapter 29

Altona, Hamburg, 1996

The family met once a year, alternating between Dublin and Cape Town. One particular time, however, they came together on a sunny morning in the Altona train station. They all intended to check in to the same hotel so that they could spend as much time together as possible over the following days.

Aunt Ceara had come from Dublin with Aidan and Paula. Daniel's mother and her sister fell into each other's arms as his father watched them with a smile on his face.

Daniel loved his vivacious aunt, who still made furniture in her workshop in Ballygall and looked nothing like a woman in her sixties approaching retirement. He recalled his disbelief when his mother had told him about Aunt Ceara's traumatic experiences and the consequences. Today, she radiated happiness; her adopted daughter, Paula, and the closeness of their family must have made a huge contribution to the change in her. Uncle Aidan had taken early retirement from firefighting, but still played music with his old friends in the Shamrock on the weekend.

Paula greeted Daniel with an impish smile.

He looked into her blue eyes. "Well, my little cousin, you get more beautiful every year. May I ask Uncle Aidan for your hand in marriage at last?"

"Why not?" She giggled. "But maybe you ought to have a word with Shane first."

"Who's that?" Daniel put on a black look.

Ceara kissed her nephew on the cheek. "It's good to see you, lad. Shane's Paula's colleague in the architecture office. He follows her around like a moonstruck puppy, but she brushes him off like a real ice maiden."

"He's ugly and he stutters, Mum," Paula replied, holding her cousin's eye for a moment. "No competition for you. But you'll be wanting a Jewish wife, won't you?"

They smiled.

Megan and Henry had arrived by then. To everyone's delight, they had changed their original plans and decided to get married that week in Altona. When would the next opportunity arise to have the whole family in one place? Paula was given the role of bridesmaid, which she undertook with great enthusiasm. The following Friday, Megan Flynt would become Mrs. Henry Johnson.

After greeting each other, they sat calmly, dressed in their best clothes, in the hotel café—and waited. They were missing someone.

When a tanned man in his midfifties entered the room carrying a small suitcase, Peter moved slowly to meet him. Watching his grandfather in his double-breasted suit and white shirt, Daniel thought what a handsome man he must have been when he was younger, one who commanded the attention of others.

"Ariel Fisch?" Peter's voice trembled.

"That's me," he said in heavily accented English and shook his hand happily. "Dr. Nathan Fisch's great-nephew, Herzel Fisch's son."

Daniel's grandfather's face was serious. "I'm Peter Dölling, although my true name is Paul Blumenthal. I was Dr. Fisch's son-in-law." He brushed a hand over his eyes. "To see you standing before me, here and now, has suddenly brought the past to life. Come with me. Let me introduce you to my family. May I call you Ariel?"

"Please do." The businessman from Tel Aviv straightened his glasses.

Daniel could see the emotion on the faces of every member of his family.

"We're all delighted you've come such a long way to be with us," Lilian said.

Ariel bowed. "I consider it an honor to be present at the laying of my great-uncle's Stolperstein. My father sends you his very best wishes. He lives in a nursing home, and I'm afraid his health isn't good enough to allow him to make the journey, but his mind's still sharp. He'll be ninety next year."

Daniel liked Ariel's open manner, and it wasn't long before they were talking like old friends, united by the bond that had first been woven between Dr. Fisch and Johann Blumenthal.

Daniel glanced at the clock. The laying of the first Stolperstein was to take place in an hour's time. He exchanged a look with Megan, then Paula. The closeness between the young women, and that between his mother and Ceara, never ceased to move him. He often regretted that thousands of miles separated them and it wasn't possible to stop by on the spur of the moment to have tea or wander around the shops.

Daniel took out his camera and discreetly snapped a few photos to remember the occasion by. His favorite subject was his grandpa—the way he listened to Ariel Fisch, leaning on his elbows; his friendly smile as Aunt Ceara poured his tea; the gleam in his eye as he watched the youngsters, as he called Megan, Henry, Paula, and Daniel himself. Grandpa's cheeks were flushed, and he sniffed noisily. Although life had done him few favors, he seemed happy and was clearly enjoying this reunion. Capturing these moments meant more to Daniel than his grandfather would have guessed. It might even be the last time his grandpa could come with them. Daniel had already discussed the possibility with the family, and they had agreed that, in that eventuality, they should meet in Cape Town, because no one could imagine the reunions without him.

A little later, the family set off. It was fortunately only a stone's throw from the hotel on Königstrasse to the Blumenthals' former home. Megan linked arms with her grandfather, while Aidan and Henry talked quietly. The rest of them walked the short distance in silence.

Peter took Daniel to one side in front of the old family home. "I don't know how to thank you for arranging this for us, my boy." His eyes shone with unshed tears. "I'm so happy and so grateful that my Clara is being honored in this way. That she won't be forgotten."

"She won't—not Grandma Clara nor anyone else from this family, I promise you." Daniel, too, was affected by the ceremonial atmosphere; it was worth every effort to see his grandfather's joy.

"If only August, Lotte, and all the others we've lost could be here to see it," Peter said, looking thoughtfully at the small, cleared hole in the pavement.

Their conversation was interrupted by the arrival of Gunter Demnig, the creator of the Stolpersteine project. He raised his broad-brimmed hat to reveal shoulder-length hair and gave them a friendly greeting. After explaining the procedure to Daniel and his grandfather, he beckoned two men over. One, in work coveralls, was carrying a suitcase and was clearly responsible for laying the stone. The second, dressed in an unremarkable suit, had a violin in his hand.

Daniel's throat tightened as he watched his grandfather, who was unable to take his eyes from his parents' house, a parade of emotions crossing his face.

They attracted curious glances from passersby, the older generation in particular maintaining a respectful distance as they stopped to watch.

When the man took the brass block, gleaming in the sunlight, from the suitcase, a murmur rippled through the family. In silence, they took each other's hands and formed a circle.

Here lived Lotte Kuipers, formerly Blumenthal, born 1887, before she emigrated to Cape Town, where she died in 1979.

The violinist played one of the Yiddish melodies Lotte had loved so much. As the artist said a few words, the Stolperstein was set into the paving stones. Peter wept.

Daniel had quietly discussed with his family whether it would be right to lay a memorial stone to Lotte in the town she had vowed never to set foot in again. But Johann's and her fates had begun here in the house on Königstrasse, before ending with her emigration. The family had agreed that Lotte's Stolperstein did belong here. They imagined the occasional residents of Altona pausing in their busy lives to look at the little brass memorial and read about her life. Maybe there was still someone who remembered Lotte, Johann, and Paul Blumenthal, and their jewelry shop.

When the music had come to an end, Daniel began reciting a Jewish prayer for the dead, *El Maleh Rahamim*, and Ariel Fisch joined in with a clear voice. As they spoke the old words, Daniel saw from the corner of his eye how his grandfather's lips moved silently.

Afterward, the assembled company made their way to the residential building a few blocks away where Dr. Fisch had once had his clinic, with the apartment where he had lived with Clara on the second floor.

They repeated the ceremony in front of the building, which now housed a pharmacy. A child pressed his nose against a window in the house next door. Daniel had to support his father as the artist spoke a few words about the persecution of father and daughter.

Daniel once again recited the prayer for the dead and looked up in surprise as an old lady, who had just left the pharmacy, joined in.

A little later, the brass stones gleamed among the pavers outside the building.

HERE LIVED DOCTOR NATHAN FISCH, BORN **1880**, DEPORTED AND MURDERED IN RIGA IN **1943**.

HERE LIVED CLARA BLUMENTHAL, NÉE FISCH, BORN **1909**, SHOT IN BREMEN IN **1938**.

This time, the violinist played an old popular song that Peter had requested because it reminded him of an evening during their flight, when he had heard it in a guesthouse with his wife and daughter. Soon thereafter, the Nazis had forbidden the popular group that sang the tune, which included some non-Aryans, from performing in public.

After the solemn ceremonies, Peter asked for everyone's attention in a voice husky with emotion. "My dear ones, I've reserved a table in our hotel for six o'clock. I'm looking forward to sharing a meal with you—my treat."

"Oh, Papa, that's so kind of you," Ceara said.

"What did my friend Friedrich always say? We're not getting any younger—let's enjoy each other's company while we can. It'll make me happy. But I will need a little rest beforehand."

"Whatever's best for you." As his grandfather left them, Daniel had a feeling he was hiding something, but kept the thought to himself.

The women took their leave. They had an important mission to complete, as Megan had not wanted to overload her luggage with a wedding dress, and it would only have creased in the suitcase anyway. So, chattering excitedly, they headed for the bridal shop, where they had an appointment.

While they were gone, Daniel, Aidan, Sam, Henry, and Ariel talked about Ariel's life in Tel Aviv, the jewelry trade, and the Blue Heart in Cape Town. Daniel told Ariel about the silver music box, which Herzel Fisch remembered to that day, and showed him the heirloom.

"Wonderful," the Israeli said. He turned to Daniel. "Have you read through Uncle Nathan's diaries?"

"They were what gave me the idea of the Stolpersteine. It's because the Jewish part of our family is growing ever smaller that I think it's important to preserve our heritage." Ariel clapped him on the shoulder in appreciation.

The afternoon flew by. As the family finally made their way to the festive table, where Peter was already waiting for them in his best suit and a colorful tie, the rays of the evening sun were making the chandeliers sparkle.

"You look wonderful, Grandpa," Megan said.

He smiled easily. "Take your seats."

Daniel and the others looked at one another, eyebrows raised in inquiry. Realizing there was something missing from the table, he set the music box between two vases of flowers. With a smile, Ceara positioned her little wooden box next to it.

Then his grandfather tapped a spoon against his wine glass and raised his voice.

"My beloved family. None of us will ever forget this day. And tomorrow we'll lay another Stolperstein in Lübeck for dear Uncle Max." He seemed to be working hard to maintain his composure. "I want to thank our Daniel with all my heart for this gift. Because that's what these Stolpersteine in honor of our dead really are—a gift." He looked around at each of their faces in turn. "The time left to me on earth is gradually passing."

"Don't talk like that, Papa," Lilian said, but Peter cut her off with a wave of his hand.

"I'm old," he continued, unmoved. "But I regret nothing, and I'm grateful for the good life I've had with you all. That's one of the reasons I want to celebrate with you here today."

Glasses were raised and clinked together cheerfully.

Lilian spoke. "What's the other reason, Papa? Don't keep us waiting."

Daniel observed his grandfather. He thought his bearing looked more upright, his eyes brighter. Whatever he had to tell them, it seemed to have an astonishing rejuvenating effect.

Peter smiled, reached into his jacket, and took out an envelope. He put on his reading glasses. "Let me read this out to you."

"What is it?" Paula said from her seat opposite Daniel.

"You'll hear soon enough." He began to read slowly.

Dear Mr. Dölling,
We're delighted to inform you that your application has been successful. We are hereby granting you the express permission to use the name you were given at birth once again, with immediate effect.

He lowered the letter, tears running down his face. "I hope you'll congratulate me. My name is once again Paul Blumenthal, son of Johann and Lotte Blumenthal, husband of Clara, and father of Margarethe and Gesa."

Daniel's heart skipped a beat. The next moment, he was hugging his grandfather.

Cries of joy rang out around the room, and Paul laughed as he found himself embraced from all sides. When he finally extricated himself, he held the family heirloom aloft.

"'Johann Blumenthal, Altona 1914. For Paul, with love.' Those are the words my father once engraved for me on the base." He was beaming. "If I could express my happiness today in a color, dear Papa, the room would be silver like your music box. *L'Chaim.* To life. Cheers, my lovely family!"

Author's Note

Dear reader,

The publication of *The Silver Music Box*, the first part of this family saga, was the fulfillment of a long-held dream for me. I felt it was one of those stories that simply had to be told. Even as I began the writing process, I knew I didn't want my novel to be a big doorstop of a book; I wanted you to be able to fit it in your pocket, so it could go with you wherever you went on the train or the bus. The complex story meant that limiting the novel to a few main characters was a major challenge. Even before I had typed the words *The End*, the idea of a sequel was developing inside me, as I wanted to give space to certain characters who kept whispering stubbornly that their story was not finished.

The second part carried on seamlessly where the first left off, in 1963. I was fascinated by the question of the inner burdens and scars carried by Jewish families after the atrocities of the Nazi regime. Was it possible for the younger generation to put the past behind them once and for all? Maybe the fate of their ancestors was also—to put it metaphorically—burned into their DNA, as the Jews have been hated and persecuted since ancient times, something that I find inexplicable to this day.

In the second part I have once again given a role to my historical figure, August Konrad, whose real surname was Kastenhuber. He lived happily until 1974, surrounded by his family in Regensburg, and played a small but central role in *The Silver Music Box*. Since I am so full of admiration for August, his courage and determination, I didn't want to leave him out. In reality, he moved to Regensburg in 1965, not 1963. I'm sure August was very proud that his son-in-law, Rudolf Schlichtinger, was a social democrat and, in addition, served for many years as mayor of Regensburg. His dear granddaughter Uschy Schlichtinger, who runs the wonderful Blaue Lilie café-gallery in Kallmünz, gave me her consent for the slight discrepancy in the dates.

Gunter Demnig is also a real person. He is the inventor of the Stolpersteine. In the Talmud it says that a person is only forgotten when their name is forgotten. True to this sentiment, since 1993 the artist has been making brass plaques with the details of the victims of Nazi persecution. They should not be forgotten. By referring to Mr. Demnig, I want to show my respect and recognition for his work. Further information about him and his wonderful project can be found at: http://www.stolpersteine.eu/en/.

Returning to the subject of apartheid seemed a logical step to me, since racial segregation in South Africa was already touched upon in *The Silver Music Box*. Moreover, Lotte Kuipers was definitely one of the characters whose story I wanted to continue. For that reason, I gave a voice to my fictional character Dede Achebe, and placed her by Lotte's side.

Fraudsters, human traffickers, and refugee smugglers have always existed. Crimes involving children being abducted and sold as a result of the chaos and misery of war are particularly despicable. No punishment is enough for those who commit them. I wanted to deal with this subject because it fits within the period of World War II, when people found so many ways to make money from the misfortunes of others, as Dr. Cook and Owen Fitzpatrick did in my story. While I was writing, I was struck in particular by their heinous motive.

Regular reports are still made today of atrocities in the name of anti-Semitism. The innumerable heroes who hid their Jewish fellow citizens, smuggled them out of concentration camps, gave them food and so much more, too often go unrecognized. Tens of thousands of Jews probably owe their lives to them. I would like to put forward Friedrich, Gregor, August, and Dr. Fisch as representatives of them all.

We are all familiar with the magic of music. It transcends boundaries and is understood all over the world. The piano piece "Dolly's Dream and Awakening" by Theodore Oesten seemed to me to be the perfect melody to transcend time, space, and continents for the Blumenthals.

Finally, I would like to mention a further detail, specifically for those who know London. In the prologue, I refer to an Underground station in Hackney. In fact there were several there in 1940, but they were all at least twenty minutes' walk from Sutton Place. For dramatic reasons, I have allowed myself to reduce the distance between Sutton Place and the nearest Tube station.

Acknowledgments

Many people have worked hard to help me transform my initial idea into this book, and I am extremely grateful to them.

My heartfelt thanks go out to: my agent, Lianne Kolf, and her assistants in Munich for their wonderful work; my lovely editor, Lena Woitkowiak of Amazon Publishing, Munich; my enthusiastic editor, Gabriella Page-Fort, of AmazonCrossing in Seattle; my copyeditor at Verlag Lutz Garnies for her sensitive editing; my proofreader for his keen eye; all the hardworking people at Amazon Publishing for their support and the wonderful cover; Silvia Kuttny-Walser and Ingeborg Castell, my two tremendous mentors, for the many years of advice and support; my dear colleague, Dr. Barbara Ellermeier, for her historical advice; my dear colleague, Dr. Melanie Metzenthin, for her specialist advice on the subject of treating trauma and psychoanalysis. She had the brilliant idea of a crossover—our more observant mutual readers may have noticed that in both our novels there is an appearance by the same character—Lieutenant Arthur Grifford.

I would also like to thank my colleagues, companions, and friends. And, last but not least, my family. Without you, I couldn't live my dream.

But my greatest thanks go to you, my readers. Your emails, in which you told me of your life histories and experiences from the Nazi period and the subsequent years, have moved me greatly. As has the message from one amateur artist for whom *The Silver Music Box* provided the inspiration for his next work.

Dear readers, you are the engine that drives me to continue telling exciting stories.

Shalom, all the best, and see you soon!

About the Author

Mina Baites has written stories for as long as she has been able to think, and she loves transporting her readers to new, mysterious worlds. She has published a number of successful contemporary romances under the pseudonym Anna Levin. She also cowrites historical novels set in her beloved Germany as one half of the pseudonymous author Gerit Bertram. Mina lives with her family in northern Germany and loves traveling.

About the Translator

Photo © 2016 Sandra Dalton

Alison Layland is a novelist and translator of German, French, and Welsh into English. A member of the Institute of Translation and Interpreting and the Society of Authors, she has won a number of prizes for her fiction writing and translation. Her debut novel, the literary thriller *Someone Else's Conflict*, was published in 2014 by Honno Press, to be followed by her second, *Riverflow*, in early 2019. She has also translated a number of successful novels from German and French into English. She lives and works in the beautiful and inspiring countryside of Wales, United Kingdom.